ACCLAIM FOR THE DEE SANDERS & FRIENDS ADVENTURE THRILLERS

3 HOUR TOUR
Book 1
Over 900 5-star reviews, 51%

"High Praise and a Must Read — This is a must read if you like an adventure story with rich deep characters and excellent scene settings. It's a fast paced story that continues to build and build with an amazing plot and ending."

"Let's Upgrade that 3 Hour Tour — I was surprised to discover this author who can capture and hold my attention cover to cover. Corny as it sounds, I would have read it in one sitting if time allowed. With that noted, characters were well developed; the story unfolds with wit, humor and enough danger to keep you on the edge of your seat."

"Hang on to your Seats — A fun, imaginative story reminiscent of adventure stories of the past, with a modern twist. After a nostalgic beginning for those of us who enjoy cruising, the author leads us into a scary voyage to a breathtakingly beautiful locale where the adventure really begins. It is totally unexpected, but I will leave it to the reader to explore. I give the story five stars thumbs up."

"Awesome — OMG, what an amazing story! I was there experiencing it every step of the way! The book provided me with a much-needed escape from reality. I will be watching for your next great adventure. Kudos for a job well done!"

"A Cruise of a Lifetime and I don't like the Ocean — This book has everything including adventure, romance, intrigue and there is no way to expect the ending, but to read the book and enjoy! I read the entire book in just one afternoon and have downloaded book #2 for in the morning: Great reading well written."

———

CABO 2 COZUMEL
Book 2
53% 5-star reviews

"High Octane Chase — This is an amazing adventure of 6 people and the crazy cartel leader chasing them. From Cabo to Panama, back to Mexico, on to Key West, then to the Canary Islands, on to Gibraltar and Seville, and back to Key West and finally Mexico City! It's a wild chase, with the group escaping the cartel leader over and over. This is a really exciting read and an interesting travelogue. You will definitely not be bored!"

"Reeled me in from Page 1! Excellent! — I normally

don't take time to read fiction, but these books are worth my time!!"

"Heart pounding Adventure — I read this book in one day. It was very exciting and had a very interesting cast of characters. I love the author's writing style. So many twists and turns made this book so fun to read."

"Like adventure stories? — Check out this series!"

———

ALL 4 ONE
Book 3
70% 5-star reviews

"Incredible reading — This is not the normal read for me but once I started reading I couldn't stop. I had to get all three books. Loved everything and would definitely recommend it. I was a little shocked at the end but loved how it ended."

"Thrilling Read — This series is an educating and thrilling read. The conflict that melded friends into family is wonderfully written. I loved reading the whole series. Two thumbs up!"

"I didn't want the book to end — Just like the first two books in this series, this book kept me glued to the pages! It was so full of adventure and excitement and I just love all of the characters! They felt like good friends and that I've been on these adventures with them. I found myself slowing down near the end because I didn't want this one to end! I hope Dee and friends pop up in another adventure soon."

"Great Adventure — You'll love reading about the adventures Dee and his friends have and love reading about the exotic and interesting places they visit. The characters are very well developed. You really must read this book and the other 2 in the series. You won't be disappointed!"

4 RIVERS

A DEE SANDERS ADVENTURE

LP SNYDER

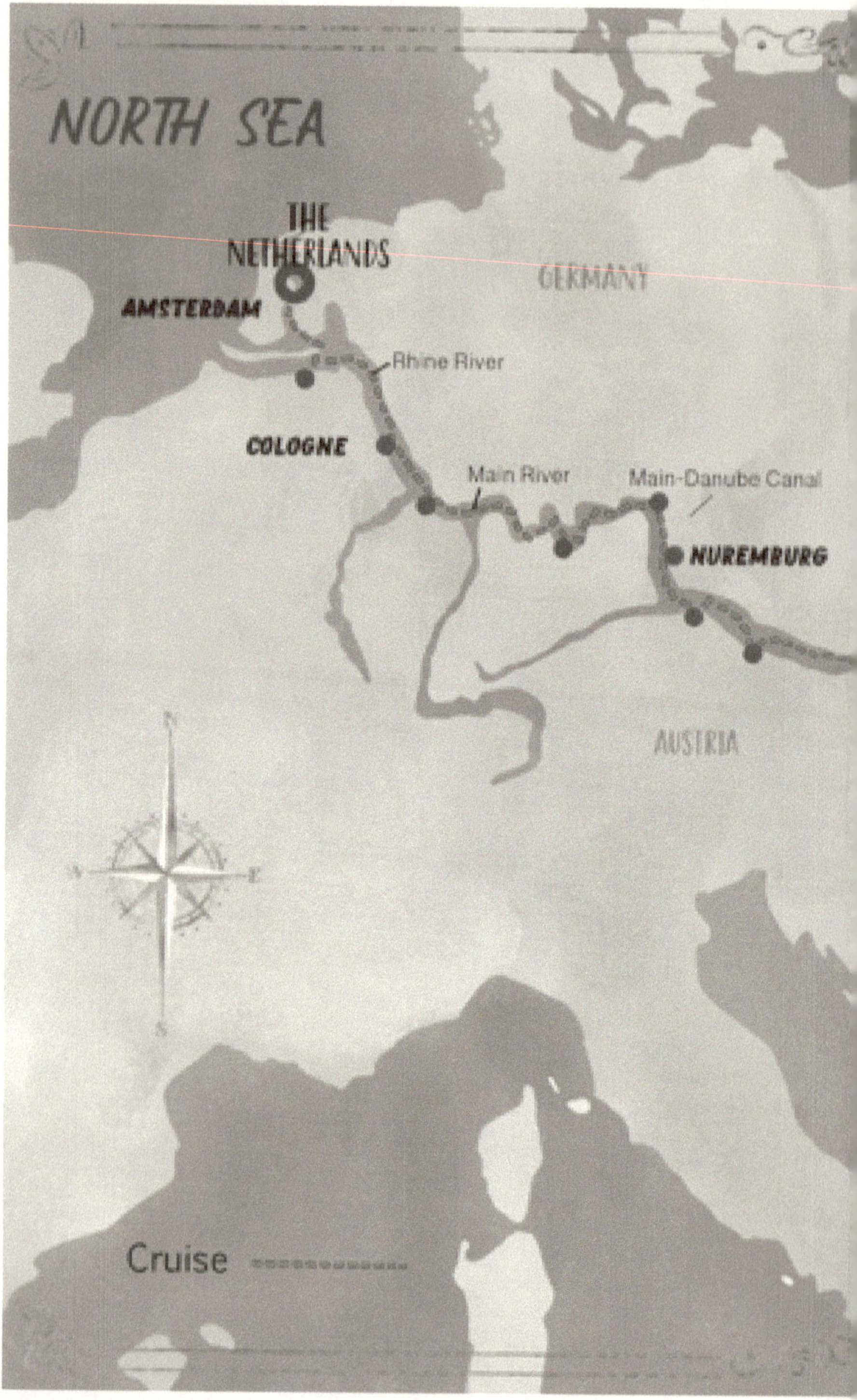

NORTH SEA
THE NETHERLANDS
AMSTERDAM
GERMANY
Rhine River
COLOGNE
Main River
Main-Danube Canal
NUREMBURG
AUSTRIA
Cruise

The Cruise

VIENNA
HUNGARY
BUDAPEST
Danube
ROMANIA
BELGRADE
BUCHAREST
CONSTANTA
CROATIA
SERBIA
BULGARIA
BLACK SEA
ISTANBUL

BELGIUM
Rene
PARIS
Aldo
Anna
METZ
Paris Trainyard
Three Trains
FRANCE

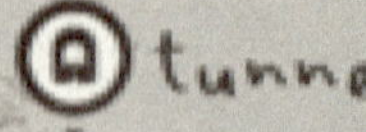

@ tunnel

NORDHAUSEN KOHNSTEIN
MITTELWERK
KASSEL
COLOGNE
GERMANY
FRANKFURT
CZECHOSLOVAKIA
PILSEN
VIECHTACH
BOHEMIAN FOREST
KARLSRUHE
STUTTGART
KUFSTEIN
NEUSCHWANSTEIN
CASTLE
AUSTRIA

2024 Sky Blue Stories Paperback Edition

www.skybluestories.com

Cover art by Vince Conti

Maps by Jamie Lee Scott

ISBN: 978-1-7355084-6-7

DEE SANDERS SERIES ORDER

Book 1 — *3 Hour Tour*

Book 2 — *Cabo 2 Cozumel*

Book 3 — *All for 1*

Book 4 — *4 Rivers*

Book 5 — *5 Days* (Coming in late 2024)

Book 6 — *6 Ways to Die* (Coming in 2025)

PART I

ANNA, ALDO, & RENE

Late 1943
Outside Paris, France

There were heavy clouds and mist alternating with light rain. The steam from the sitting locomotives blended in and made visibility nearly impossible. Anna Simone was trying to locate her companions. They were French Resistance, freedom fighters and anti-Fascists, at the depot early that morning to make things difficult for the departing Germans.

Anna moved carefully along one of the trains, stopping to glance about and look for her friends. She could see very little and couldn't risk calling out as she saw several German officers scurrying about the station platform.

The two men she was looking for seemed to have vanished.

Edging further along the train, Anna suddenly felt a hand across her mouth as she was forcibly pulled backward into a strong body. She wanted to scream but turned instead, her eyes wide, and saw the face of Aldo Anouilh, one of her companions.

He nodded at her as she recognized him, and he slowly removed his hand.

"Have you seen Rene?" he asked.

Still startled, Anna only shook her head in response.

Aldo continued, "There are three trains and each of us will need to shadow one of them. We were not anticipating this number and are forced to split up."

Hearing a "hiss" they both turned. Rene had appeared a few feet behind them. "What do we do?" he asked.

"Each one of us boards a train. We go with them," Aldo replied.

"We'd better hurry," answered Rene as the engineers released the steam, indicating their imminent departure.

"Rene, you go to the far track, I'll go to the middle, and Anna you stay with this one. We think they all are heading for Berlin. Best case, we'll meet up there. But, do any damage you can between here and there and be sure you know where you are when the train finally stops."

Rene and Aldo slipped off into the darkness without so much as a goodbye, leaving Anna alone.

Dee & Friends
Current Day

We stayed at the hotel on the Black Sea for several days after the wedding. Everyone went sightseeing, ate well, lay by the pool, and talked nonstop. But it had to end. Diego and Eve, the archeologist-historians that had helped us with the Egyptian artifacts, flew out to return home, and the rest of us gathered to consider our next adventure.

"Where do we want to go?" asked Keno.

"How about further south into Africa?" replied Jamal.

"Too hot this time of year," answered Angelic.

"Someplace cooler, and scenic, would be good," said Gina.

"Do we want to cruise?" asked Dee.

No one objected. "How about a river cruise, take a break from the deep water? Europe would be scenic and have comfortable temperatures. We could cruise from here on the Black Sea to the North Sea; get a look at a good chunk of Europe."

There were nods of approval. "How do we get all the way to the North Sea?" asked Mike.

"To get from here to there, we take several rivers that interconnect and end in Amsterdam, Netherlands. We'll pass through six or eight countries and sightsee along the way. The river cruises stop most evenings and allow passengers to disembark in many of the ports. It'll take us a while to complete, but there's a lot to see," said Dee.

"I like it. Let's do it," said Jamal.

Everyone agreed.

"I'll go to work on booking it in the morning," said Dee.

Anna
Late 1943
Outside Paris, France
In the Train Yard

Anna stood silently beside the train, the rain falling heavier now. She pulled the hood of her jacket tighter to her head and adjusted the collar. She had to decide. The others, Aldo and Rene, had gone to the adjacent trains. It was a good ten hours of travel time from Paris to Berlin, assuming they could keep moving and that was where they were going. There might be obstacles, or damaged or destroyed track, air attacks from the Allies, or local resistance. The Germans were definitely losing the war now and in full retreat. The French population was not as frightened as it had been earlier in the conflict. Towns along the way might take a stand against a German train. Perhaps she could enlist some help.

Anna reached in her pants pocket and felt the garrote she had fashioned from bamboo stems and razor wire. She had it wrapped in a small piece of flannel but all she had to do was grab one of the handles and shake it. The other handle would pop out and she could quickly grab it and stretch the wire tight. She had practiced, a lot.

There was a Luger in her other coat pocket, and she could use it as well. Anna hoped not to as the gun was noisy, especially inside a train car. She had debated carrying one of the captured MP-40 German submachine guns. But as a woman, she felt, if discovered or captured, there'd be a more convincing story if she wasn't heavily armed. Anna could plead some sort of ignorance or stupidity or insanity. She could whine and wail. It might be useful. If Aldo or Rene were spotted or captured, they'd be shot on sight.

Moving along the side, she paused and pressed flat

against one of the boxcars. German soldiers were climbing down a short ramp from the railcar to the platform below. They turned and pulled the ramp away, leaving the freight door open. Anna saw her chance and with the receding steps of the soldiers, she quickly ran a few paces and jumped into the car. She could only hope all the soldiers were gone.

Anna landed on her feet, hands gripping the Luger. There was nothing, only stillness, silence inside the car-the rain now beating on the roof, and there were boxes—wooden crates full of something, probably stolen from local families. She slipped into the back corner of the freight car as she heard steps, and then there was the sound of the freight door sliding shut, and darkness. Once again Anna found herself alone.

Dee
Booking the Cruise

Dee went downstairs the following morning and was directed to a complimentary communications center. Looking online, he found several companies offering European river cruises. After a few minutes of searching, Dee confirmed they could sail from the Black Sea to the North Sea. He'd gambled on the possibility when selling the idea to the group.

They'd take a ferry from Istanbul a couple hundred miles up the coast to Constanta, Romania. From there, after crossing a short canal, they'd reach the Danube River. Traveling up the Danube to Vienna, the ship would pass through eight eastern European countries. It would take seventeen days. From Vienna they'd sail further up the Danube until reaching the Main-Danube Canal, a little over one hundred miles later the ship would arrive on the Main River. After a couple of days there, they'd sail on to the Rhine River and into Amsterdam. That leg of the trip would be an additional twelve days. The ship would pass through Germany and Netherlands. The trip would take about a month from when they first set sail.

It was really three rivers and a canal that they would cross, but the "4 Rivers Tour" on the website sounded a lot more impressive. There would be three days to get ready before the ship, the company actually called it a "Longship", would set sail. Dee expected the group would need that time to get ready.

Leaving the center, he joined the others at a late breakfast. Mike was yawning and Jamal was playing with his phone. The women were all chatting.

"Hey guys," said Dee, pulling up a chair and setting down. "Here's the deal."

He explained the times and places to mostly nods and shaking heads.

"What's the story on the longship?" asked Jamal.

"It's four hundred and fifty feet with four decks, holds 200 people versus the 2000 people we've been cruising with on the ocean liners. I booked us three luxury cabins with balconies. It should be scenic. There are multiple restaurants, bars, sundecks, a small pool, a library, and no one under eighteen. It should be a relaxing trip."

"Why does it take so long?" asked Keno.

"There are excursions in every port; the ship travels primarily at night, lots of sightseeing, time moves slowly."

"So we're going to stop and get off a lot?" asked Gina.

"Only if there's something to see, right?" replied Angelic.

Anna
Late 1943
Paris
On the Train, Leaving

Anna huddled in the corner of the boxcar, felt the train gain and then reach speed. It chugged along endlessly. She glanced about, not sure what to do first. There were boxes, contraband, stamped "Property", while there were others stenciled with the names of artists, "Renoir", "Van Gogh", and then a "Picasso". That box caught Anna's attention as the Germans were not known to be fans of modern art. It gave her pause. Perhaps it was better to rest for a moment, gather her thoughts.

She settled back against the wall of the boxcar and exhaled. *It seems so long ago. I was only twelve, but had developed early and seemed older in my appearance. One day my father came back to the house from town with a man about his same age. He was a bold, loud man and I huddled behind my mother as my father and the man came into the kitchen.*

"Anna, this is Pablo. He would like to meet you," said my father.

My mother pushed me forward from where I'd been standing behind her leg. I nodded at the man.

Pablo gazed at me for a moment and then at my mother and father before he spoke. "I saw you and your parents in town the other day and was taken by your beauty."

"She is but a child of twelve," replied my mother.

"Ah!" said the man. "Who would have known? When I saw your father again today, I asked if I might meet you. I am a painter of some renown. Gratefully your father recognized my name. I would like to paint your portrait."

Mother raised her hand to her face. "I don't know?"

"Please," the man replied. "I am an abstract, modern painter; there

will be little physical resemblance to your daughter, only her spirit and her beauty will shine through."

My mother looked at my father. "I think it will be fine," he replied.

"Tomorrow then?" said Pablo.

Both parents looked at me and I nodded slightly. Then they turned to Pablo and added their agreement.

He returned the next day with paints and easels. Pablo set me up in the living room on my mother's favorite couch. My father or mother was with me at all times. Pablo prepared the painting; first with a blue tint and then with a rose. To me, neither looked anything like how I pictured myself. In fact, I wasn't sure what the painting looked like. But then Pablo surprised us all.

"With your permission, I would like to paint a portrait of Anna, for you, her family."

He had my mother wrap me in a plain white sheet with only my shoulders and legs visible. Then he had me recline along the couch with one arm beside my torso and the other along the back of the couch. Pablo asked my parents to stand to the side, beyond where they could see his easel. He worked for a day and a half, covering the canvas when he took a break, and taking it back to town with him when he left for the evening.

"What do you suppose all that is about?" my mother asked my father over dinner.

"I really don't know, perhaps some sort of creative artist thing. We'll see soon enough. I hope it looks a little more like her."

When Pablo finished the next afternoon, he invited my parents over to see the painting. "I took some artistic liberty, but I took no visual liberty."

My father's eyes widened and my mother's hand went to her lips. I couldn't stand it any longer, so I grabbed the sheet and jumped from the couch, running over to see the portrait. It took me by surprise.

Looking at the painting, in perfect realistic detail, I was reclining along the couch, but I was completely naked, nude. I stifled a giggle and smiled, my eyes sparkling.

"It is my gift to you, for being so generous and allowing me to paint your daughter, as she really is," said Pablo. "I hope you like it."

My parents kept the painting, after much discussion, putting it in a back bedroom on the same wall as the door so that it would not be easy to see.

But I loved it, and I've kept it to this day.

The train's whistle screeched and brought Anna back to the present. She glanced around again. There was work to be done.

Dee and Friends
Packing for the Trip

"What will we need for this trip?" asked Gina as the group sat at breakfast the next morning.

"Whatever it is we'd better get it," replied Angelic. "We only have today."

The group chatted for a few moments and then Dee raised a hand. "What about we get a few basics and buy the rest of it as we need it? The ship docks almost every night. Maybe we can get a better idea of what we want."

"We won't have to drag so much stuff with us," added Jamal.

"I like the sound of that," said Mike.

"Makes it easy," added Keno.

"Let's make a quick trip for anything we need immediately and relax for the rest of today," said Dee.

———

The next morning they caught the early ferry. It was approximately two hundred miles and would take a half day to get to Constanta. After disembarking, they'd have the afternoon to wander about and then spend the night in a hotel by the dock. The following day they'd go aboard.

———

It was a short trip to the longship, and they checked in quickly and found their staterooms.

"Won't take much time to wander around this one," said Keno to the group as they reconvened on the sundeck.

"That's Romania, isn't it?" asked Angelic, pointing to the land beyond.

"Yes," replied Jamal. "And if we walk around to the port side, we can see Bulgaria."

"And we didn't have to leave the ship," said Gina. "I like it, should be easy. I hope we meet some interesting passengers."

Anna
On the 1st Train, En Route

The train was rolling steadily along and Anna felt comfortable moving around the boxcar. She stepped among the crates and studied the walls for anything that might be useful. The only light came from just below the roof line and cast shadows across the car and the boxes. There didn't appear to be anything in the boxcar but the freight. Anna wasn't sure what kind of disruption she could create. Nor was she sure where the train might stop. It would be midday before, moving north, the train got to Belgium, and even later when it crossed into Germany at Dusseldorf on its way further north to Berlin.

It would be nice to know where I am.

Anna climbed up on one box and was woefully short of the ceiling. She stretched her arms up and sighed. Then looking in the far corner toward the front of the car, Anna saw two crates stacked one upon the other. She made her way to them. The one on top was long and thin. She hefted it and the weight was light.

It must be paintings. Then she saw the name stenciled on the box—*Murillo.* She smiled and turned the box on its edge. *Now if I can just climb that, I should be able to reach the opening and the roof.* There was a cross brace on the front of the box and by holding one hand on the top edge and balancing herself, she inched up the brace and stood atop the box. She reached a hand and steadied herself against the ceiling. Feeling more secure, she looked out the opening. Farmland beyond Paris, but it looked flatter than what she remembered of the trip toward Belgium. *It's still early and hard to see.*

Glancing again, she thought more light might be helpful. Below the opening at the roofline, the next board was splintered. Taking a firm grip on it she tugged. There was a creak from the wood and it rebounded back into position nearly pulling her from the crate and causing her to fall. Anna recovered her balance and caught her breath. Pausing for a second she looked down. The lower box was stenciled —*Property*. Anna knew that meant contraband of some kind which was heavier and more durable than the paintings, also why it was the bottom box. She had a quick thought, *If I grab the board firmly and jump off my crate to the one below, it might be enough force to crack the board.*

Anna took a firm grip, lining her hands with the bottom of her jacket, and jumped from the crate she stood on to the one below. She hung in the air for a moment, then there was a screech and a crack and she tumbled to the crate below with a four-foot piece of board in her hands. Looking up she now saw a larger space to see outside. Plus, maybe she could do something with the board, a weapon, a tool, something. She climbed back on the upright crate and glanced out to the countryside. Daylight was breaking and she could see clearly.

Dee and Friends
Onboard

The group stood on the sundeck and watched others stroll aboard. With passengers this few in number, it would be a lot easier to remember faces and maybe names. While passengers could turn over at any dock, many would probably sail through, at least to Vienna.

There was an assortment of people, but as the website had said, no one under eighteen. Mostly they were older couples, looking wealthy and/or retired.

"I guess younger people would want more excitement or more activities," said Angelic.

"Or other singles," added Gina.

"You should know, girl," said Keno. Gina punched her lightly on the shoulder.

"He found me," she replied.

"Lucky for him," said Angelic. "He and Jamal about choked over the sight of you in that blue bikini."

"Hey, look," said Keno, her arm extended and finger pointing. The group followed her line of sight.

"It's a really old woman in a wheelchair," said Gina.

"She's being pushed by a ship's officer," added Angelic.

"She looks to be alone," said Keno.

The group watched the woman roll aboard. A few feet behind was another crew member with a large cart chock-full of luggage.

"Looks like she might stay for a while," said Mike.

"Maybe we can get to know her," added Gina.

Aldo
On the 2nd Train, En Route

Aldo had boarded the second train in the line of three at the Paris station. He had slipped into an empty boxcar, which confused him greatly. Why would the Germans leave an empty car, unless they planned to pick up something else?

That could be a problem. I'll need to be alert at whistle stops for the Germans on-loading additional freight. There is nowhere to hide. If they open the door, I could shoot as many as possible and try to run. But that seems doubtful. It's better if I could find a way out of the car. For now I feel safe but need to remain alert. Perhaps I could talk to them, but the Germans would probably shoot first.

He had had little time as the steam engines fired from the train station one immediately after the other. Anna's had been first, and he hoped she had gotten aboard. Aldo had to jump quickly in the first open car he had seen and held his MP-40 at the ready, but the car was empty. He just barely got out of sight when the freight door was closed. There was nothing in the car and he could see very little as there wasn't much light. He felt the train change directions several times, causing confusion about what direction they were headed. The information he had indicated that all the trains were going to Berlin.

Aldo found by standing in just the right spot beyond the door there was enough light to see his watch, a Flieger chronograph he had taken off a dead German aviator. The face of the watch had some light cracking and the leather band was distressed, but the watch kept good time and Aldo relied upon it. Time to the Belgian border would be three hours if they didn't stop, or if they were in fact heading that way.

Rene
On the 3rd Train, En Route

Rene had been lucky to have a little more time than the others. He watched Anna's train pull away while he was still on the ground. Rene couldn't find an open car and as Aldo's train rolled forward, he'd done the only thing he could. There'd been a flatcar with three large partially open-ended metal cylinders chained to the surface. Rene had crawled inside one cylinder and hid behind the metal flange at the mouth of the cylinder. He could only hope that no one would see him. If Rene could stay concealed until the train left the station he'd be okay, cold in the open air, but okay.

As the train began rolling, he could see both Anna's and Aldo's trains take a switch connector and head due east, rather than north toward Berlin. That did not agree with the information that Aldo had given them.

Then he felt his train change headings onto another track, and he was going northeast. Rene watched Anna and Aldo roll away.

It's cold and damp; it had been the coldest year on record, and I'm steaming off in a different direction from my friends. Inside the cylinder, the air is still and solemn. Watching them recede in the distance, I wonder if I will ever see my friends again.

Anna
On the 1st Train, En Route

It definitely doesn't look like the terrain heading toward Belgium. The countryside is sparsely populated and flatter than I remember. I guess, from the sunlight and shadows, that the train is heading almost due east. It switched tracks just outside the rail yard in Paris. That must be the answer. Maybe there was an issue with the route—bombings, or a disruption of some kind.

Anna knew she'd have to keep watch on her location, to see if it corrected and went north. Also, what the problem might be. Perhaps it was something that could help her derail the Germans. She felt confident the train still headed for Berlin.

Settling back against the boxes, Anna tried to get comfortable. She wasn't sure how long it might be before the train rerouted or what stops it might make along the way.

Dee and Friends
First Night, Dinner

They spent the afternoon touring the ship, meeting the crew and some passengers, and going through the safety drills. The ship disembarked early in the evening.

Assembling in the main dining room, they saw more of their fellow passengers.

"Where do we stop first?" asked Keno.

"I think its Pleven, Bulgaria, where we spend tomorrow," said Dee.

"Anything we want to see?" asked Angelic.

"I don't know, maybe we can look after dinner."

"Hey," said Gina, "it's the older woman in the wheelchair. A steward is rolling her toward us."

They all looked up to see the wheelchair approaching their table.

"Would you mind if I sat here at the end of the table?" the woman inquired as the steward came to a halt just beyond them.

Jamal was the first to respond. "Please, we'd love for you to join us."

"Thank you." The steward adjusted her chair to the table, nodded, and turned away.

The woman looked up at the group gathered around the table. "I am Anna Simone. It is very nice to meet you."

Anna
On the 1st Train, En Route

It had been several hours, and the train had chugged along in what felt like the same direction. There had been no abrupt turns. Anna felt like there was a new destination. She'd glanced out the car several times and had seen no sign of her location.

Anna's stomach was grumbling. It was full daylight and had been for quite some time. She guesstimated three hours from when they had departed Paris. Anna pulled a small sandwich from her pocket and nibbled. It was all she had, and she felt bad about eating it so soon. It was going to be a long ride. She'd thought the three of them would be together. Aldo had a watch and Rene usually had a little extra food. Plus, just their companionship sometimes kept her mind off of eating.

Then she heard it, the train whistle. Anna scrambled up the box to look outside. She could see a city in the near distance and then a simple rail siding sign that said "Metz".

So, we're still in France but coming up on Germany. We'll probably turn northeast toward Frankfurt and then on to Berlin. The train came further south taking this route, adding time to the length of travel. I wonder why they did that.

Anna felt the train slowing, and the whistle screeched again. They clambered to a stop in the train yard in a pile of steam and squealing brakes. Anna scrambled off the box, flipped it back on its side and slipped into the shadow in the front corner of the car. She reached inside her pockets and felt the reassurance of the Luger and the bamboo handles of the garrote. The train moved slowly forward and changed directions.

Must be on a side rail, are we going to pick something up or drop something off? This can't be the final destination.

The train eased to a stop and lurched. Seconds later the door to the car opened.

Rene
On the 3rd Train, En Route

Judging from the location of the sun, Rene could tell he had been traveling for several hours. It was three and a half hours to the Belgian border and from the stations the train had passed through, he knew they were getting close. So far they'd shown no signs of stopping or even slowing down. Only the train's whistle as they passed through the villages. He guessed they headed for Bonn and then on to Berlin.

He was cold, sitting on the open car; the metal only offered shelter when the wind or the train was moving in certain directions; when they weren't, he was freezing. Rene knew it was only going to get worse as they got nearer to Berlin.

He had studied the train's length when they had rounded several slow curves. There were a few boxcars but mostly flatcars with various pieces of machinery or equipment. A couple of half-tracks, trucks with wheels in front and treads in back, sat two railcars in front of him. Rene thought he might hide in the cab of one if he could work his way forward. He would be less likely found if he hid in the bed, but probably not much warmer because of the open canopies in the rear of the half-track. Being in the cab meant more likely to be spotted when the Germans went to unload, but being in the open metal cylinder wasn't any better. They'd surely see him, and he'd probably be so cold as to be incapacitated, if not frozen.

Aldo
On the 2nd Train, En Route

Aldo checked his watch again; he was three hours out of Paris. He felt the train moving at a steady speed and decided to take a chance. Aldo found the levers for the freight door and switched its position to allow the door to open. He walked the door back slowly, allowing it only a few feet. He leaned forward and felt the wind in his face. He saw nothing that caused him to hesitate. Pulling his face back inside the car, he stood with the door propped open and surveyed the passing countryside. Aldo should have been in Belgium if the train had gone north. He checked the time on his watch and after fifteen minutes was ready to close the door. Then he saw them. The signs along the track read—Karlsruhe, Stuttgart. He was in Germany, or about to be. Aldo quickly pulled the door closed and dropped to a squat.

The train has gone almost due east and slightly south. It could go to Berlin this way but it isn't very direct. Maybe it has to do with the tracks or separation from the other trains as a security measure, or maybe it's the empty car and something else to be collected. I really need to get out of here before the train stops.

Aldo looked around the car, in pitch darkness again.

I'm going to have to open the door to see, and I'd better do it quick.

He reopened the freight door and glanced around the car, concentrating on the roof. It was still dark inside, which he decided might work to his advantage. Even with the door fully open, Aldo felt that only the middle of the car had light. Looking down the track, he could see the train was on a flat stretch so that the door shouldn't move. He stepped away and walked to the back corner of the car. Peering upwards he could just make out some cross braces at the corner of the roof.

If I can get to those, and they're strong enough, I could lie on them and hide. The Germans won't likely look up and probably won't see me if they do. Or, I could shoot them.

Anna
On the 1st Train, En Route

She could hear voices as the freight door opened. Anna had the Luger in her hand. If the soldiers saw her, they would be across the car from her and shooting them would be her only choice.

She saw another crate being shoved inside the car. The soldiers on the ground were trying to wedge the new crate on top of the one directly in front of the door. Anna slunk further back against the wall.

The soldiers continued to wrestle with the crate and their voices grew louder and angrier. Finally, Anna saw hands grab the door frame and felt the car shake slightly as one soldier pulled himself up and inside. His eyes hadn't left the crate so far.

Anna heard what she thought was cursing and watched as the soldier kicked at the crate. There was a sharp voice from outside and the soldier stopped kicking and bent over and lifted the edge of the crate upon the one below it. Anna saw the hands of the other men below pushing the top crate further inside.

The soldier stood up and as he turned toward Anna, there was more shouting and another crate appeared in the opening. This one was thinner and upright.

It must be paintings, and the other must be contraband.

The soldier slid the crate in Anna's direction and then walked it around beside the now double-stacked crates in front of the door. He looked up as he finished and Anna felt certain he had seen her. The soldier stood motionless for a minute. Anna's heart raced, and she felt like she could hear it beating, a hundred beats a minute, pounding out in rhythm a symphony the soldier was sure to notice. There was more shouting, and he turned quickly and jumped back to the platform below.

Anna let out a sigh of relief and pocketed the Luger as the door closed.

Aldo
On the 2nd Train, En Route

Aldo wondered about the other trains.

Where did Anna and Rene go? Berlin was still a possibility but seems less likely now.

He had to get busy, sensing that the train would surely make a stop sometime soon, now that they were inside of Germany. Aldo made his way to the front corner of the car where he had seen the cross braces in the corner of the roof. He held his arms up, too far below them. Aldo looked around for several moments but came up with only one idea. He secured the MP-40 over his shoulder and tightened the strap so that the gun pressed firmly against him.

Stepping back toward the middle of the car, Aldo lined up in the dark as diagonally as he could from the corner of the car. He'd seen what he was about to try several times and had successfully done it himself on a couple of occasions, all at lesser heights.

Aldo jogged a couple of steps and then broke into a run. As he approached the corner, Aldo leaped as far up the left wall as he could, keeping his feet under him. When he hit, Aldo pivoted and bounced over to the right wall. Then he pivoted again and jumped for the rafters.

He felt them in his hands but could not get a solid grip and tumbled to the floor of the car below. He landed with a crack, the rifle burying into his shoulder.

That hurt. He exhaled and climbed slowly to his feet, brushing off his arms, legs, and shoulder. Aldo looked up to the ceiling and could barely see the rafters. He'd been close and had worried too much about his feet, and not enough about his hands and making a firm grasp.

One more time and then I'll have to try something else.

Aldo stood silently in the middle of the freight car. He breathed in and out, again and again.

This is it.

He made a big push off and ran full speed for the wall. He caught his stride and launched into the jump. This time he didn't look at his feet but at the other wall where he headed and as he reached it, he set his eyes on the rafters and lunged valiantly.

Aldo felt his fingers contact the wood, and he grabbed it tightly. Aldo hung there for a moment, swinging slightly as the train moved.

I couldn't do that too many times. I'll need to stay up here until I get a better idea of what's going on.

Aldo slowly pulled himself up and kicked a leg until he secured it around one of the other rafters and eased himself upward. He flipped over on top of the rafter so that he could look down. The rafters seemed stable enough. There was little to see looking down into the car, but there was a small gap between the freight car wall and the roof. He could finally see outside, if he peered closely.

Dee and Friends
First Night, Dinner

Dee, Jamal, and Mike all rose to their feet.

"I'm Dee Sanders," he said and pointing a hand, "and this is my wife Gina." They both nodded to the older woman, and she smiled and returned the nod.

As Dee seated himself, Jamal jumped in, "I'm Jamal Jones and this is my wife Angelic."

"I should hope she is young man," replied the older woman. Angelic smiled broadly as Jamal sat down.

The older woman looked up at Mike. "And last but not least."

Mike smiled at her. "Mike Williams and my wife Keno." Then he seated himself.

"Thank you for that," Anna replied. "I appreciate your courtesy." She adjusted her silverware and looked up at the group. "Are you all together?"

"Yes ma'am," said Gina.

The older woman smiled. "No need to call me that, I'm just Anna. How far are you sailing?"

"We're going all the way to Amsterdam," replied Mike.

"That will be lovely," said Anna. "That's where I'm going, where I live now."

Anna
On the 1st Train, En Route

Anna heard the whistle, and the train pulled slowly away. She quickly adjusted the painting crate and climbed to the roof. The train was moving along a side rail and heading back to the main track. *Surely they'll turn north now.*

She wondered if there had been other crates placed in other cars. It seemed a long way to travel for just a couple of items. Anna got down and made her way to the two new crates. The larger one said "Property" and turning to the thinner, upright crate she saw "Rembrandt" stenciled across the side. Anna smiled to herself. *That might explain the detour and the stop. The Nazis love the "old masters".*

The train slowly gained speed as Anna realized they had departed the rail yard and were back on open track. *We should turn anytime now and head for Frankfurt.*

Aldo
On the 2nd Train, En Route

Aldo settled in on the rafters. He was sort of comfortable but knew he'd get stiff soon in the prone position he was resting. Glancing out the opening, Aldo sensed only that he was well inside Germany. The train went into a long slow turn and he could tell they were now heading in a more northerly direction. *Perhaps Berlin was the destination.* Aldo made himself lie as still as possible and tried to rest until something developed.

He closed his eyes and thought back in time. *Anna seemed so young when I first met her. I wasn't much older, a couple of years, but I'd been fighting for what felt like a lifetime. I joined the French Resistance and worked in the area around Paris. When I came into contact with Anna and Rene, we forged a small and effective group. It had been hard not to be attracted to Anna, as was Rene, but Anna, after a short time, chose me. She and Rene had been about the same age and I felt that being a year or two older had made the difference for me. Anna saw me as an established hero. Rene had just been getting involved, the same as Anna. We've worked well together for the last two years. I maintain contact with the local organization and lead the activities our little group gets involved with. Sometimes I go out to scout missions alone, but I always go back and collect the team when there's a job to do.*

The train clacked along the rails and Aldo's eyes soon closed and his head drooped to the side as he slept.

Rene
On the 3rd Train, En Route

Rene noticed the train was on a long straight stretch and climbed out of the metal cylinder where he had been stationed. He could see nothing along the train; half expecting guards perched at various intervals, Rene kept low to the platform.

He slowly made his way toward the half-tracks. Getting to the edge of the car he was on, Rene thought at first he might have to climb down and then back up from one car to the next. But gauging the distance, he felt he could comfortably span the areas between the cars. Plus, it was miserably cold in the open and it would be faster to jump so that he got re-hidden before someone saw him. Surely the guards had pulled inside to make the train less conspicuous to observers. Rene covered the distance of the second flatcar and jumped to the third with the half-tracks.

Approaching the vehicles slowly, Rene worried that there might be someone else, trying to stay out of the cold, housed inside the cab. He saw no sign of anyone in either truck. Slowly he tried the door of the first cab, his MP-40 at the ready.

Opening it, he saw the truck was empty. He quickly climbed inside and closed the door behind him. While it was still cold, he was out of the wind and, in a moment, he realized that his own body heat would warm the contained space. It was far better than being outside.

He could lie across the seat and rest. With a small motion, Rene could raise his head and glance out the window to determine his location. He sighed in relief and rubbed his hands together.

Something to eat would be good now, he thought as he reached inside the pocket of his jacket. He was in Belgium and he had some time to rest. He lay back and closed his eyes.

Anna and I were so young when we met Aldo. I adored Anna, but she quickly fell for Aldo. He was older and experienced. Anna was so beautiful, and such a fighter. It was fun, if you could say such a thing about war, to fight and work with them. There really had been little fighting, only a time or two. Most of our missions were to distract, disable or misdirect and, most importantly, to not get caught or killed.

Anna
On the 1st Train, En Route

Anna walked around the car again, looking at crates with property or painters' names stenciled upon them. That was the entire contents. She sat on a crate but then thought to check her location. Making her way to where she could climb and see, Anna thought for a moment about the others. *Where were Aldo and Rene? Why were the trains separated? Hopefully, we will all get together again in Berlin.*

She climbed up the crate and looked outside. Watching for a moment, Anna observed the shadows and noted that the train was still moving due east. *I'm going to rest for a bit and check again later.* She felt a little woozy as she climbed down and lay upon the large property crate beneath her.

Anna closed her eyes. We *have come so far, moving around all the time, the three of us hopping from job to job. Slowly becoming better friends, we spend all our time together. I feel bad for Rene as Aldo and I grow closer and became intimate. Rene is always left out, but he never complains. His passion keeps him warm.*

Dee and Friends
First Night, Dinner

"Did you sail down from Amsterdam?" asked Gina.

Anna paused for a second, looking at each of them. "No, I flew into Bucharest, Romania, to see some friends who were there visiting. I stayed for several days. We went to the Black Sea, toured the city, ate well, and caught up with each other."

"That must have been fun," said Angelic.

"It was. But it made me want to slow down a little and take my time getting home. I saw this cruise and here I am, with you lovely people."

"Simone sounds like a French name. Are you from Netherlands?" asked Dee.

"You're quite astute Mr. Sanders."

"We're always teasing him about that," said Mike.

"You just have to tell him to be quiet," added Keno.

Anna smiled. "I love inquisitive minds. He's quite right. I am originally French, although I have lived in Amsterdam for many years. I enjoy being on the water."

"So do we and there's always room for one more," added Jamal.

"Thank you. Then we should have quite a good cruise. I'll enjoy hearing each of your stories."

"And we'll want to hear yours as well, if you want to tell it," said Gina.

Anna smiled at the group and raised her glass in a toast. "New friends."

Aldo
On the 2nd Train, En Route

Aldo nodded in and out as the train slowly rolled across Germany.

He allowed his mind to wander back to the first mission they were assigned. *We were to disrupt a convoy of Nazi supply trucks delivering food and weapons to an outpost near the border of Vichy, France. The plan had been simple—Anna was to stand by the road in peasant girl attire and then wave to flag down the convoy. When they stopped, she would dive into a nearby ditch and Rene and I would send a rocket into the first and last trucks in the convoy. It might have worked if there had been only two trucks, but there were four and the two in the middle were full of German troops.*

Anna stood by the side of the dirt road attired in a tight fitting blouse and a long skirt with a high slit. Her hair was down and she smiled and waved seductively at the first vehicle in the convoy.

"Bonjour, Bonjour!" she cried out.

The truck rolled to a stop. Anna stayed in place and the passenger door opened and a soldier climbed down. As he took two steps forward, I unleashed the first rocket on the truck. Anna dove in the ditch and I heard the second rocket go off.

German soldiers began pouring out of the two middle trucks.

"Schnell, Schnell!" one of them cried out as he waved his MP-40 at the scattering soldiers.

I stood and fired several rounds from my MP-40 at the advancing troops. Then I dropped and ran. Rene did the same at the other end of the column. We disappeared into the forest beyond.

The soldiers surrounded Anna, who was still lying in the ditch. The closest one fired a round of slugs in the bank beside her. Anna threw her hands up to her face as dirt and gravel cascaded on top of her.

"Halt," screamed the officer as he stepped toward Anna. The group of soldiers drew closer, surrounding her.

Another officer stepped through the group waving a pistol. "Ruckzug, ruckzug."

The soldiers moved away. The officer took Anna by the arm and helped her from the ditch. Then he motioned with his pistol toward the remaining trucks.

Rene and I watched through binoculars from a nearby treetop.

The Nazis climbed into the remaining two trucks, Anna in the front of the lead truck with the officer, and the remainder of the convoy drove away.

Dee and Friends
The First Night

They finished dinner and offered to escort Anna back to her cabin.

"The crewman that rolled you up to the table, shall I call for him?" asked Gina. "Are you alone?"

"Yes, but not really. I have my dog Ate, that's short for A8; he is my only traveling companion. He's never let me down. It's no small trick to get him onboard, but he travels with me everywhere and I have used this ship line many times."

"Allow me," said Mike while rising to his feet. He positioned himself behind her wheelchair.

"I'm ready," said Anna.

Making their way out of the dining room, they moved forward on the ship and at Anna's direction took the elevator from the middle deck to the upper deck.

"I only use this chair for longer walks. I can navigate around my cabin and for short distances."

She pointed to a stateroom they were coming upon.

"You're just down from us," said Angelic. "We have the three staterooms at the end of the hallway."

"That's excellent, my dear. We shan't have far to go to visit with one another. I really enjoy sitting on my balcony during the day. You all shall have to come and see me when you have some time."

"When would be good?" asked Gina.

"Anytime in the afternoon would work. I sleep in a bit at this stage of life but I'll look forward to seeing you all." Anna opened her stateroom and rolled inside, waved, and closed the door behind her.

"I bet she's got some stories," said Jamal.

"And I bet we'll get to hear them," replied Dee.

Aldo
On the 2nd Train, En Route

Aldo jolted awake and rose quickly, nearly falling from his perch before remembering where he was. He steadied himself with one hand and rubbed his eyes with the other. Aldo stretched his shoulders and observed that he was already stiff. Glancing out the small open space, he studied the terrain for a few moments. There were no signs, and he appeared to be between villages. The shadows told him he was moving north.

We should finally be on the way to Berlin. Why didn't the train go through Belgium? Maybe there was a problem of some kind? Perhaps it had been safer to stay in occupied France and then cross into Germany. Frankfurt should be the next major city and I can confirm my location.

Aldo laid his shoulder back on the crossbeam. He listened to the clatter of the rails. There was still a long trip ahead of him.

The first job with Anna came back to mind. *Rene and I were stuck in the treetop as the remaining convoy pulled away. We climbed down and went to examine the remainder of the two trucks we'd rocketed. Moving in slowly, with our MP-40s drawn, we quickly checked the area. Dead soldiers and more dead soldiers, there were no supplies, but there was a moan.*

Rene ran to the second truck, and a Nazi was crawling from the wreckage. I raised my MP-40. Rene held up a hand and I slowed for a second. Flipping the man over on his back, Rene saw a neck wound and a massive chest wound. Rene placed a pistol, a confiscated Luger, to the man's temple. The man had looked up, into the sky, and then his head rolled to the side. Rene felt for a pulse; there was none. He put the Luger away.

"No use drawing attention to ourselves and wasting ammunition. Where are the supplies?" he asked.

I could only shake my head. The information passed on to me said the convoy would travel this way on this day toward the outpost near Vichy, France. Our job was to intercept it and, if successful, to contact the surrounding locals and make off with everything we could.

Then we heard sounds in the distance and froze in place. I turned the binoculars down the road beyond the ridge, the way the original convoy had come. There was another one coming.

So there'd been two convoys, and we'd attacked the one transporting troops. I'd have laughed if they hadn't carried Anna away.

Rene and I retreated into the bushes. We each had one rocket left. There were three trucks this time and they weren't that far behind the troop trucks. If the order had been reversed, the supply convoy could have radioed for help if we'd attacked them and the troop trucks would have been all over us. We got ready.

I hit the first truck in the engine, and Rene hit the third truck. The second truck tried to pull around, and I jumped from the bushes and sprayed the cab with my MP-40. The truck bounced to a stop. Rene came out of the bushes and we approached slowly.

This was the supply caravan. I had Rene inventory what was on hand and I walked back into the woods to radio our local contact for backup and removal. Now we had to go and get Anna.

Anna
On the 1st Train, En Route

Anna opened her eyes. The train was still steadily rolling along. They'd been in Metz when the train stopped. Surely they were in Germany by now.

Have we turned north?

Anna climbed up her box and looked outside. There was nothing but open country as she watched the shadows; they were still moving east. Anna tried to determine how long she had napped but couldn't get a good estimate.

We'll have to turn soon.

Anna lay back down, determined to stay awake this time. Her mind wandered.

The first job Aldo, Rene, and I went on, I was captured. It was so embarrassing. I jumped in a ditch and German soldiers surrounded me. Originally thinking I would be shot or raped, I was surprised when an officer pulled me up and placed me in a truck, taking me with them.

It still wasn't good. They'd thrown me in a makeshift cell at the outpost near the Vichy, France border. Many of the officers eyed me throughout the afternoon and early evening. I knew I was an attractive young girl and steeled myself for what was to come. Hopefully, there might be some moment when I could escape.

Several of the men had spoken to me in German. I recognized the language but did not speak it. When I'd shrugged my shoulders, they'd laughed at me. They didn't search me, which was surprising, and maybe they would yet, but in the meantime I had a knife strapped to my inner thigh. Feeling a little better about that, I waited for them to come to me.

Dee and Friends
First Night, After Dinner

"Meet in our cabin?" asked Gina. "Let's sit on the balcony, I think there's some wine in the mini-fridge."

They moved through the stateroom and onto the balcony.

"What about Anna?" asked Keno. "I bet she was a live wire in her day."

"Why do you say that?" asked Angelic.

"Just something about her, an aura, a mystery, I don't know. She just seemed a little different."

"In a refreshing way," said Jamal. "This could be a long trip and while I'm sure there will be lots to see, there may be some slow days. I bet she'll be good entertainment."

"Dee, where was it you said we are headed tomorrow, Pleven?" asked Mike. "What's that about?"

"It's about 200 miles; we'll be there in the morning, to the dock. The city is about 50 kilometers inland. We'd have to take transport."

"Is it worth it?" asked Keno.

"Pleven looks like a municipal center, an older city— architecture, churches, cathedrals, museums, that kind of thing."

"Will it be as interesting as Istanbul?" asked Angelic.

"Probably not," replied Dee.

"I say we skip it," said Gina, "Let's rest on the sundeck in the morning and talk to Anna in the afternoon."

There were nods around the group.

"There'll be lots of stops along the way. We can take it easy," replied Dee.

Rene
On the 3rd Train, En Route

Rene raised his head slightly to see out the window of the half-track. Time of day suggested he was still in Belgium. Sitting up, he scanned the horizon for any signage. There was nothing he could see. Rene expected the train was headed for Bonn or Koln, where perhaps they'd stop, once back inside Germany.

He was slightly warmer now and realized he'd been dozing.

If there was any sort of activity on the train, I would likely be trapped. I could come up shooting, but I probably wouldn't get many. But suppose it was only a couple of guards and I shot them first. What would I do? If the train was still moving, I could jump off to an unknown fate. But worse perhaps, if the train stopped inside Germany and I could get off unharmed, where would I go? What would I do? I see no options in Belgium.

Lying back down, Rene tried to get comfortable. His mind wouldn't stop racing.

The Germans had carried off Anna on our very first mission. It had gone so badly; we were lucky all three of us weren't killed, attacking a troop convoy! Then we'd hit the supply trucks a few minutes later. There was food, ammunition, medical supplies, a radio, and some clothing. Aldo had contacted the local Resistance fighters, and they had materialized out of the woods and carried everything away. The group led Aldo and me to an abandoned farmhouse they used occasionally to meet and plan. They explained where the Germans camped, wished Aldo and me luck, and disappeared into the night. The only good news was that the camp was just being set up and our earlier attack had misdirected many of the supplies, along with our attack on the troop convoy reducing the number of soldiers on hand.

Aldo and I caught a ride with a farmer headed toward the former Free Zone. Surprisingly, we rode in the front of the truck as the farmer was eager to help us and felt confident the Germans were all holed up in the new camp. He dropped us off a mile from the camp and chugged away into the night.

"What now?" I asked Aldo.

"We go get her."

"Are you crazy? They'll kill us for sure, and Anna."

"Anna may already be dead."

"Surely not. They'll keep her alive."

"For their own entertainment, perhaps?"

I hadn't thought of that. It made my skin crawl. "We have to go get her."

Aldo glanced at me. "Yes, we do."

Aldo
On the 2nd Train, En Route

Aldo stirred again and remembered where he was this time. Stretching slowly so he wouldn't dislodge himself, he glanced out the railing for several minutes. Shortly he saw a sign along the rail bed, "Frankfurt".

So, I'm moving north and likely headed for Berlin. There's still a stop somewhere for whatever contents go into this car. Surely they wouldn't just leave it empty. Germans are too efficient for that.

Laying back Aldo felt he had some time before the train arrived in Frankfurt, if that was where they stopped.

It had looked like it was going to be a disaster trying to get Anna away from the Germans. Rene and I made our way toward the outpost. We didn't have much of a plan—scout the location, hope she was still alive, look for an opportunity, and try not to get killed.

We traveled by foot, after being dropped off by a farmer, and made our way near the perimeter of the Nazi camp. Noting it was still being established, with partial buildings erected, some tents, and a few shelters, we hoped that would be helpful. We approached the camp slowly. There didn't appear to be any guards, which struck me as odd. The Resistance had been overrun when the Nazis had swept through the remainder of France, disrupting the Vichy regime. Apparently the Nazis still felt safe, at least for the moment.

I debated us sweeping in from two sides, in a pincher movement, and shooting everyone we saw. But I didn't know how many men were present. There were at least two trucks of troops from the first convoy, which rendered that idea rather foolish. We were standing there in the dark trying to decide what to do when I heard a sound.

Anna
On the 1st Train, En Route

There was a change in the sound of the tracks and Anna scrambled up the crate to look outside. They were crossing a river, from Metz heading into Germany; it had to be the Rhine. It seemed odd to her that the train still headed east and didn't turn and follow the river north. Feeling confused Anna climbed down and returned to her position on the crates. She had taken off her outer jacket to make a pillow. Her sweater kept her somewhat warm and lying down helped take her mind off of being hungry. Her stomach churned.

Where are Rene and Aldo? Where am I headed? What am I going to do when I get there? Her mind swam in circles. She tried to calm herself by remembering how she had handled trouble in the past.

The German officer had come to my cell. It was a cage really, like one you might see in a carnival or a zoo. I tried to lift it or even move it but the weight had been too great. I had observed that the cage was in a shelter rather than an enclosed structure. I could see partially into a camp that appeared to be under construction.

The officer who had put me in the truck arrived with two other officers and a soldier that unlocked my cage.

"You may leave us now," said the officer to the three others. They retreated outside the structure and disappeared into the dark.

I didn't move to leave the cell. I wanted the officer to come to me. I hadn't had time to grab the knife when the party of soldiers had entered.

The officer moved around the cell, examining me from all sides. I stayed still and let him look.

"They'll come back when I call to them. You will need to entertain us all. But first, I think you will entertain me alone," said the officer. "My name is Heinrich Schmidt and you are?"

"Anna."

"That's a lovely name for such a lovely young girl." He continued to circle the cage and this time I turned and stayed face to face with him as he did. "I like it that you are so attentive."

He stepped forward to the cage door and slowly pulled it open. I did not move.

Heinrich stepped inside. Still I did not move. He stepped closer to me and pressed his arms around my shoulders, drawing him near to my face, his breath in my ear.

"I'm sure you're quite skilled, as I've found most French girls to be," he whispered.

I closed the distance between us, my lips finding his. I breathed into his mouth and found his tongue while my hands moved at my sides.

Heinrich pulled me tighter to him.

I kept my stance, with my bare leg straining the split in my dress.

I reached one hand down slowly and drew the knife silently from its sheath. Then I raised both hands behind his back, as if to caress his shoulders, and squared myself to him. Leaning forward, I pressed my body against his. I felt him respond and relax into me.

I raised the knife and as he leaned forward, lowering his head to embrace me more fully, I plunged the blade into his neck at the base of his skull and twisted my wrists.

There was a soft gurgle and I felt Heinrich collapse. He was still alive, but not for long, and not functioning.

I struggled getting him to the floor of the cage due to his weight. I looked up for any sound or movement. Apparently the other men were expecting Heinrich to take a little more time with me.

I pulled the knife out, wiped it on Heinrich's uniform and put it back in the sheath. I liberated his sidearm and with that in hand I stepped from the cage and pushed the door closed, which made a slight click as it relocked. I paused again, looking and listening.

I slipped out the far side of the shelter and stayed in the shadows. What noises I could hear came from across the camp. Now I needed to get to the road, or better yet the forest, and disappear.

There was a motorcycle with a sidecar just beyond the shelter. I *toyed with taking it, but the noise at this time of night might be unexpected. I passed it by but had a thought; perhaps I could push it down the road a few kilometers and then start it and ride away. Good thing it's dark. The bike was heavy and I struggled to get it rolling. I was thankful for the downhill grade and the burst of adrenaline or it would have been impossible. Which way to go was my next thought.*

Rene
On the 3rd Train, En Route

Rene lay in the half-track, the train rolling steadily along, nothing had changed.

Aldo and I had retreated to the road outside the camp, unsure of what to do next. Then I heard it, a motorcycle started up not too far from us. We dashed to the side of the road and peered ahead toward the camp. I saw the bike, no headlight and a flapping of cloth or something in the wind. It only took a moment. I jumped up and ran into the road. Aldo tried to stop me but I moved onward.

"What are you doing?" called Aldo.

"It's Anna," I replied. I stood in the road and waved my arms, trying to keep my face in the moonlight so that she might see me.

The cycle faltered for a second and then died down but didn't cut off.

I ran toward her waving my arms and calling softly, "Anna, Anna."

She recognized me, stopped the bike, and hopped off to hug me tightly.

Aldo ran up, and as Anna and I swung around, I saw he had an unhappy look on his face. I released her and pointed. "Look, it's her." She stepped forward and hugged Aldo. I saw him smile.

"Let's get going," she said. "They'll be after me shortly."

I climbed into the saddle and pointed to the sidecar for the two of them. It was good we were all skinny.

Aldo
On the 2nd Train, En Route

Rene and I jumped to the side of the road as the sound of a motorcycle became clearer. I feared a German courier and possibly an escort but it looked like a single rider. Suddenly Rene ran out onto the road. I tried to stop him as he rose but he shook me off.

He waved down the rider who slowed to a stop. It was Anna.

She and Rene hugged, and I admit, it made me jealous. But she and I rode together in the sidecar while Rene drove, and it was good to hold her near me.

We had done what we were supposed to do, and had been told it was customary after a mission to disappear for a while. I had an idea.

I motioned to Rene at the next crossroad to continue north until we reached the ambush site. Once there, we grabbed a couple of Nazi helmets and a couple of jackets for camouflage. Then we turned back south, found a parallel track to travel and headed for the city of Vichy.

Anna
On the 1st Train, En Route

I pushed the motorcycle from the camp onto the road and headed north, to return the same way the truck had brought me. The bike was just outside the circle of light from the overhead posts when I heard men talking and dropped to the road.

It was an active conversation and after a few seconds, as the sound grew no closer to me, I raised my head and looked across the saddle of the bike to see the two men, the tips of their cigarettes glowing in the darkness. If they looked down the road, they would surely see me. I decided to crawl into the bushes and hide on the far side of the bike.

The men kept talking, their voices growing more in volume. Then they ground out their butts and turned toward the camp, still engrossed in whatever they were arguing about.

I leaned against the bike for a second. Now to get moving before anyone else showed up. I pushed hard to get the cycle rolling again and almost reached a trot as the road grade broke slightly downhill.

Rounding the bend away from the camp, I pushed another kilometer as the grade wound down and the road began to rise. Now was the time. I'd ridden motorcycles as a young girl. This was a BMW R75, a heavy duty and capable off-road machine. I'd seen them before. These were the biggest, the baddest, and the heaviest motorcycles the Germans rode.

I hoped the bike would start. I could have rolled it off the grade perhaps but it was too late for that now. I spun the key into position, primed it once, and kicked the starter. It fired the first time, fortunately for me. These were smooth, quiet running machines, and I hoped there were no keen-eared guards, other than the two arguing that I'd already seen.

I pulled my dress up, straddled the seat, and rolled away. The wide handlebars, which I had struggled with while pushing and trying to keep the bike on a straight path, were almost more than l could handle and they caused me to lean forward against the gas tank and air filter. My dress flapped in the wind behind me.

Anna shook the thoughts from her mind and rose to check her location. Scrambling up the crate, she glanced out and saw that the shadows of the train and surrounding countryside indicated she was still headed east.

What is happening?

Rene
On the 3rd Train, En Route

Aldo had me travel north until we reached the ambush site. There we grabbed a couple of Nazi helmets and an officer's cap. Also, a couple of tunics, one soldier and one officer, and a leather jacket for Anna. We had come from the north, home was to the north. But Aldo had me turn at the next crossroad and head east.

"Turn and find the next road to the south, we are going toward Vichy," he said.

I wanted to ask him why but I didn't feel comfortable slowing down and giving away any advantage we might have in escaping. I could only imagine the Germans would expect us to go north and perhaps by going south we could avoid them. Aldo had always served as our leader and I trusted him, so I turned. Let's see what lies ahead.

Aldo
On the 2nd Train, En Route

I knew it was 4 or 5 hours to the southern coast, to Marseille. A few days in the sun, even if it wasn't that warm, and some time by the water would be a nice break. I could use the opportunity to shore up my relationship with Anna. Rene might enjoy it as well. I doubted either of them had ever been to the ocean. I could impress them with my knowledge of the sea and the beach. It would be fun.

Aldo stirred and glanced outside the train to verify his position. He knew it was 4 or 5 hours from Frankfurt to Berlin and glancing at his watch it had been nearly an hour since he'd seen the sign. The train was still traveling north, and he wondered where or if they would stop.

After turning south, we ran a parallel track some miles east of the camp road and eventually turned back west for Vichy. All of France was occupied by the Germans at this point in time and I felt confident we could take the motorcycle all the way to the coast and back. The only issue might be an aggressive Nazi trying to confiscate it.

We stopped outside Vichy and hid the bike in the forest. We walked into town on foot so that we wouldn't be noticed and could better blend with the locals. Once in town, we ate at a café and went shopping. We bought some more food, water, and goggles for the bike. Our plan was to ride through to the beach. We looked the part and I would hide Anna at my feet and cover her with blankets when necessary. After trekking back to the bike, we got underway. We'd stop on the southern outskirts for fuel. It would only take a couple of tanks to get to the coast. If the bike didn't work, we'd do something else, maybe ditch it once there and take a chance on the train coming back or catching a ride.

Rene
On the 3rd Train, En Route

I thought Aldo was crazy taking us south. I admit I was curious, but scared, and I had to drive. We continued on for several hours and it appeared we were heading toward Marseille. The road was mostly empty, and we encountered no problems, just open countryside. Anna sat on the floor of the sidecar and while she felt the road more than Aldo and I, she could hide easily if the need arose.

Stopping at a small village just north of Avignon, we wanted to stretch, eat a bite, and look for fuel. The Italians and Germans occupied Avignon at this time and Aldo felt it best to avoid the city.

Back on the road again, we circled Avignon and continued south for Marseille. Aldo had found a map in the pocket of the sidecar. He directed me along smaller roads that would bring us into town from along the beach.

Anna
On the 1st Train, En Route

Rene jumped onto the saddle of the motorcycle, and Aldo and I climbed into the sidecar. We took off north, toward home. We only went as far as the ambush site. They gathered up some helmets and jackets. I was grateful. It was cold on the bike, even in the sidecar. After only a short distance, Aldo pointed for Rene to go east and then south, back the direction we had come from, on a parallel track. I glanced up to Aldo and motioned him toward me. He leaned over to hear.

"Why are we going south? We'll surely be caught."

He smiled at me and then whispered, "Trust me, Cherie." Aldo squeezed my shoulder affectionately.

I didn't really have a choice and smiled back weakly. I hoped he knew what he was doing.

We drove for a time and stopped outside Vichy, where we ate lunch and bought a couple of things for the trip.

We continued again for a couple of hours before stopping outside Avignon where we refueled the motorcycle. From there, we took back roads to get to Marseille.

Anna's head jerked at a bump on a trestle. She shook the old thoughts away and rose to check her position. Climbing to the top, she glanced out to the German countryside. Deciding to stay vigilant for a while, she tried to plan for when the train stopped. From what she could see the train was still moving east. She watched for what seemed like a long time. In the distance she thought there was a sign along the railroad berm. Anna watched intently as the sign drew nearer. She squinted to make it out. At last she could read, "Stuttgart".

It makes no sense at all. We're headed toward the Black Forest and maybe beyond, to Bavaria. Could the art be heading for the Neuschwanstein Castle?

The Nazis, specifically the Einsatzstab Reichsleiter

Rosenberg or ERR as it was known—the German art-looting organization, managed all the confiscated and stolen art from their location at the castle.

Hitler had plans for a great museum, filled with what he considered the world's finest art. *I'm growing desperate now. The castle was remotely located in southwest Germany, in Bavaria. Could I hide on the train? If I managed to escape, it would be a long way from Paris or Berlin, alone. How could the information the Resistance passed along have been so wrong, or so incomplete?*

She climbed back down and laid her head against the jacket pillow she had fashioned. It was still a couple of hours to arrive in Munich and the castle was beyond, so it would be longer before they arrived. Anna lay still, trying to think.

Do I try to get off the train? I can't sabotage the art. What damage, chaos, or confusion can I cause? How do I get back home? I will surely die here.

Anna was stiff and tired from the long ride. She was very hungry and felt nauseated. The clatter of the rails soon drew her back to sleep and to her dreams.

Dee and Friends
Second Day

We started on the sundeck late in the morning, after breakfast in the main dining room. The food was good, and we weren't nearly so crowded as on the big cruise ships.

"I think I like this," said Jamal.

"How's that?" replied Mike.

"I have a fair amount of room. I slept well, breakfast was good, and the weather is nice. I'm with my lovely wife and friends."

"Doesn't get any better, does it?" said Keno.

"Another day in paradise?" asked Mike.

"You people are all crazy," added Gina with a smile. "Let's go talk to Anna."

"Why don't we bring her up here?" asked Dee.

"Great idea," answered Gina. "I'll go check with her."

"I'll go too," said Keno.

"I'd better supervise," added Angelic.

The three of them rose from their chairs on the sundeck and started for the elevator.

"I suppose she'll be in her wheelchair, perhaps we'd better grab another umbrella," said Dee.

"If she comes up?" added Mike.

"I think she'll be along," said Jamal. "Those are three persuasive ladies."

"I agree, but I think it'll be her choice. I sense she can hold her own and makes decisions based upon what she wants to do," replied Dee.

"Maybe we shouldn't let the women around her too much," added Mike.

Jamal threw a pillow at him. "Help me get the umbrella."

———

A few minutes later the ladies reappeared, Angelic pushing Anna's wheelchair and Gina and Keno scurrying along on each side.

"Gentlemen," Anna called out as the group rolled up to the loungers. "It's so nice of you to ask me to join you. It is so beautiful up here and I had planned to get out earlier. But this worked out well.

Let me get everyone something to drink." With that, she raised her hand and the steward immediately appeared.

Jamal and Dee looked at one another quickly, sharing the quiet thought of *that was impressive.*

The group settled in a semi-circle around Anna with their drinks in hand.

"Tell us about yourself," said Gina.

Aldo
On the 2nd Train, En Route

Aldo rubbed his eyes and glanced outside the train. They were still moving north. He felt the engine decelerate slightly and craned his head to see further down the tracks. There was a sign in the distance that read "Kassell". Located there was the Fieseler aircraft plant and Henschel & Sohn manufacturing facilities for the German Tiger tanks. It was an important town for the Nazis. Perhaps there was something to pick up.

He felt the train continue to slow and was sure now that they would be stopping. Aldo glanced about the car again and reminded himself how dark it was and how little he or anyone else could see. That was his only defense, or start shooting. But with his curiosity aroused now, he wanted to know what the Nazis would bring aboard. Aldo felt the train continuing to slow and he could see it was easing into a small station with a couple of warehouses beyond the tracks.

The train came to a complete stop and Aldo did his best to make himself small. He checked his legs and feet, making sure they were securely on top of the crossbeams. He held the MP-40 beside him so that he could rise and fire quickly, if needed.

The doors to the car opened, and soldiers quickly jumped inside. They didn't look up.

We are deep in Germany; they have no reason to be suspicious. I just hope this goes quickly.

The soldiers moved several heavy wooden crates into the car. Aldo could see the boxes were stamped with "aircraft parts". There were also several metal tubes, similar to the ones on the train Rene had been on. Then there were boxes of supplies. Aldo couldn't read the labels from his position. The soldiers had filled the car from the middle and left only a few feet of space at each end. Aldo had been grateful for that.

It made sense, but it didn't. The aircraft plant is here. Why would the Nazis be moving parts? Could it be another airfield, onsite repairs, a different plant, or maybe something different? Maybe it wasn't really aircraft parts and what about all the supplies and the metal tubes? He dismissed that thought quickly as several engine blocks were dollied aboard, then more boxes. The car was almost full.

Aldo was watching intently and leaned forward on one of the cross beams to see better. The board groaned softly. One soldier had just stood up and turned his head toward the sound. He was near the door and what little light there was shifted to darkness between him and Aldo. The soldier stared up into the corner for a long time.

Aldo dared not to breathe. He didn't even blink. If the soldier made a move toward him, Aldo was prepared to pull the MP-40 forward and open fire. It was the only way.

The soldier stared for several more seconds, a lifetime to Aldo. Then his companion bumped his shoulder.

"Schnell!"

They turned together and started for the cargo door. As the soldiers jumped to the ground, Aldo allowed himself to breathe. It was a slight sigh but it shuddered across his entire body. The door clanged shut and darkness returned.

Rene
On the 3rd Train, En Route

Rene woke as he realized the train was slowing. He glanced over the dash of the half-track, trying to stay low and out of sight.

We must be in Germany by now. I'm not surprised they're stopping.

The train pulled into a station and slowed. Rene couldn't see where they were. He had a couple of guesses but was afraid to move in the open cab. Lying quietly, Rene waited and listened for sounds. He heard some shouting, engineers or train workers. They sat for several minutes and the train moved again.

It had either been a fuel or water stop, or whatever had been taken off or put on was done quickly.

Rene rose slightly and looked around him. There were a few scattered buildings.

There, on the side of that one, "Koln". The train continued east and I assume it's still on its way to Berlin. I lay back down. There were several hours to go. Rest while I can.

We were outside Marseille, traveling along the water. It was cold, but beautiful. The motorcycle didn't help, and we'd been riding long enough now that I wasn't sure I could walk a straight line when I got to get off the wretched thing.

Aldo and Anna were both covered by the blankets and were holding each other. I only had my jacket which had proven tight and I'd had to unzip it somewhat to handle the big bike. Leaning forward had helped some, but I was ready to get off the monster.

Aldo punched me in the shoulder and pointed to the side of the road. I pulled off behind some trees and we climbed slowly off the bike and out of the sidecar.

fifteen, but my parents were elderly and fearful for their own lives. I think my parents felt George would care for and look out for me when they were no longer able. I didn't completely agree with that thought, but I married him. We were mounted on horseback and stood in the middle of the creek while the minister read us our vows from a little promontory. My parents stood on the shore.

"It only lasted a short time. My parents died early in WWII. I think it may have scared them to death, as they'd seen the horrors of WWI. When the Germans invaded France, the Nazis arrested George for growing the garden. He shared the produce with our neighbors instead of providing it to them. When he denied their accusations and argued with them, he was gunned down and the garden burned. They saw him as a broken old man for whom they had no use. I held him in my arms, blood coursing from his body and covering mine. I watched the light flicker from his eyes. At that moment, it was the hardest thing I had ever done."

"That's so sad. How did you manage?" asked Angelic.

"Afterwards, I joined the Resistance to avenge my family —my parents and my husband. I met, worked with, and eventually fell in love with a young Frenchman. He was slightly older than me and while I loved my first husband and always will, there was something intoxicating, enchanting, and enticing about the Frenchman. We grew close. We worked together and played together. We had a purpose."

Aldo
On the 2nd Train, En Route

The train moved slowly forward. Aldo couldn't resist. He dropped from his perch to examine the new contents. He held the MP-40 at the ready as he moved among the boxes. Glancing about, he saw crates marked aircraft parts and machine parts, loose tubing, tank treads, stray things he didn't recognize, as well as pieces of several aircraft engines.

It makes little sense. The aircraft plant and tank plant are here in town so the pickup must be for field sites. We're still heading northeast. It's another four hours to Berlin. I would think they'd want replacement parts closer to the front lines, not closer to the capital. There is time to sabotage these items. If nothing else, I can open the doors and push them out of the boxcar. I might have to jump too. I was hoping to ride all the way to Berlin and slip out in the big rail yard there, maybe meet the others. Time to decide.

Rene
On the 3rd Train, En Route

We strolled slowly along the road in the sun. It wasn't very warm, but it felt good to walk after that long ride. I could smell the salt spray in the air. I knew we were close.

After a mile or so, an old truck chugged up behind us. We had heard the sound and could tell that it wasn't the Nazis, just a farm truck laboring along the way.

Anna waved to the driver while Aldo and I stood silent and still beside her. As the man slowed to a halt, Anna approached the passenger window and spoke to him before waving us over.

We sat on the back of the bed, our legs dangling inches above the road as the farmer drove slowly into town.

He let us out in the old city square and chugged away with a wave of his hand.

"Let's go down to the water," said Aldo. "The main pier and beach are just beyond those steps. Follow me." It was something we were good at.

We went down the steps quickly; neither Anna nor I had been to the ocean or a beach before. We came from farm families and they traveled little, especially between the great wars.

The waves were rolling in and they seemed massive at first glance. I learned in the few short days that followed, while we were at the beach, such waves were common and rather ordinary, with the incoming tide.

Aldo ran for the water and Anna and I followed. He shouted and threw his hands in the air, running about in circles. At that moment, an observer would never have known there was a war going on.

The train rattled over a trestle, and Rene woke with a start. Glancing out the window of the half-track he saw a town that lay just ahead. There was a sign that said Kassel. There were aircraft and munitions plants located there.

I wonder if we'll stop. What might we offload or take on? I'd better be prepared.

With that, Rene rolled into the foot well and crouched below the dash, his head positioned so that he might pop up and take a quick look when needed.

The train slowed almost to a stop and then gathered speed and pulled through the station. Rene leaned against the seat and exhaled.

For sure, I thought there would be a conflict there.

The train continued northeast toward Berlin. Rene lay back in the seat, his legs feeling the strain from the squat where he had crouched.

Anna
On the 1st Train, En Route

We were walking along the road, Aldo and I holding hands. The air was light, and it smelled of the sea. I would have been content to walk into town but a farmer in an old truck picked us up and then dropped us in the town square. Aldo led us down to the ocean. As we descended the steps, I looked up and saw the water for the first time. The tide splashed onto the beach and the sun shone off the waves in a brilliant rainbow. The air was cool, but I felt warm inside. It was magnificent.

We ran along the beach and I just wanted to stay there by the water forever, never to return home, no more problems, no more war. I wanted to be free.

We strolled for a time and then made our way ashore. It was late afternoon, and we were hungry. Stopping at a small café, Aldo purchased bread and cheese that we shared at a small table off the street.

"It's getting late, where will we stay?" asked Rene.

"We should be able to find a hostel," replied Aldo.

"How will we afford it?"

Aldo smiled at me. "I have enough money for a couple of rooms for a couple of days."

Rene looked curious. "Where did you get it?"

"I took it from one of the dead soldiers in the convoy. He didn't need it, and we did."

Aldo
On the 2nd Train, En Route

I really can't decide what to do about the crates. I feel like it will be a few hours before reaching Berlin. Aldo sits on the floor and leans back against one of the aircraft engines and drifts off again.

We ran along the beach, wonder and amazement written on Anna's and Rene's faces. The wind whipped our hair, and the waves crashed on the shore. We spent the afternoon there and then ate at a small café. I led the way to a small hostel on the boulevard above the beach.

"We'll take two rooms for two days," I said to the hostel clerk, an elderly woman with gray hair and glasses. She was thin with a pinched face and a sniffle as she handed me one key and Anna the other.

As we moved down the hall toward the rooms, I took the key from Anna and handed it to Rene. Then I took Anna's hand and led her to the first room.

Anna
On the 1st Train, En Route

When Aldo took the key from me and handed it to Rene, I wasn't surprised. I'd been expecting him to approach me for some time. I allowed him to take my hand and lead me into the room.

We closed the door and turned to each other. Aldo embraced me and we kissed, softly at first and then more intently as he pulled me closer to him. I could feel the heat from his body and the rising temperature of my own.

Aldo was a couple of years older than me and I had wondered about his experiences with other girls. I doubted there had been any women, probably just hopeless flirtations and foreplay. I, however, had been a married woman. I knew what I was doing. I only hoped that he did as well.

There was a change in sound and Anna shook herself awake. She quickly climbed to her observation point and looked out. After a moment she realized the train was crossing a river. Coming out of Stuttgart, it must be the Danube, which meant they headed for Munich.

Rene
On the 3rd Train, En Route

I stood in the hallway as Aldo led Anna away. The moment had been coming for some time. I had seen it, felt it. Saddened, but not surprised, I made my way next door. I stepped inside and sat on the empty bed. At least we had private rooms. Aldo had paid for them, now it seemed obvious why. We could have ended up in a common room with bunks.

I got up to go to the community toilet at the end of the hall. There was a tall water closet visible through the open door and a very shapely pair of legs emerged. Perhaps Aldo wouldn't be the only lucky one.

A skirt fell in place, and I realized someone had been bent over. Approaching slowly, I made my way toward the room. Just as I arrived, a young woman came out. She was quite beautiful; her face angelic, like some paintings I had seen as a boy, but she was shorter and rounder than Anna. The young woman smiled. Her teeth were green with decay. She nodded at me and moved down the hall. Perhaps I wasn't so lucky, but then maybe I was.

Rene woke and rose slightly in his seat. The train was steadily moving along to the northeast. It was growing colder and he could feel the air seeping into the surrounding cab.

Hopefully, we'll get there soon.

Anna, Dee and Friends
Second Day
On the Sundeck

Anna shook the ice in her glass. "I seem to have finished my drink. Would anyone like another? I believe I'll have one more." She raised a finger to the waiter, who responded immediately. "Anyone else want something?"

No one raised a hand. They were immersed in Anna's story and had ignored their drinks.

"I think you had us mesmerized," said Angelic.

"It's an old story from long ago. I'm sure you have other interesting things to keep you busy."

"We'd love to hear more," replied Gina.

Anna sat back in her chair as the waiter placed the new drink in front of her. "Our first mission with Aldo was really a mess. I ended up getting captured, then escaped and reunited with the others. We went to the beach to celebrate."

"Give us the details," said Keno. "At least the ones you want to share."

Anna sighed and then smiled.

Aldo
On the 2nd Train, En Route

I decide to open the railcar doors and push out whatever I could budge, then jump out after and try to make my way back, perhaps another train bound for Paris.

The engine slowed, and Aldo froze in place. It had only been an hour since leaving Kassel. That put their location near the Kohnstein. He listened intently.

The Kohnstein was a mountain that housed an underground factory. The purpose was to protect it from the Allied bombers, but the practical reason, for the war effort, was to build V-1 bombs, V-2 missiles, rockets, 162 jet fighters, all kinds of nasty things. It was rumored to be the headquarters for all the Nazis attempts at new and improved technology. There'd been talk of atomic energy—a bomb big enough to end the war. Also mentioned were chemical and biological weapons, a throwback to the First World War, or something newer and deadlier.

Could this have been the destination all along and not Berlin? I am beginning to have serious doubts. If the train ends its journey here—I'll never get out of the tunnel alive.

Aldo had noticed the darkness falling as the train had left Kassel. It should have been pitch dark by now. He had been traveling all day. But there was light outside the car, a weak iridescent that probably came from overhead lighting or spotlights. Aldo breathed the air, and it was thicker and no longer smelled of the countryside or the train. There were mixed mechanical and chemical odors. The train continued to slow and then ground to a halt.

Anna
On the 1st Train, En Route

My stomach is clenching, from hunger I presume, but I also feel nauseated, probably from the long ride and the constant motion. If the train is headed for the art castle, I have no idea how I'll get back to Paris. I'm not likely to find any Resistance that deep in Bavaria. Maybe I can make it to Switzerland but crossing the border out of Germany will be difficult.

———

Aldo had been clumsy but strong and energetic. The two days passed quickly, and we left the room only to grab some food. I was quite satisfied with our relationship when we headed back for the motorcycle and our return home. Only then did I think to wonder what Rene had been doing all that time.

Rene
On the 3rd Train, En Route

I only saw them once in the next two days. Aldo came out of the room and gave me some money to buy food. Then he disappeared again. I ate at the small café where we had stopped before. I chose odd hours to keep away from crowds. I toured the city in a similar fashion, staying hidden as much as possible but curious to see the sights and the ocean. I sat on the beach for hours and watched the docks from a distance. There was a great deal of Nazi activity, both coming and going. I wasn't clear on the latest Nazi or Allied offensives but knew enough to stay far away and unobserved. I also spent some time walking about the Old Town. It was a beautiful place, and I hated to leave to return to war. But I was lonely and no one ever lies about being lonely or alone. I was ready to go home.

The train slowed, and Rene popped up to look. It had been about an hour since the train had last slowed in Kassel.

What now? Berlin would be a couple more hours.

Then it went dark. Rene had looked up just in time to see the train pull into a tunnel. But it kept going and then there were overhead lights and noises and people moving about.

We're in the Nazi mountain stronghold. That's where this stuff is going, not Berlin. I'll never get out of here alive. I hope Anna and Aldo went to Berlin. Maybe they can find one another.

Anna
On the 1st Train, En Route

We walked back to the bike, and nothing had been disturbed. Rene seemed happy to see us, if a little tired and perturbed.

"Let's get home."

Aldo nodded and replied, "Same arrangement. You drive, I'll ride, and Anna will sit in the floorboard or my lap."

Aldo couldn't keep his hands to himself on the trip home, and I didn't stop him. I'm surprised we made it as Rene was the only one paying attention to the road.

I think we went back the same way we had come, except at Dijon we ditched the bike and hitchhiked the rest of the way to Paris. It was a great trip, a big adventure. We were now definitely in the Resistance, in the war.

Anna, Dee and Friends
Second Day
On the Sundeck

"That was just the first of our missions. After we returned to Paris and to our homes, we took part in several more over the next two years. Aldo and I remained a couple. Rene never settled down. We did everything together, all three of us. I think Aldo took a certain pleasure in holding me over Rene but Rene never let on that it bothered him."

"That must have been difficult," said Angelic. "It appears that you were quite fond of Rene."

"Oh, certainly that's true. But it was more like we were sister and brother."

"Did he see it that way?" asked Gina.

"I doubt it. But I was, not really in love, but certainly infatuated with Aldo." After a pause she added, "I was young. I thought there'd be more time."

The cruise was rounding a bend in the river. The sun came from behind a cloud and washed over them in a dazzling display of light, igniting the shore along both sides of the ship.

"It's beautiful on the river," said Gina.

"Yes, it is. I've always enjoyed the Danube."

Rene
On the 3rd Train, En Route

As the train slowed to a stop in the middle of a switch yard, Rene peeked from behind the dash of the half-track. There were several other trains and as his pulled abreast of them, Rene saw identifying numbers on the engines.

There, "5258", it's one of the engines I saw in Paris. They were all the big Nazi war locomotives, steam trains. Was it Anna or Aldo on that one? Can't remember, but surely one of them is here. Maybe together we can find a way home.

Rene crouched back down in the floorboard.

I need to find a way off this thing. How will they unload? Surely everything was coming here and the train won't go on, or who knows where it might go afterward. I'm in the middle of the switching station. Maybe now is the time to crawl into the back of the half-track and hide. Look for an opportunity to bail out of it while in transit. But what about Anna or Aldo, how do I hook up with them? I need to get to that other train.

Aldo
On the 2nd Train, En Route

Aldo climbed swiftly back to his perch as the train came to a halt.

This time was easy. I had a lot of motivation. If they see me they'll kill me, no time for explanation.

He sat motionless on the rafter, his legs wrapped tightly around the boards and the MP-40 clutched in his hands, ready to fire.

The car door slid open and a group of Nazi soldiers jumped into the car, laughing and shouting to one another in rapid fire German.

I wish I knew the language. I'll have to settle for observing their actions and attitude.

The soldiers moved quickly about the car and collected the crates and parts in an assembly line, then moved to the dock outside. As the car emptied, none of the soldiers glanced up.

Aerial is a great point of view.

The soldiers departed, jumping from the car. The last one stopped and another man, an officer, jumped up and inside.

"Was ist los?" asked the soldier.

Looks like a problem of some kind.

The officer glanced around the car without looking up. He held up three fingers. "Drei lokomotive, Paris?"

The soldier shook his head. "Zwei lokomotive, Paris. Eins, München."

That sounds a lot like two trains here and one to Munich. I bet Rene is on the other, the equipment train. He's the one who should be here.

Anna, Dee and Friends
Second Day
On the Sundeck

Anna put her second drink down, now empty. "Well, I've enjoyed your company, but I think I'm about talked out. I'd better get back to my room and rest."

"We'd be happy to take you back," said Keno, glancing at the other two women.

"I'd like that."

The three women rose and Angelic, with Gina alongside, rolled Anna's wheelchair while Keno led the way back to her room.

"Those were quite some stories," said Dee.

"You don't believe her?" asked Jamal.

"Absolutely I believe her. I expect she gave us the sanitized version for mixed company and new acquaintances."

Mike laughed briefly. "What makes you say that?"

"You don't live to be ninety-plus and not learn something from the mistakes you've made and from the things you've seen. She's a survivor—someone who's done what they had to do, in a hard place and time."

The three women were approaching on their return from Anna's room.

"Wasn't that exciting?" said Gina.

"An amazing story and background," added Angelic.

"I'm awed," said Keno.

"I think we all are," replied Dee. "I expect she can keep us entertained throughout the journey."

"All we have to do is pay attention," said Jamal.

Aldo
On the 2nd Train, En Route

Aldo stayed in position on the rafters for a few minutes. Both soldiers had departed and the car door stood open.

I guess that lets them know the car is empty.

Aldo dropped to the floor of the railcar as quietly as he could, taking the shock in his knees as he landed. He eased to the door and peeked out to one side without revealing himself. There was another train on the next track and several others farther away.

Changing positions, to the other side of the freight door, Aldo could see down the track and more of the other train. It was the equipment train. Aldo remembered the large piping and the half-tracks.

That's Rene's train. Where would he be?

Aldo checked in both directions and, seeing no one, slipped out of the car he was in and quickly crossed over to the other train. Moving slowly along the track, he stayed crouched and close to the train.

Rene should be hidden, what were the options? There weren't many boxcars, mostly flatbeds with equipment stacked, parked or chained.

Aldo moved farther along the rail. He was coming up on the half-tracks when suddenly he froze. Coming from his left were a group of three soldiers. They were in some kind of discussion. Aldo stood still as a statue. He didn't even breathe.

The soldiers were chatting animatedly and Aldo would swear one of them's eyes passed right across him. But there was no recognition.

Sometimes you don't see things if you don't expect them to be there. The soldiers are in a hidden underground fortress deep in their own country.

Aldo finally exhaled as the soldiers moved farther away.

Rene

On the 3rd Train, En Route

Rene sat in the half-track for some time, trying to decide what to do.

Anna or Aldo is here. I can't leave without them.

Rene raised his head cautiously over the dash and looked about. There were three soldiers approaching in his direction and, just as he was about to duck, he saw it.

Just behind the soldiers was Aldo, frozen stiff as a statue against the train. Rene ducked as the soldiers approached. He could hear their voices as they passed. Quickly he raised his head again and Aldo was still standing there. Rene glanced quickly in both directions and could see no one approaching.

He slid open the door of the half-track just enough to slip out onto the flatbed. Rene, crouched low, took a couple of steps, enough to put him in Aldo's line of vision. Then he waved one hand slowly, hoping to get Aldo's attention but not to startle him.

Aldo
Mittelwerk
In the Switching Yard at the Underground Factory

Aldo was trying to decide what to do.

I can't stay here. I have to be moving. Wait!

He saw the hand waving, and as he expanded his field of vision, realized it was Rene. His adrenaline spiked. He nodded in the direction and the hand motioned toward him.

Aldo looked quickly in both directions and then took off in a low crouch for the half-tracks and Rene.

Rene
Mittelwerk
On the 3rd Train in the Switching Yard

I motion Aldo in my direction when he finally sees me. We can hide in the half-tracks and plan what to do next.

Aldo reached the flatcar and Rene lowered a hand to pull him up and onto the deck. They both scurried for the half-track and piled into the front seat floorboard.

Aldo and Rene
Mittelwerk
On the 3rd Train in the Switching Yard

They clasped hands and hugged one another briefly.

"What are the chances we actually find one another?" said Aldo.

Rene nodded. "Where's Anna?"

Aldo looked down for a moment. "I think she's on her way to Munich."

"What?"

"I overheard two soldiers on the other train talking, two trains here, and one to Munich."

"How will she get back? How will we help her?"

"I think right now we better help ourselves."

Anna
On the 1st Train, En Route

Anna could no longer sleep and after turning over several times on the crate, got up to check her position.

Climbing slowly to the top of the car, she felt weak all over and very much alone. Reaching her position, she studied the landscape. The train was following along a river.

We crossed the Danube a while back. We'd not be running along beside it now. This must be a tributary, which means we're probably running due south and no longer southeast. That must mean we are going to the art castle. It can't be very far. Where can I hide? I can't be sick now.

Aldo and Rene
Mittelwerk
On the 3rd Train in the Switching Yard

"What are our options?" asked Rene.

"We can retreat or we can fight. Fighting won't take long, we'll be dead. Retreating, we might have a chance. We can stay in this half-track, hide in the back. When the Nazis offload it, we see where they take it. Maybe they drive right out of here," replied Aldo.

"Or maybe they park it in a corner."

"Maybe."

"Shouldn't we try to do damage? Isn't that what we were sent for?"

"There's damage and there's suicide."

"Yeah, but look at this place. The secret underground headquarters for development. We could make quite an impact."

"Or we could live to fight another day. Might be more helpful in the long run."

"Are you afraid?"

"It would seem the wisest course of action."

"I'm not. I'm not afraid to die."

"I'm the team leader, you follow me. We get out of here."

Anna
On the 1st Train, En Route

Anna felt the train slowing and then ease to a stop. One more time she climbed to her vantage point. Looking out, she could see the castle. It was enormous and very grand, very ornate. Sitting on a promontory no doubt made it seem even larger as there was tier after tier climbing into the sky. The train sat on the main line, steam still rising from the engine. There was a single rail line that ran down a small gorge to the foot of the castle. The train pulled slowly forward.

Anna backed into the corner of the car and positioned herself behind one of the crates. There was absolutely nowhere to go.

So, I'm going to die in a damp, dark, smelly boxcar in southern Bavaria, miles from home. It seems like such a waste. There was nothing I could do to the art. Destroying it would have been worse than stealing it. I'll miss my friends.

Dee and Friends
Second Day

After sitting on the sundeck for another hour, the group had broken up and gone to their staterooms to prepare for dinner. While in Istanbul, they had slipped into the habit of dressing for dinner, but having very little in luggage with them, they had to make do with the clothes they had.

Dee stood, watching his wife Gina slip into a V-necked pullover and an expensive pair of jeans. He knew she would add heels, partly because she was short, but it also completed her desired look.

I am so lucky. When we first met on that Pacific cruise, I was single. Formerly an accountant and human resource manager at a large metropolitan television station, Dee was widowed and had decided to take a cruise. He met and made friends, then later married one of them, Gina.

They, the group of friends, had been on a slice cruise, where travelers leave from one port and eventually arrive at another at their journey's end. The ship they were on had a mechanical issue and several passengers were transferred to a nearby sister ship. Unfortunately for Dee and his friends, their lifeboat was caught by a rogue wave and washed away from the cruise ships. They were not recovered by nightfall and a huge storm hit, carrying them away. After the storm subsided, the survivors on the lifeboat drifted onto a deserted island where they remained for approximately four months until being discovered by the Coast Guard. As a result of the adventure, and some recovered treasure, the group decided to stay together and travel in search of new adventures.

What an adventure it had been, across the Pacific, the Gulf of Mexico, the Mediterranean, and then North Africa to Istanbul. Now here they were on a river cruise on the Danube.

Gina knew Dee was watching her get dressed. He was always watching her. She knew he loved her and she appreciated the attention. It hadn't always been that way.

She had spent a decade of her life, after her mother was killed in a car crash, raising two brothers and a sister to adulthood. She had managed this by first becoming an exotic dancer and then an adult film actress. She had not yet graduated high school at the time she took on the task. After getting her siblings out of the house, she slowed her career and tried to decide what was next in her life. A short time later she took a vacation; it was the slice cruise where she met Dee and the others.

Gina slipped into her shoes and nodded to Dee. "Time to go."

When they arrived, Mike, Keno, Jamal and Angelic were already seated.

"Fashionably late I see," said Jamal.

"Just slow," replied Dee.

"It was probably me. Too many years of showbiz prep," added Gina, followed with a grin.

"Hey, a girl's got to do what a girl's got to do," said Angelic.

Sliding into her chair, Gina replied, "Where's Anna?"

"I stopped and checked on her," said Keno. "She said she was still tired and would dine in her cabin, that she would see us tomorrow sometime."

"That's too bad," replied Angelic.

"We don't want to wear her out," added Jamal.

"What's on tap for tomorrow?" asked Mike.

"We should reach Vidin, in the northwest corner of Bulgaria," answered Dee. "Then we'll cross into Serbia."

"Both sides of the ship?" asked Gina.

"Just port side, starboard is still Romania."

"Anything to see in Vidin?" asked Keno.

"It's the capital of a province, a part of the old trade routes from east to west, controlled by Romans, Celts, Germans, Bulgars, remnants of all those civilizations—forts, churches, government buildings, ancient architecture."

"Is it on the water?" asked Keno.

Dee nodded.

Keno looked at Mike. "Let's go shopping."

"We can talk to Anna in the afternoon," added Gina.

Aldo and Rene
Mittelwerk
On the 3rd Train in the Switching Yard

"Let's get in the back," said Aldo, jerking a thumb toward the rear of the half-track. "Surely they'll offload it and park it before anyone else would get onboard."

"Better hope so."

They cautiously exited the cab and quickly clambered into the rear of the half-track. There were several blankets in a pile on the bed floor.

"We can hide under those when they unload," said Aldo.

Rene nodded.

I think Aldo is more interested in saving himself than fulfilling the mission. While I don't really want to die, if I'm going to I want the sacrifice to be worthwhile. Not shot like some dog hiding under a blanket. Let's see what happens.

They didn't have to wait long. Troops of soldiers appeared and with cranes, forklifts, and ramps they unloaded the flatcars.

Aldo and Rene couldn't see much. Aldo had found a small gap in the back curtain and observed some of the activity.

"I think they are coming for the trucks," he whispered.

A few moments later they heard footsteps and talking. Then the truck shook a little as a driver opened the door to the cab and climbed into the front. The half-track moved and then dropped steeply as the truck pulled down the ramp. Aldo and Rene felt the front wheels land on the ground below and pull away from the train. They didn't go far.

"I told you they'd park it somewhere close," said Rene.

"For now," replied Aldo. "We wait and watch. Try to find a gap in the canopy where you can see."

I don't know about Rene. I don't need him to be a hero. I'd never have time to explain to the Nazis. We'd both be dead. I've got to keep a close eye on him and find a way out of here. It's madness. Italy has already surrendered. The Allies have taken back the port at Marseille. The war is almost over, unless the Germans can do something big here, immediately.

They waited and watched. There was consistent activity around the trains for the next several hours. But then both of the trains pulled away, deeper into the tunnel.

Aldo tapped Rene on the shoulder.

"It might have been good to stay on board or to have gotten back on, but hard to tell when or if they'll come back out."

"Perhaps they go out the other side."

"To Berlin? Not my first choice."

"Besides, we had no way to get back onboard. There was too much activity. We'd have been seen."

"Maybe we could drive this thing out?"

"We don't know where we are. We'd be lost in seconds."

"Just a thought. We'll wait to be driven out."

They sat for a long time and didn't see anyone. Aldo stifled a yawn and leaned back against the wall of the bed while stretching his head even further back and poking the canvas. Rene glanced over at him, noting the outstretched arms and audible sigh.

Rene dropped back down and looked out his peephole again. There he was, a single German sentry armed with an MP-40 just like the ones he and Aldo had. The sentry moved slowly toward the half-track, the MP-40 at low ready.

Tapping Aldo on the arm, Rene pointed outside the truck and then motioned for the blankets. Aldo's eyes got big. They got on their bellies against the cab of the truck and covered themselves with the blankets. Each of them lay in an opposite direction, their MP-40s covered but pointed toward the rear of the truck.

In a moment they felt rather than heard the sentry. He had soundlessly lifted the flap at the back of the truck and swung his shoulders and arms, with the MP-40 in front, into the back of the truck. He stood silently for several seconds.

There's nothing here but a pile of old blankets. I pity the fools they send out in that truck for the Russian front. Those blankets won't ward off the cold.

The soldier rubbed his eyes and looked at the blankets for another moment. He swung around, let the flap back down, and walked away.

Rene and Aldo heard his feet shuffling on the concrete as he receded into the distance.

Catching their breath, they slipped out from under the blankets. Sitting for a moment, they resumed their watch.

"Here we go again," said Rene. "There's a group, looks like five soldiers approaching from down the tunnel. They're headed this way."

They crawled back under the blankets. In a few moments, they heard footsteps approaching. There was a long moment of silence and then an earsplitting scream.

"Aufmerksamkeit! Kommen sie, schnell."

The sound was right on top of them. Neither moved. The command was repeated. Rene felt a gun barrel poke into his ribs. He rose slowly, his hands in the air, the MP-40 hanging from the strap around his neck. He saw Aldo doing the same.

The Nazi soldier motioned with his rifle toward the tailgate of the truck. Aldo and Rene emerged from the blankets and moved slowly in that direction. They dismounted from the bed and stood on the concrete in front of the soldiers.

The one who had poked Rene took one hand from his MP and slowly removed the MP from around Rene's neck.

It appears that I'll die quietly, like a dog in the night.

Everything happened quickly. As the other soldiers watched their comrade remove the MP from Rene, Aldo seized his own MP and shot.

Rene felt the bullets rip across his chest and dropped to his knees. He looked up, his hands trying fruitlessly to clutch and stop the wounds. Aldo pulled his hands away from the MP-40 and raised them in the air.

Rene felt a cold chill of air and crumpled to the concrete.

Anna
On the 1st Train, En Route

The train pulled to a stop at the bottom of the gorge. There was a small platform for off and on loading at the castle. The train moved forward in slow jerky motions.

Unloading the cargo I presume. It's not really taking that long between moves. I'd have thought it would take more time. Or, there's a good size crew doing the unloading, which means I have even less chance of not being discovered or killed.

The train pulled forward again. The door to Anna's car opened and several soldiers climbed inside. Anna shrunk in the corner, Luger in low ready. It was all she could do to hold her hands steady.

To her surprise, several more boxes were loaded, right on top of those already in the middle of the car. Then Anna saw it, her coat. It was balled up as a pillow and lying on the next set of crates beside the soldiers. Anna changed her position slightly, to have a better field of fire she told herself, but it was mostly to keep from shaking so badly the soldiers would hear her.

They loaded four more crates and exited the car. None of them had noticed the coat. The door slid shut with a clang. Anna leaned back against the wall of the boxcar and shuddered so violently that had she had her finger on the trigger of the pistol, she'd probably have shot her foot off. The train moved slowly forward another car length.

What is going on? Are we adding more crates to move around to the other side of the castle? This is where the Nazis keep their stolen art. Why aren't we unloading?

Anna scrambled over and grabbed her coat and put it on. She had grown colder in the valley of the castle. Her stomach had begun a steady rumble, and she felt her knees go weak.

She woke sometime later. Anna had collapsed in a heap where she stood and was sprawled against one of the crates. It was dark outside, and she had no idea where the train might be going. It was moving at full speed and appeared to have yet another destination.

From the castle, the train could be headed for Munich or Berlin or anywhere, to the south lay Austria and Switzerland or, if they went far enough, Italy. But that makes no sense. The Allies have retaken Italy. Why would they go south? Surely we're headed deeper into Germany.

The train hadn't traveled long after Anna woke. She felt it slowing, a switch of tracks, and a sharp turn. They picked up speed but not like it had been before. It was more like the train was suddenly trying to find its way in the dark.

Several minutes passed and the train's progress got slower and slower. Finally, it ground to a halt. The train sat for several moments, although Anna could still feel life in the engine and a slight sway in the cars. Then they moved again. There was loud screeching and brake exhaust and finally the train sat still and Anna felt it go quiet.

She sat in the car for a long time. The cold and the stillness crept inside and surrounded her. She climbed back to the observation post and could just make out a single light against the wall of what must be a tunnel.

Where am I? Where is everyone? I can't see or hear anything, just the quiet stillness of the night. I'll wait a bit longer. My stomach is churning so I place a hand upon it.

Awaking again sometime later, Anna rechecked the areas she could see outside the train. There were no sights and no sounds, just the solitary light and the silence.

Anna made her way to the door of the boxcar and slowly opened it. There was a slight screech, but no one came running. She pushed the door all the way open and climbed out.

Standing on a rail spur, Anna noted her train was on the

spur and off of the main track. There was room for another train to pass. Perhaps it wouldn't even notice the train she came in on, sitting there quietly.

It was a tunnel, and there was only room for the main line and the single spur.

There doesn't seem to be anyone here. It's as if they walked off and abandoned the train. Maybe there were only the engineers.

She stepped onto the main track and looked in both directions. The tunnel existed for a short ways and then everything disappeared into darkness.

Do I take a chance with the unknown and continue down the track? Maybe there's a town on the other side. I don't remember there being one on the way we came into the tunnel.

Anna put her head down and started back the way the train had entered. She saw no way that it could have been turned around, so this must be the correct direction. Anna started walking.

I've never been afraid of the dark, at least outdoors. However, I don't care for tunnels much, never been in many. What if another train comes? There's not much room on either side of the tracks.

She continued on, picking her steps carefully and constantly observing her surroundings, which were largely never changing.

We can't have come that far into the tunnel. We were going slowly. She bent to examine the tracks more closely. *They were rusty, very little metal sheen. This rail line isn't used much. It's a great place for hiding something.*

Anna continued to walk, and then she noticed. Off in the distance, she heard the sounds of the night. There didn't appear to be much more in the way of light, but if she could at least be outside, it would be such an improvement. Her steps quickened slightly, and she stumbled but caught herself.

Slow down, breathe deep. If it's out there, it's not going anywhere.

She continued along, choosing her steps with more care

and the night sounds growing louder and clearer. In the far distance, she thought there might be some twinkling light, stars, in the open sky.

Please let it be so.

A few more steps and she could feel the night air open up the proximity of the tunnel. There was more light and she could feel the outdoors surrounding her.

Where am I? How do I get home?

When Anna broke free of the tunnel, the false darkness, she breathed a sigh of relief and disappeared quietly into the night.

PART II

———

ANNA & ALDO

Dee and Friends
Third Day
Vidin

"Nothing like shopping to recharge your batteries," said Keno as the group boarded the longship after a morning of cruising Vidin and picking up supplies.

"I got to admit, it's fun," added Gina.

"And educational," said Angelic, followed by a laugh. "I mean look at all those cool historical buildings the shops were located inside."

"All right ladies," said Dee.

"Relax," replied Keno. "You know we're just pulling your chain."

"Amazing, isn't it?" said Mike. "Large major metropolitan cities the world over, all got the same stuff."

"I don't think Vidin is really a major metropolitan city in the world we know," replied Dee.

"Yeah, but it looks like a major metropolitan city for the world we're in now," said Jamal.

"We found what we needed," replied Angelic. "It was major enough."

"Lunch on the sundeck," called Gina. "Maybe we can coax Anna out with us."

After putting all their new purchases away, the group convened at the grill on the sundeck. The day was beautiful, much brighter, with clearer skies than the day before.

As they sat down Mike spoke, "Where do our travels take us tomorrow?"

"Dude, don't you ever look at the map?" replied Jamal.

"I could, but I'd rather hear it from Mr. Travelogue," he replied and then turned to Dee.

"We'll be at Donji Milanovac in Serbia. The Danube rolls out in that area and we'll be on the right bank of Lake Derdap. Maybe we can get in some water sports or touring."

"Why don't we get Anna right now and worry about tomorrow then?" said Gina.

Dee looked up and noticed that while he and the guys had been jabbering, Keno and Angelic had slipped off, presumably to get Anna.

Gina's phone binged, and she picked it up from the bar and scanned the message.

"They'll be up in a few minutes, let's find a table."

Ten minutes later, the ladies appeared, rolling Anna in her wheelchair. She waved at the rest of the group as the three of them approached the table.

"So good to see you all again. I hoped I hadn't bored you to death last time."

"You left us wanting to hear more," said Mike. "It was a treat."

"You are all so kind to take an interest in an old lady like me. I spend most of these cruises sitting on my balcony talking to my dog Ate."

"I bet he's a good listener," offered Jamal.

"He is, he's marvelous in fact, but it's so enjoyable to chat with interesting people. Angelic and Keno have told me a little about your adventures. My, they do sound exciting."

"Mostly they have been," said Dee. "And several times there's been an air of danger. But for better or worse we chose that. I suspect you've seen danger that wasn't of your own choosing."

Anna smiled before speaking. "You're a perceptive young man. But danger has a mind of its own and will find you whether you are looking for it or running from it."

"Tell us more," replied Dee.

"Shall we order lunch first and I'll offer a couple of thoughts if you still want to hear them?"

Jamal waved the waiter over, and they ordered.

———

"My last mission was a train ride into Austria. There were three trains in Paris and each of us took one. We were told they were going to Berlin. I found out later that was bogus information but at the time we took it as fact.

"The train I was on was full of stolen artwork and contraband, mostly taken from Jewish families. Did you know there were over 30,000 pieces of stolen art that were never recovered from the Nazi thefts? Anyway, my train went south from Paris and after a time I figured out that it was going to the Neuschwanstein Castle, also known as the fairy-tale castle—despite its dark history—but then some fairy tales are rather grim. It's located in southern Bavaria. That is where the Nazis had accumulated all their stolen artwork. And we did in fact go there. But only to pick up more art.

You see, the war was turning, and the Nazis were on the run. We didn't quite realize it. We stopped and picked up more works and then kept going. We crawled into Austria, the Führer's homeland, and made our way onto a tiny, remote, seldom used train track that ran through some western mountains near to Germany or Switzerland. The train pulled into this tunnel under one mountain and was abandoned. I walked out of the tunnel, into the night, a long way from home."

"It was full of all that artwork and valuables, and it was abandoned?" asked Gina.

"Not for long, it was part of a plan. The Nazis took abandoned or seldom used train tracks in rural areas and hid trains in the tunnels. Then they blew up the mountain to close the tunnel and pulled up the track back to the main line. It was their way of hiding things for the future."

"That's unbelievable," said Mike.

"It would seem that way, but you have to remember communications in that day. The world was seen as much larger, more remote locations, places to hide, and time to recover."

"What happened to you?" asked Angelic.

"Fortunately, I was on the first train they parked, on the spur line in the tunnel. The engineers staged the train and left. I eventually walked out of the tunnel and began my trip home."

"What about your other two friends?" asked Keno.

"I never saw them again, at least not for a long time and there was only the one of them by then."

"What about coming out of the tunnel?" asked Jamal.

"That's another story."

"We have time, if you do?" said Gina.

"I'll tell you that and then I'll have to go rest."

"Memories take a lot of energy," said Dee.

"Yes, they do. You are correct. I expect you know from your own experience."

"Nothing like what you're telling us."

Anna leaned back in her chair. "I walked out of the tunnel in the dark. I thought it would never end. Once outside I was in the deep forest. There could have been a town in any direction, the engineers and any others had gone somewhere, but I didn't know where. So I followed the tracks until I got back to the main line, where the rails were shiny and the right of way was much bigger. Then I followed the main line until I came to a crossroad. At that point I had to decide—do I try to catch a westbound train, do I look for a town? I was really hungry, tired, and sick. I retched multiple times on that walk and feared dehydration or hypothermia if I passed out. Knowing I didn't have enough energy to run down a train, unless it just stopped, I elected to look for a village. Following the road, I tried to stay out of sight. In the end I was lucky. Leaning against a tree, so I wouldn't fall over, a man on an old swaybacked horse approached me.

"You look like you could use some help," he said.

"I couldn't even reply and I was afraid he'd leave me. I held on to the tree and nodded but still slipped to the ground.

"The next thing I remember was waking up in a big soft bed with two little faces staring at me. I nearly screamed and was so startled that I pulled back from them until I was against the wall. A woman came running into the room and held her hand up to me.

"She said, "It's okay, you're safe with us. Let me get you some water, some food, and tell my husband you're awake."

"Wow," said Keno.

"So this was the wife of the man on the horse?" asked Jamal.

"Yes, and his family. That's when I learned I was in

Austria. They had migrated from Bulgaria and were settling a small farm. They were so very good to me. I slept in the big bed, which belonged to the man and his wife, and they brought me food and water and new, to me, clothes that fit. I seemed to gain weight despite everything that had happened."

"Gaining weight?" asked Mike. "They must have been feeding you really well."

"Actually, it was right after that, the man's wife…she told me I was pregnant."

Aldo
Mittelwerk
In the Switching Yard

I thought the Nazis might shoot me. But I was counting on them being curious. It appeared they were.

The guard who had been relieving Rene of his MP-40 turned his own weapon into Aldo's face and placed it right under his chin.

I could see his finger tightening on the trigger. Perhaps all for naught. I was just about to speak when he did.

"Marsch!" And he poked the rifle into my neck.

One of the other guards grabbed my MP-40 and cut the strap with his knife, then pulled the gun away. We walked further into the tunnel.

I wonder if one of them is the same man who had looked in the half-track earlier. It had to be.

They walked perhaps a hundred yards and came upon an office. The soldiers stopped, in formation, surrounding Aldo. The one holding the weapon on him went into the office. He reemerged shortly with an officer.

"Vas ist los?" demanded the officer. He repeated it. Aldo shrugged.

"You do not speak the mother tongue?"

Aldo nodded. "I speak English."

"Why are you here and how did you get here? I'll only ask you once," said the officer while withdrawing his pistol. He placed it beside Aldo's jaw.

Aldo swallowed hard. "I hitched a ride on a train. I was lost. Where is here?"

The German officer smiled. "I don't believe you. The last trains to come here were from Paris, moving from west to east. Why would you jump on an east-bound train?"

"I just wanted out of where I was."

"And you chose to come into the lion's den?"

"It's where the train took me. Besides who says I was on the last train?"

This time the German officer laughed. "Three of my men saw you standing beside the train. My guard knew you both were in the back of the half-track. Did you really think your presence would be unnoticed for any length of time? Why did you shoot your comrade?"

"Who said he was my comrade?"

"It was some charade to buy you time, but I'm afraid it failed." He slid the pistol to Aldo's temple. "Goodbye."

"Wait."

The German officer paused. "Why?"

"Perhaps I can be helpful to you?"

"In what way?"

"I could spy for you."

The officer laughed again. "Doubtful. We let you go and you run off? You could never be trusted."

"I have something to tell you."

Anna, Dee and Friends
Third Day

"Pregnant?" said Angelic.

Anna smiled and then whispered, "Yes."

"How did she know?" asked Gina.

"The symptoms, the morning sickness, the swelling, a slight fever, she had two of her own, been there before."

"How far along were you?" asked Keno

"Seven months."

"And just a slight swelling?" asked Angelic.

"Again, you must remember the times—there was little to eat, we were constantly on the move, I was skinny anyway, and frequently missed periods. It never crossed my mind."

"What did you do?" asked Gina.

"The man and his family were kind enough to put me up for the remaining time. I tried to help but was frequently sick and lost all energy. I'm afraid I wasn't very helpful, but they were so gracious."

"What happened then?" exclaimed Angelic, causing the men to smile.

"I expect she had the baby," replied Jamal.

"Yes, a little blonde girl. I stayed for a month afterwards and tried to nurse but wasn't successful. I was just too scrawny. The wife was still nursing her youngest, and she took over for me."

"Took over?" asked Gina.

"Yes, she could easily feed the girl. I named her Elise, for my mother. It made it simpler for me. I'm afraid I wasn't a good mother. I wanted to get home, to get back to Paris, to Aldo and Rene. I had no way to feed the child, no money, didn't know how long it would take me. I wasn't prepared to be a mother."

"You could have stayed with the family I'm sure," said Keno.

"They offered, tried to insist, but I saw how easily Elise took to the woman. How caring and compassionate she was. I knew these were good people and they could offer Elise so much more than I. It broke my heart but I felt it was what I had to do, right or wrong."

"How long did you stay after you made your decision?" asked Gina.

"Only a couple of days, to prepare for the journey. They provided me clean clothes and some food. They offered a little money, but I refused to take it. I got their information and gave them mine—so I could try to stay in touch at some point in time."

Aldo
Mittelwerk

They led Aldo around the factory; it was enormous. Mittelwerk was German for 'Central Works' and it contained everything the Nazis were developing—mechanical, technical, scientific, biological, chemical, and atomic. *It looks to me like they could still win the war.*

There were tunnels and cross tunnels, each with a different function. German scientists, engineers, and technicians managed the work, while all the manual labor was performed by prisoners or slaves from the nearby concentration camps. The barracks were chock-full of the laborers, who all looked underfed, overworked, and near death. There appeared to be an endless supply of them as they walked about the tunnels.

Each of the areas, one in each tunnel, seemed to work independently without interference from the others. The tunnels were numbered 1-20 and then the cross set were numbered 21-46. They were extensive. *How long did it take them just to excavate the space? The mountain has to be enormous.*

There were V-1 bombs in one tunnel, V-2 rockets and missiles in another, A-4 missiles in the next and on and on— jet engine fighters, anti-aircraft missiles, a liquid oxygen plant with generators for producing propellant for the rockets and missiles, jet fuel production, and an oil refinery. That was just the mechanical section.

As we walk past one tunnel, I notice my escorts speed up.

"See that man in the white lab coat over there?" hissed the soldier near me.

I nod.

"That is Werner von Braun. He is the chief scientist working on developing a bomb containing radioactive waste. It will be devastating when he's finished. It should be soon."

"Is that what he does?"

"No, it's just one part. He's working on intercontinental ballistic missiles, and is in charge of developing many other new weapons, including atomic. It's supposed to be a very powerful bomb."

As we walked past, I wandered what else the Nazis could be working on. It didn't take long to find out.

In the next tunnel, the escort whispered, "This is the biological and chemical sector. They are refining gases and poisons from the First World War and are also developing new strains of virus, something like the 'Spanish flu' only worse, much worse. They finish these and turn them loose, the war is over, everyone else will be dead."

"How long have they been working on this stuff?"

"Since before the war, sometime in the late 1930s. Hitler put a group of scientists on the project not long after he took power."

Suddenly there were screams and cries from beyond the scientist.

"What is that?"

The escort pointed toward the far wall beyond the scientists and technicians.

"Those are the test subjects, live tests on some laborers."

I followed the direction of his hand. There were a dozen laborers lined against the wall being sprayed with various substances by three different mask-clad technicians. The laborers writhed in pain and screamed. I turned away. We kept walking, quickly.

We were coming to the end of the tunnels. There was one large area left. As we drew closer, I saw stacks of corpses piled along the tunnel walls.

"Those are the laborers who failed to complete their shift."

"They died, or they were killed?"

"They expired."

"What are they doing to them?"

"The doctors drain the blood from the bodies before they are burned."

"Why?"

"The biologists perform various tests or experiments on the blood. They type it, store it, and document the effects upon completion."

"Charming."

———

There were troops everywhere, very tight security on the entrance and exit. But the Nazis seemed otherwise fearless, immune to the Allied bombing, deep in their underground lair. I studied their movements for several days, watching and waiting.

Anna, Dee and Friends
Third Day

Everyone sat silently for a moment. A slight breeze picked up and blew across the sundeck. Anna shivered.

"How long did it take for your curiosity to get the better of you? To check on your daughter," asked Dee.

Anna thought for a moment before speaking. "I was very consistent in those days, the war effort and my friends were my focus. Consistency and curiosity don't often go together, one seems to exclude the other. But then I suppose there is a consistent curiosity, although I'm not quite sure that's a virtue." She paused and looked straight at Dee.

"Well, I think I've probably been out long enough for today. I'd better be going." She glanced about for a waiter or steward.

"We'll take you back," said Gina.

"Thank you."

All three of the women assembled and rolled Anna away.

"You said she'd be colorful," observed Jamal to Dee.

"I had no idea."

"But ninety plus years is a long time, time for a lot of things, you said that too," added Mike.

"Yeah I did, and I'm also saying, did you notice she didn't answer the last question?"

Aldo
Mittelwerk

Troop trucks came and went constantly. They would group the soldiers and then load them on the half-tracks. There were many comments about "Russland", which I take to mean Russia. Those troops were going to the front, which explained why their departures were the least supervised or the most ignored.

There was a locker room where the soldiers exercised and bathed. Aldo carefully slipped inside one day not long before a troop truck was scheduled to depart. He observed the men entering the area. Seeing one the correct size, he waited until they were all on the exercise floor. Aldo went to the locker room and rapidly changed into the man's uniform.

The man was a private, a Gefreiter, with plain sleeves on his jacket. *That makes it easier, no need to speak, just follow orders, imitate what you see.*

Striding out of the locker room, Aldo saw the troops being assembled for the half-track. He waited until they were at attention and then slipped into the back row.

Aldo kept glancing, eyes only, toward the locker room where the soldier had recently entered.

I hope he was planning a long workout.

In a few minutes the half-track arrived and the soldiers loaded from the front of the ranks. That put Aldo at the rear of the truck, likely the coldest place as the half-track approached Russia. It suited Aldo.

The truck rolled down several long corridors.

Rene was right, we'd have never found our way out of here.

Finally reaching the entrance, the half-track stopped only briefly, as everyone knew its destination and the driver felt confident no one would be onboard that hadn't been ordered to be.

They rolled out of the tunnel and toward the forest

beyond. It was late in the afternoon and would be dark soon. Aldo could tell from his position in the rear of the truck and the position of the sun, they were heading north.

Perhaps a stop in Berlin for the night, one last opportunity for a good time before we die. I could wait until then and see what's possible or maybe I should go as soon as I can. Watch and be ready. As they grow tired or sleepy, maybe there will be an opportunity.

The truck bounced along for several hours. Aldo peeked at his watch, which he'd kept carefully hidden so he didn't have to explain why he had an aviator's watch as a private in the army, in a language he didn't speak. He estimated it was still another hour or more to Berlin. There was no dinner and so the soldiers did what most soldiers do when they can, sleep.

The truck crossed a bump or a rut and bounced heavily. The soldiers bobbed around but continued snoring.

This is my chance. The truck has slowed so there must be worse road ahead. Next bump I'm going out the back.

The truck rocked, and the soldiers bounced again and suddenly there was one less of them as the half-track continued down the road.

Aldo rolled over the tailgate on that bump. *I positioned myself by leaning on the top edge of the metal gate, the curtain above flapping in the wind. It was a hard fall, and I tucked and rolled quickly to the side and into the ditch, which was half full of water. I was wet and bruised but out of the truck. I got up and ran in the opposite direction, back toward the mountain hideaway.*

Dee and Friends
Fourth Day

They woke early, had breakfast, and took an excursion around the lake. Getting back late that afternoon, windburned and sunburned, they retired to their cabins to clean up.

This time dressed for the occasion, they met for dinner. But they were more an exception, as most of the passengers were casual.

"I thought we had enough getting sunburned in North Africa," said Angelic to her husband Jamal. When he didn't reply she glanced across to him and he was staring out the glass, lost in thought.

It's hard to tell about him. He can be so many different things at different times. Jamal had played football all of his life, from the peewee league onward. He was an All-American wide receiver for the University of Georgia and then drafted into the NFL. Jamal didn't enjoy the "pro" environment and left the team to buy a corporate gym in downtown Atlanta, where he trained overweight executives. *We had taken a cruise where we met Dee and the others and got stranded on the island before being rescued. Then he spent all that time researching the gold bell he and Dee had found in the Sea of Cortez. Then art and archaeology work in North Africa, Spain, and France with Diego and Eve.* He could be anything at any time and Angelic wondered what would be next.

Studying his face, she thought, *Here I am, a Nurse Practitioner in Oncology. I have believed in helping people all my life and worked hard to get through undergraduate and medical school. Then I met Jamal, and we got married. The cruise where we met the others was a vacation we felt we had earned for our hard work. Look at us now.*

Angelic noticed that Jamal was looking at her.

"What are you thinking of?"

"Just wondering what comes next."

"Only one way to find out, go for it."

"Go for what?" asked Keno, who had sat down beside them.

"Whatever comes next," filled in Mike who was also sitting down.

"That's what we do," added Dee who was sitting across from them.

"Put a sock in it," said Gina, sitting across from Keno.

"No Anna tonight?" asked Dee.

"Not tonight, she's resting," replied Gina. Moving her finger between the three women, she added, "We may stop in and check on her later."

"Better not wait too late," said Jamal. "She might be in bed."

———

After finishing dinner, the three women started for Anna's room. The men adjourned to an outside bar.

"Text us or come by," called Dee. "We'll be right here."

———

Gina knocked softly on Anna's door, then a little louder. There was a rustling from inside and the sound of a small dog barking.

The door opened partially, and Anna's face appeared. "Hello, I'm so glad you came by. Do come inside." Anna stepped back and opened the door fully. She was on her feet but making her way to the couch.

"Please have a seat. How was dinner?" she asked.

Gina sat beside Anna on the couch while Angelic and Keno sat in the two chairs opposite the couch.

"It was quite good. We've enjoyed the longship so far," replied Angelic.

"I've always found them to be comfortable and accommodating." A small dog, a terrier of some breed, ran to Anna's feet and sniffed about her ankles. Sensing another presence, the dog stopped and glanced at the women.

"It's alright Ate, they're friends. They're really very nice." Speaking to Gina she said, "Lean forward and let him sniff your hand."

Gina did so and after a moment the dog licked her hand. "You passed," said Anna with a smile. The other two women rose and approached the dog in the same fashion. Each time he licked their hand and then his tail wagged furiously.

"See I told you they were good people." She pointed at the tail that was still wagging. "He likes you. A dog's tail never lies."

"He's beautiful," said Keno. "Did you say his name was Ate?"

"Yes, it's actually A8 but I call him Ate. A8 is short for Aldo #8. I've had seven other of these dogs over the years and each of them was named Aldo. The dogs have never let me down, never failed me. They make great companions."

Not touching that one, thought Gina. She looked to the others and saw slight, almost imperceptible, nods.

"We just wanted to check on you and see that you were okay and that you got some dinner," said Angelic.

"Oh yes, they are gracious to bring it to my room. I typically have always eaten in until I met you lovely people."

"We won't keep you. We just wanted to say goodnight and that we hope to see you tomorrow," said Gina.

"I'd like that. I think we may be coming up on Belgrade, Serbia. If you get a chance to go ashore, go see Belgrade Fortress. It sits at the conflux of the two rivers, on top of a labyrinth of tunnels the Romans built. It's been around since 300 BC, contains a lot of history."

"Really?" asked Keno

"Yes, I think you'd enjoy it. I spent some time in the city years ago. It's full of mystery and intrigue. Some of it might rub off on you," she replied and then smiled.

"That sounds fascinating," replied Angelic. "We'll tell the guys, they'll love it."

———

"You want another round?" asked Jamal.

"No, I'm good. I don't think the ladies will be too long," replied Dee.

"Where we headed tomorrow?" asked Mike.

"Belgrade."

"Is there anything to see?"

"It's the capital city of a small country, trade route destination, there's an old fortress from before the time of Christ. There are gardens, churches, architecture, public spaces; it's somewhat typical of eastern European cities. They're all beautiful to look at and full of history. It just depends on what you're looking for."

"Why adventure, of course," replied Jamal.

"Don't let the women hear you say that."

"Say what?" said Keno as the three women walked up to where the men were sitting.

"How much fun shopping was this morning," ad-libbed Mike.

Keno rolled her eyes at him. "We going ashore tomorrow in Belgrade?"

"We can, if you want."

"Let's do it."

They paired up in married couples and retired for the
night.

Aldo's Adventure

Aldo hadn't gone very far when he heard a train whistle. His left ankle had twisted under him when he rolled out of the truck. The slow jog he'd been in had helped straighten it out somewhat. Still, with it weak, Aldo wasn't sure he could catch a train.

Which way is it going? What speed is it traveling? Can I run fast enough? If not this one, maybe another one. How often will they come by?

Aldo made his way toward the sound, walking now and flexing the ankle, testing. The rail line wasn't far. He stood in the bushes and watched as the train sped past, very rapidly.

No catching that one. At least the line is moving east and west at this point. It could turn at any time and I'd end up back in the underground mountain. I'll sit here for a while.

Aldo made his way to a flat stretch, where he could run and try to board if he got the chance. He also picked the spot that was closest to the track, again to save time. He huddled between two trees and tried to make himself as small as possible to ward off the cold and minimize the wet spots from the water in the ditch.

Watching my breath float away in the chilled night air when I exhale, I wiggle to keep from going numb. We weren't even to Berlin. I can't imagine how cold Russia must be. I wonder about Anna, where is she? Is she still alive? It was unfortunate about Rene. I liked him. But it was the only way to stay alive. Concentrate on this moment or you will freeze between these trees.

Then he heard it, far in the distance, a train whistle, long, slow, mournful. Like something that labored in the night. It wasn't a Nazi steam train. This was something old and tired. Aldo moved from between the trees, got himself in a ready position.

In the distance he could see a faint light. The train did not appear to be moving quickly.

This might be my best chance. If it's a civilian train, it will surely stop in a village where I can hide, find food, steal a vehicle, something.

The train approached, moving at a slow steady speed. The engine flashed past and Aldo broke from his spot to run alongside it. There were several passenger cars and Aldo did not approach the train until they passed. Then there were the boxcars and an open door. Aldo picked up his speed, the ankle beginning to really throb, and moved closer to the train.

I hope there's nobody on board. I'm in a German uniform and they'll kill me.

Aldo reached the open door and grabbed the edge of the flooring of the car. With a last push on his good ankle, Aldo plunged into the car, rolling to the middle and preparing for the worst.

Nothing but silence, it's empty, thank goodness.

Aldo got to his knees and crawled to the edge of the car. He leaned against the siding and watched out the open door for a sign of civilization.

Dee and Friends
Fifth Day

They assembled that morning for the excursion into Belgrade.

"What do you guys want to see?" asked Dee.

"The Belgrade Fortress," replied Keno.

"How did you know about that?"

"I looked at the map, isn't that what you always say?"

"Actually, Anna told us about it. Suggested we might enjoy it," interjected Gina.

"Really?" said Jamal.

"Why would she think that?" asked Mike.

"Anna seemed to know a lot about the place, about the city as well. I got the feeling it meant something to her. Said she'd been here before," replied Angelic. "It can't hurt, right?"

"The fortress is probably the biggest tourist attraction in town. It's been here for centuries, lots of history."

"Let's go take a look," said Jamal.

———

They returned in the late afternoon, weary from their efforts.

"We walked all over that fortress," said Keno.

"And under it," added Gina.

"There was a lot to see, what do you suppose Anna had in mind?" said Angelic.

"She's supposed to meet us for dinner later. We can ask her," replied Gina.

A couple of hours later they were all assembled at one of the tables in the main dining room. Again they had dressed for dinner, as had Anna, who sat at the head.

"It's so nice to eat with people who dress for the occasion.

I must admit that I have a lot of really nice things that I rarely get to wear. It's a treat."

"As was the fortress, we saw a lot of history," replied Angelic.

"Was there something specific we should have looked for?" asked Gina.

"Did you know that Attila the Hun, one of the most grisly figures of history, was buried there? And he's not alone, there are many others."

"I don't think we saw that grave or marker," added Keno.

"But we saw the passage of time, the passage of empires, good and evil across the centuries," said Dee.

"One can see many things if one looks closely enough."

"What did you do today?" asked Keno.

"I kept Ate company, and rested and read. I love history, so full of intimate details. Shall we dine?"

Aldo's Adventure

He'd been riding for about twenty minutes, seeing nothing but countryside. Then Aldo felt the train slow even more. Sticking his head out the open door, he thought there were lights in the distance. Aldo moved further back in the car.

Should I stay on board, if possible, maybe keep traveling west? Or do I get off here to avoid the Nazis, find something to eat, figure out where I'm at?

The train slowed again, and Aldo heard air brakes and screeches from the tired old rails. He stayed in the darkness.

Let's see what happens.

The train shuddered to a stop, and Aldo could see several buildings across a small street. Nothing was marked.

Where is this place?

He waited another minute, and nothing happened. No one approached, there was no sound. Everything was quiet and defeated.

I have to look.

Aldo eased across the car and glanced down the side of the train. He saw nothing. Moving across to the other side of the door, he looked the other way. Another train, a Nazi steam train, heading east.

Where would they be going? It's all boxcars. I don't think it's a troop train. Maybe supplies to the Russian front. I don't want that. Maybe it's from Mittelwerk. Where would that be going, Russia? Might be interesting to see. Could that be valuable information? The train is on a spur line; the engine isn't powered.

A group of uniformed Nazis crossing the rail yard interrupted his thoughts.

I am in uniform although it's not in very good shape. I could pass for one of them as long as I don't have to speak.

Aldo slid out of the rail car, straightened his uniform as

best he could, and made for the other train. The engine was cold to the touch. It wouldn't be leaving soon.

Aldo saw a small café. It looked unoccupied.

Something to eat? No money, how do I order?

Aldo started digging in the pockets of the uniform, something he hadn't done before. There'd been no time. In the breast pocket, he got lucky. There were several folded bills, Reichsmark—the German currency. In denomination, there were a couple of 2s, a 5, and a 20. It seemed our private was a frugal man.

Currency in hand, Aldo moved toward the café. As he got closer, he could see there was an older gentleman in civilian clothing sitting in the corner.

I have to take a chance. I'm starving. I must go inside.

Hesitantly Aldo entered and then saw the cook set a sandwich in the window for the waitress. Aldo hurried to the counter, and the waitress turned away from the sandwich and in his direction. He smiled at her and she returned it with a smile of her own.

Aldo pointed at the sandwich and held up two fingers. The waitress smiled again and made a note. She tore the ticket off and hung it in the window. Aldo moved to one side as she grabbed the sandwich sitting there and took it to the older gentleman.

He sat away from the old man but near enough the counter that he could see it clearly.

In a few minutes, the waitress brought him the two sandwiches. They smiled at each other again and she left him to eat.

He sat there for a few seconds, not trusting his hands to touch the sandwich without spilling it or stuffing it in his mouth. His stomach groaned audibly, causing him to look around quickly. No one noticed or seemed to care. He moved slowly and took the first bite. *I'm not sure exactly what it is, except good.*

Aldo ate one and began the second. As he was doing so, the old man walked to the counter and nodded at him but didn't speak. Aldo nodded back and then watched the man closely. He handed the waitress a Reichsmark with a "2" on it. She handed him some coins in return. He nodded and pocketed the coins.

Aldo glanced to the table where the old man had sat as the waitress approached it to clean. Aldo could see no paper or coins on the table. He watched the waitress clean the table; her face sad.

Aldo finished the second sandwich and rubbed his stomach.

A nap would be good, a nice bath, some clean clothes, might as well wish for the world.

The waitress was back behind the counter.

Probably best if I go before anyone else arrives.

Aldo walked to the counter with the Reichsmark "5" in his hand and gave it to the waitress. She went to dig for his change and as she looked up at him he held up his hand and pointed to her while nodding. She smiled just before he turned away.

That was close. What to do now. I don't like being in this uniform. It could be handy, given where I am, but it could be a problem, depending on where I'm going.

He walked down the street a short distance while keeping a sharp eye for other foot traffic. Small houses appeared. Aldo could see into the backyards.

There was a clothesline, with clothes hanging on it. They must have forgotten to take them inside. Never leave clothes hanging at night, you know what happens.

Aldo grabbed a pair of pants and a shirt.

Would have been nice if there'd been a jacket or coat, better grab another shirt. Good thing there was no dog, probably inside or they didn't have one, couldn't afford them with a war going on.

Aldo slipped back to the train he came in on. He could see the Nazi steam engine warming up.

If I'm quick I might get over there and open a boxcar and get inside. What would it gain me? What do I have to lose?

Aldo bundled his new clothes and walked carefully over to the steam train. He looked in both directions and, seeing no one, pulled himself up on the car and tried to open the door. There was no lock but the handle wouldn't turn.

I can't beat on this thing, someone will hear.

He pushed and shoved but couldn't get any movement. He glanced in both directions again, still no one and then placed the bundle of clothes between his knees, freeing both hands. He grabbed the handle and jerked hard. It gave way with a slight groan. Aldo looked around, nothing. He pushed the door open enough to scramble inside and quickly closed the door behind him.

The car was full of crates, with artists' names stenciled on them. Monet, Manet, Degas, Rembrandt, Picasso—that one was a surprise. This was an art train, probably headed to the castle outside Munich, maybe towards Anna. He threw his bundle of clothes on the crate and fashioned it into a pillow. *Now for a long nap. I'm taking this train.*

Dee and Friends
Fifth Day

Back in their stateroom after dinner, Dee and Gina changed out of their formal clothing.

"You want to sit on the balcony with some wine?" she asked.

"Yeah, that'd be nice. It was a long day. I'm tired."

"What's the matter, getting old?"

He stepped across and squeezed her bare shoulders. "Not just yet."

There was a knock at the door. They grinned at one another and Gina went to answer.

It was Angelic. "You and Dee want to join the rest of us on our balcony, have some wine?"

"Yeah, we were just talking about that."

They followed Angelic down the hall, into her room, and onto their balcony.

The others were seated loosely around. Angelic did the honors, and they toasted.

"New friends and new adventures," said Jamal.

They clinked glasses and took a sip. Everyone sat back and relaxed.

"Was there something we were supposed to see today?" asked Mike.

"I was wondering the same," added Dee.

"Anna was kind of coy at dinner," said Angelic.

"Do you think she was coy or being careful?" replied Gina.

"About what?" asked Keno.

"That crack about Attila the Hun and others being buried there, that got my attention," said Dee.

"She's probably just playing with us. She's been here or

lived here and just wanted to give us something to do. Give her some time to herself," added Jamal.

"Do you think she's getting tired of us? Are we pestering her?" asked Angelic.

"I don't think so. She seems clearly energized when we're around, more like she's playing a game, entertaining herself and us," replied Dee.

"I don't know, how about some more wine?" said Keno.

Aldo's Adventure

He slept for several hours. After verifying the time, Aldo estimated they still had three or four hours to Munich. He laid back and rested his head.

A trainload of art, likely for the Neuschwanstein Castle. Probably where Anna ended up. Where would she hide? I don't see her fighting. She'd be fierce, but she'd surrender. She's too clever to die or let them kill her. They'd keep her alive, just out of curiosity. How will I find her? I found Rene.

Aldo grew tired of thinking and got up to rattle around the boxcar. He examined each of the crates, noting the artist.

Who knows how much all this is worth. The Nazis had good taste.

Then he saw the crate marked "Picasso".

That's not like them, too modern.

Aldo moved closer. It was a small crate.

Maybe only one painting? Maybe someone's personal favorite? Let's have a look.

Aldo sat on a larger crate of Rembrandts and studied the container holding the Picasso. He flipped it over in his hands. It was nailed securely but being smaller than the other crates, the slats weren't as thick.

He set the crate down and rummaged around the car looking for any tools. There was nothing.

Maybe there's another way.

Aldo turned the crate over in his hands again and settled on what he thought was the thinnest slat. Fortified by his dinner and nap, he flexed his shoulders and wiggled his fingers.

If I push against the crate and pull against the slat, maybe the crate will give away or the slat will snap.

He pushed and pulled, nothing. He tried again, still nothing.

Maybe I could stomp the slat, but I might damage the painting or paintings.

Aldo exhaled and concentrated.

Remember jumping up the walls in the boxcar, focus.

He exhaled loudly, counted off in his head, and gave a tremendous effort. There was a creak, then a snap and the slat gave way in his hand. Aldo released the slat for a moment and flexed his hand again. He turned the broken slat outward and pried against the frame of the crate. After several strong tugs, the slat came loose. He repeated the process for the other broken slat.

With both halves of the slat in hand, Aldo chose the longer one to pry on the next slat in the box. After several attempts he was successful in removing that one.

One more slat and I should be able to lift a painting out.

He busied himself again, this time with the full slat he had just removed. It went quickly and the third slat fell away.

Now, let's see what we have.

Aldo carefully reached inside the edge of the crate and felt the frame of a painting wrapped in a soft cloth. He pulled it out slowly so as not to damage the frame or the canvas. Once free of the crate, he laid it carefully on the container of Rembrandts.

Unwrapping the cloth from the painting, Aldo's eyes grew wider.

It was a figure study, a woman, it appeared. But, it didn't look like any woman Aldo knew or had ever seen. *I wonder who liked this.*

Aldo turned the canvas over and once again his eyes grew wide. There was a name, and a date painted on the back.

Anna, it says Anna and there is a date.

He flipped the canvas back again.

It couldn't be. She told me about the painting, even described it. The colors, the shape, it was just like she had said. After I got to know her, and she told me the story, and showed me the realistic portrait Picasso had done for her, and yes it looked like her, this was unbelievable.

Aldo sat and stared at the portrait for several minutes. Then he re-wrapped it and put it back in the crate.

I'm keeping this one.

Dee and Friends
Sixth Day

They met for breakfast the next morning. There were eyes being rubbed and yawns all around.

"Where are we today?" asked Keno

"Novi Sad, still in Serbia," replied Dee.

"Smaller than Belgrade?" asked Gina.

Dee nodded.

"Let's stay on the ship, I'm tired. Yesterday wore me out," said Angelic.

Dee looked to Jamal and Mike.

"Okay by me," replied Mike.

"Let's chill on the sundeck, watch the world go by, instead of going after it," added Jamal.

They whiled away the day until early afternoon when the women couldn't stand it anymore.

"I think we'll go find Anna, check on her. Maybe she'll tell us some more of her story," said Gina.

"See if she'll come up here, we'd like to hear it too. I've been watching countryside landscapes all morning. A good story would be a nice change," replied Dee.

They returned shortly, Anna in her wheelchair, sporting a big sunhat and wraparound sunglasses.

The men stood up as Anna rolled up to their table.

"Aren't you all polite?"

"We try," replied Mike.

"You're looking very fashionable," said Dee.

Anna smiled. "You're quite the observer."

"Never mind him," said Keno. "Tell us some more of your story."

Anna paused.

"What happened after you left the farm?" asked Jamal.

She leaned forward and looked each of them in the eyes.

"Did they tell you that all the city of Belgrade once existed only inside the walls of the fortress? It was immune to outside forces, self-contained from the world, like many people keep their emotions. Like I have always kept mine. I am old now, so I will tell you my story. You may think the worst of me when it is through, and I will understand."

"It can't be that bad," said Keno.

"We shall see."

"Tell us, please," added Angelic.

"The farmer took me to town when he and his wife conceded to let me go. He introduced me to a friend of his that owned a supply store. The man knew many people and what was going on around the area. The farmer thought the man might best be able to help. I wanted to go straight home. I bid farewell to the farmer and then had a long talk with the store owner. He convinced me I'd never get across the border or across Germany on foot with no money or weapon."

"That must have been very discouraging," said Gina.

"Yes, I didn't want to hear it. But the man offered another plan. He suggested I go to Vienna. That I get a job there, save some money, then maybe I could go by river or by train and get to Paris."

"There's no direct river route, is there?" asked Mike.

"No, it would have just been partway. The train was the best, most direct, option, but the river might have been easier for me to cross back into Germany."

"How were you going to accomplish all of that?" asked Dee.

"The man was from Vienna. He had family there, and he made several trips each year to visit and to purchase supplies. He didn't tell me and I never learned for sure but I think he was involved in resistance efforts."

"Wouldn't you have been aware of those efforts?" asked Jamal.

"It wasn't like that. There was no one central organization, just little groups here and there. No one knew who to trust, people didn't want to get far from their own homes. It was more like overlapping fields of operation spread about the continent."

"Please continue," said Gina.

"The man was making a regularly scheduled trip in a few days. So he had me hang around and help with the store. He put me up, fed me, and paid me a few dollars. There was a company truck he took and on this trip he took his own daughter as well as me. The plan was we were his children on their way to see their grandmother in Vienna while he did business. If he thought we were going to be stopped, he wanted us both to get in the back and hide."

"That's across the country in the wrong direction from Paris, isn't it?" asked Dee.

"Yes, and very much why I didn't really want to do it. But I understood how difficult it would be to cross Germany on foot and I just didn't think I was physically able. I trusted this man for some reason. He knew nothing about me and I worried he would turn me over to the authorities. But, it was where I suspected his sympathies lay which allowed me to follow him. We spent the first night in Salzburg with someone he knew. The action was on the Russian front and to the west. The Italians had lost, and the Allies were coming up from the south. There wasn't that much activity where we were and we traveled with no incident. Still the man was cautious. We got back on the road the second day and arrived in Vienna."

"Were you scared?" asked Keno.

"Absolutely, I had very little money, I didn't know these people, and I was heading the wrong direction, all I had was a bit of trust in the man, and faith in myself. We got to Vienna and went to a nice home in the oldest part of the city. I was welcomed as if I was family. I ate a big meal, slept in a nice bed, bathed, but was getting worried. I thought perhaps they were fatting the calf."

"What were they doing?" asked Mike.

"Being gracious in a time of need. The next day the man took me to one of the grand old hotels downtown. He had found me a job, as a chambermaid. It provided a small room in the eaves to live in, a uniform, meals, and a tiny salary."

"That doesn't sound too bad," said Angelic.

"It really wasn't. It would have been a good place to ride out the war. But I felt it was my duty to return home and to find Aldo and Rene, especially since I'd left my daughter behind to pursue those things. The problem was the money. There wasn't much after everything else they provided."

"But you could rest and recover, and plan," said Dee.

"Exactly. I wasn't happy, but it looked like my best course of action. I thanked the man, and he went away. I never saw him again."

"What happened then?" asked Gina.

"I worked in the hotel for about three months. I learned my duties, kept mostly to myself, but made friends with the managers and tried to blend in as best I could. I picked up a smattering of other languages. It was where I first learned English and German, and a little Italian."

"But you were planning?" asked Jamal.

"I was trying to, but the money was so small, and I was comfortable. I couldn't come up with anything, except frustration."

"Something happened," said Angelic.

Anna smiled for a moment. "Yes, it did. I met a man who wanted to help me. By the time I'd been there three months, with food provided, I'd filled in a little. I had my figure back. I'd been married, as I said, I knew what I was doing."

Gina clapped her hands together. "Tell us," she said.

"I could see he was moon-eyed around me and I made sure to smile at him often. He lived in the hotel, some sort of businessman. It was really quite simple. I drew him in by almost giving him what he wanted. I wasn't happy with myself for doing it, but I felt my cause was justified. He seemed to enjoy it."

"How long did this last?" asked Dee.

"Long enough. We dated, discreetly of course, the hotel would have seen it as scandal. I told him my dream was to get to Paris, to see the world. He was quite taken with the idea. The conflict was peaking, the Germans were losing, and the Allied invasion was imminent. It was early 1944. He smelled opportunity, and he thought Paris was a good possibility for generating more wealth after the war."

Aldo's Adventure

Aldo napped again, because there was little else to do.

Be rested, always the best plan. Sleep or eat when you have nothing else to do.

He opened the door slightly, as he sensed it was getting light outside. The train was moving through the mountains and appeared to be heading due south.

Perhaps we are going straight to the castle and not to Munich. That would make sense. Saying Munich would make a nice misdirection but most people know the art is being kept at the castle, which lay southwest of Munich.

By the time it was fully light, Aldo felt confident he was not headed for the city.

I have no weapon, only a little money, the castle is quite remote, Anna may or may not be there. I'm playing with fate yet again.

The train slowed and came to a stop on the tracks. They were on a promontory looking off to the mountains.

Why here? Let me look out the other side of the car.

Aldo closed the door he had opened and moved to the other side of the boxcar. He worked the lever and opened the door slightly. He could hear no sounds but surely people, soldiers, were afoot.

There it is, the castle sat on a promontory of its own across a small gorge.

The train began moving slowly down the gorge and stopped only briefly at the bottom.

I need to be prepared for when they come aboard. My best opportunity seems in one corner behind or beneath the boxes. Perhaps they won't take them all. But why wouldn't they?

Aldo surveyed the corners, trying to pick which one might best serve him. The train moved again and climbed out of the gorge, continuing until it had reached full speed.

What happened, that was just a brief stop. Why didn't they unload? Where are we going now? What about Anna? It's too late. The train is at full speed. I can't jump off.

Dee and Friends
Sixth Day

Anna stopped for a moment and looked at the group. "I'm really suddenly quite tired. I think I'll skip dinner and go back to my room. Reliving old memories can certainly wear a person out."

"We'd love to hear more," said Gina.

"Perhaps later, after I rest."

"Can we take you back to your room?" asked Keno.

"That would be nice, I enjoy your company."

The three women dutifully rose and accompanied Anna to her stateroom.

"So, what do you think?" asked Mike, as the women rolled away.

"She married the rich guy and lived happily ever after," said Jamal.

"I don't think so. She'd have told us if it had been that. Why would that make you tired? I think there's more, perhaps a great deal more. It didn't seem like she loved him, just wanted to get to Paris, to Aldo, to Rene, to the war effort, to her daughter," replied Dee. "I think there's a lot more, maybe she'll tell us."

Aldo's Adventure

An hour later, by his watch, Aldo opened the boxcar door just enough to spot the sun. They were traveling northeast.

We should be in or around Munich if we were on a main track. Where are we going?

As the train pulled through a slight turn, Aldo retreated into the car but kept a line of sight on the top of the cars in front of him.

There are no guards. This is very low profile. What are the Nazis up to?

Aldo watched for another half hour and the train moved deeper into a heavily forested and mountainous region.

We are in the furthest regions of Bavaria, maybe Czechoslovakia. Where are we going? There is nothing out here.

Not long afterwards, the train turned onto an even smaller rail line, a branch line, and moved directly toward the mountains. In one last slow turn, Aldo could see the mountain directly in front of the train and the entrance to a tunnel.

We are in the middle of nowhere.

The train slowed and entered the tunnel. It traveled only a short distance inside before slowing again. Aldo had left the door cracked.

It probably wasn't a smart idea, but it was helpful to see.

A hundred yards inside, as most light had slipped away, the train curved in a small arc and there was light from overhead. Aldo could now see. It was a good size switching station, holding six trains plus the main rail. Including Aldo's, all the spur lines were now full.

They are all the big Nazi steam engines. What is this place? They all look like boxcars; it's not a troop location.

The train stopped, and steam momentarily filled the air, blocking Aldo's vision. Moments later he could see again.

There's very little activity here, very few personnel. Something clandestine, are they all art trains? It would be helpful to know. Maybe Anna's here.

Aldo waited until his train had been sitting quietly for several minutes before he considered getting off.

How best to handle this? I have clothes and a small crate. Inspiration.

Aldo tied the lower part of the extra pants legs to the upper part of each leg. It created a small circle with the butt of the pants at the top. He then ran each of one of the shirt arms through a couple of the belt loops and tied them off. If he slipped the pants leg on each arm, with the butt up and pulled the shirt over his head as a collar, it made a pack. Aldo slipped the other shirt in first, as padding, and then the small crate to the outside and slid the whole thing on his back. It was a little tight.

Better than a little loose. At least the painting should stay in place, and the whole thing will probably loosen up as I move.

Creeping down the tracks to the next train, Aldo stayed in the shadows but saw or heard no one. When he got to the nearest boxcar, there was a lock on the door.

None of the other art was locked up, why now? Or what else could be in there?

He moved to the third train and found an unchained door. Climbing up the side of the car, he worked the door open and stepped inside pulling the door behind him.

The car was stacked with crates. They were all stenciled "property".

What kind of property, generic art? Nazis were always specific. They had extensive lists of everything that interested them.

Aldo glanced around the car and for once there were a couple of tools hanging on an inside beam, two crowbars, some gloves and a pair of tongs. He grabbed a crowbar.

I need to be careful prying this off so I can put it back.

He worked around the top of the nearest crate, slowing prying the lid loose as he moved along. Reaching the last point of contact, Aldo gave a little extra push, and the top slid off.

Oh my word, I've heard about this.

The box was full of small gold nuggets, about the size of dental fillings. Aldo ran his hand through the nuggets and lifted a few for closer examination.

Unbelievable. They were fillings, taken from the dead. Well, they won't need them now, the dead or the Nazis. A little shudder ran across my shoulders. Still, enough to fill two pants pockets. I can trade them if needed, or maybe cash them in if I survive the war.

The business of the nuggets concluded, Aldo carefully replaced the lid on the crate and moved to the door. He thought to keep the crowbar.

I should check another car. I still wonder why the one was locked. I'm going back to it.

Aldo moved slowly along until he returned to the boxcar with the lock.

Instead of prying the lock off, which would be obvious to anyone later, let me try prying the door. If I can get it open, later perhaps they might think it was never closed properly, or not.

Aldo pried on the bottom of the door opening and made a little headway. Realizing he didn't have enough leverage from there, he climbed up into the doorframe and carefully balanced his pack—so as not to fall; he leveraged the door right behind the lock. It gave way. He opened it just enough to get inside.

I have to let my eyes adjust. Glancing around the car, I am confused. It looked like a room full of supplies. Slowly things sorted out, and I realize it is a rolling laboratory.

Taking a few cautious steps, Aldo moved around the car. There were instruments, containers, tubing, glass in various sizes and shapes, and many boxes labeled with exotic looking words Aldo didn't recognize, chemicals or compounds of some kind.

I might try to sound the words out. Maybe it would strike a bell. It looks like the lab is ready to go but nothing is currently going on. I should examine the contents of the boxes more closely.

Then he heard it, the sound of a whistle, another train approaching the tunnel.

Better get out of here, where do I hide?

Aldo jumped from the boxcar and pushed the door closed. He crouched near the wheels of the car, blending into the darkness of the switching yard floor.

The new train came steaming into the yard on the main track and screeched to a halt, the engine still rumbling.

It doesn't look like they're going to stay. Perhaps I should catch a ride. But they're headed east, there's nothing out there until well into Czechoslovakia. I'd really like to get home, find Anna, no telling where she is if her train didn't stop or stay at the castle. She might be here but I think I'd better get on board.

Aldo made his way toward the main line. About four cars back he saw an open boxcar. He ran quickly and scrambled up into the car. There were a couple of pallets of explosives in the middle of the car and the rest of it was empty, save for some scattered straw piled up in one end.

That might make a good hiding place. Sniffing the air, he walked to the straw and grabbed a handful. It had a machine oil smell to it. *Well, so much to cover any scent I might have if they get up in here.*

A couple of minutes later the train rolled slowly forward. Aldo sat at an angle where he was hidden but could see out the door. It was a long tunnel and for some time there was only darkness before emerging in the forest on the far side.

I have no idea where I am or what's going on, just along for the ride, as they say.

Aldo could see back down the tracks behind him. As the

final car exited the tunnel, Aldo realized it was a fully loaded troop carrier.

There could, or would, be soldiers everywhere. I'll never get off this train.

The train exited the tunnel by several car lengths and came to a stop. The soldiers streamed off of the troop carrier flatbed.

Did someone see me? Are they coming for me? They're approaching this car.

Aldo quickly scooped up a couple of hands full of the hay and hid under it in the corner of the boxcar.

Dee and Friends
Seventh & Eighth Days

The next two days went by in a blur for the group. Anna didn't feel well and didn't want to meet for dinner or talk. The women worried about her constantly and checked on her daily.

The longship stopped in Vukovar, Croatia, and Mohàcs, Hungary. The women weren't interested in the smaller villages and preferred to keep their vigil over Anna, who assured them she was fine, just needing to rest for a few days. None of them wanted to be very far away.

The men sat at the bar on the sundeck and watched the countries slide by. It was relaxing.

Aldo's Adventure

There were feet pounding on the gravel, and then they were in the car. I'll die like a farm animal in a barn.

There were muffled shouts and grunting.

The sound seemed to stay in the middle of the car. The explosives? What are they doing?

Aldo dared not move. He lay there for what felt like an eternity, but no one came over to him. Seconds ticked away. When the sounds had receded for several minutes, he peeked out through the straw. The car was empty, all the explosives gone. Aldo lay there another minute.

I have to see what's going on.

He slipped from under the hay and gingerly moved at an angle toward the door. Easing in beside it Aldo could see down the tracks toward the tunnel. The soldiers were busy uncrating the explosives and carrying them into the opening. Another group was uncrating detonators and cable.

They're going to blow up the tunnel. Surely not to destroy the trains. The Nazis are notorious for not leaving anything behind. But we're deep in their own country.

Aldo looked back to the tunnel and noticed something strange. Another group of soldiers were prying up the tracks and pulling away the ties at the mouth of the entrance.

They are camouflaging the location. They want to come back in the future. It's like a cache—wealth, art, weapons, supplies and whatever else, the laboratory. It's a fallback plan.

He sat by the door and watched for the next hour. The explosives were set, the rails and ties loaded on the flatcar, along with the troops. An officer approached the detonator and glanced back to the train; he then turned and depressed the plunger. There was a small explosion.

I thought it would be louder but then I heard several more muffled explosions. They staged the charges back into the tunnel so that it collapsed for some distance without being a massive explosion. Easier to get back inside in the future. Clever fellows.

As the dust settled Aldo was expecting the train to pull away.

But there was another surprise.

Two men with sergeant stripes on their tunics appeared from the woods above the train. Each cradled an MP-40 in their arms. They took two steps toward the flatcar and opened fire, executing every soldier from the work detail.

Aldo sat in stunned silence for a moment.

None of them will be telling any secrets.

Dee and Friends
Eighth Night

They were all sitting at dinner, finished eating, just chatting and watching the day slide past.

"Good news," said Gina. The group glanced in her direction. "Anna said she'd come down to our room and chat. After a couple of days in her own suite, she's ready to get out."

"When will she be along?" asked Keno.

Gina glanced at her watch. "We probably should be going."

They trooped down to their staterooms only to find Anna sitting in her wheelchair by Gina and Dee's door.

"I'm so sorry we're late. Let me get the door," said Dee.

"Nonsense, I was early, just ready to get out of my room for a while. I think Ate was glad to be rid of me as well."

Angelic, accompanied by Gina and Keno, rolled Anna into the room and out onto the balcony.

"I notice you dress up for dinner even without me."

"We like to make an occasion of it," replied Jamal.

"I think that's wonderful. And if I might make a suggestion…" She paused.

"Please do," said Keno.

"I believe we are approaching Budapest, Hungary, tomorrow. Since you like to dress for the occasion, something you might really like, with appropriate surroundings of course, would be a visit to the Hungarian State Opera House. It's quite grand. They have a performance of 'The Magic Flute' that I think you would really enjoy. Get the best seats you can find."

"Isn't that Mozart?" asked Dee.

"Yes, it is," replied Anna.

"I thought it was the Beatles, Ringo maybe," said Mike.

"That's the Magic Christian," replied Jamal.

Anna cackled. "You men are really too much."

"Aren't they though?" said Angelic. "They overdose on stupid regularly."

"Oh, come on," said Gina. "Tell us more of your story."

"I don't know if I can keep up with the Magic Christian."

"I'm sure you can," replied Keno. "Plus, it will shut them up."

"You were making arrangements with the businessman," said Gina.

"Ah, yes. His name was Lorenz Muster. He was a financier, a banker, and a developer. The idea of Paris postwar intrigued him. The Allies were winning and would soon invade the continent from England. We just had to wait for the liberation of Paris, hopefully by the end of the year. Turned out it was in August and Lorenz wasted no time in getting us there."

"I bet you had a little something to do with that," said Gina.

"Maybe a little, maybe a lot, but he was in a hurry anyway. The man could smell money. That made my life easier for a time."

"Only for a time?" asked Dee.

"Don't jump ahead," she said, followed by a nod. "He wanted to get married, and I dangled that proposition in front of him but never let us act on it."

"Weren't you afraid you might lose him?" asked Keno.

"There was always that possibility but he was badly smitten and accustomed to having his way."

"That's a fine line to tread," said Gina.

"Absolutely," Anna responded and winked at Gina.

"Let her tell the story," said Angelic.

"Eager for the details," said Jamal to Angelic. She rolled her eyes at him.

"I spent from early 1944 until we left for Paris working on my language skills and feeling guilty over my daughter, Aldo, Rene, my failure to fulfill my war efforts. I was a bit confused and thinking I'd lost everything. So yes, I did cling to Lorenz, which made him very happy."

"You couldn't just stay with him permanently could you?" asked Jamal.

"No, I couldn't. My life would have been very different if I had, but ultimately unsatisfying, probably rather quickly. I had a purpose for Lorenz, but no passion. We got to Paris and fortunately he was very busy looking for opportunities which allowed me to search for answers of my own."

Aldo's Adventure

The two sergeants climbed aboard the train, and it pulled away. Not long afterwards the train came to the main line and made the turn north.

I have a feeling those mountains were in Germany and if we're heading north, we must be going into Czechoslovakia. I am a long way from home.

Aldo noted the time on his watch but within an hour the train was slowing again. Since the doors of the car had been open, Aldo had left them and hidden in the corner under the hay while the train traveled.

They were in heavily forested mountains again, and Aldo could see the tunnel as it approached.

Are we going to have a repeat performance here? Surely not, they killed everyone.

This time Aldo could see out the other side of the tunnel as the train slowed and then switched to a spur rail. This one was much smaller than the previous tunnel.

As close as he was to the front of the train, Aldo could hear the ticking of the engine and feel the steam dissipating into the cooler air.

Apparently we're really stopping this time. I'm going to sit right here and wait.

A half hour later Aldo stuck his head outside the car. Even though there was a light on the tunnel wall beyond the spur line, the tunnel was so short there was natural light at both ends. There did not seem to be anyone about.

Aldo walked slowly and softly along the train. His first destination was the flatcar at the end. As he progressed, Aldo felt more and more confident that the area was uninhabited.

Anyone remaining on the train must have gone on to the next town. It can't be far.

He got to the flatcar and stopped to survey it. There weren't as many soldiers as he remembered.

We must have lost a few along the way, on the trip from there to here, wherever there and here are.

Aldo climbed onto the flatcar and searched. He accumulated a small pile of items—several MP-40s, several more magazines for MP-40s, a couple of backpacks, which he went through before emptying, and a single helmet. Then he began going through the pockets of the remaining soldiers. Aside from a good collection of Reichsmarks, he found a Vacheron Constantin pocket watch, a solid gold signet ring, and a pinky ring with a two-carat diamond.

Those soldiers must have been from some old German families to have items of that value on them and be little more than laborers, dead laborers. The Nazis are getting desperate.

Aldo took off his homemade backpack. He untied everything and shook them out as best he could. He changed clothes standing on the flatcar. He put on the gold ring and slid the watch, the diamond ring, and the Reichsmarks into his pockets.

He was just able to get the painting into one backpack. Then he went through the weapons. Selecting the cleanest of the MP-40s, he dropped the magazine it held and entered a fresh one. He stuck three more fresh ones and his other things in another of the backpacks.

I feel better about being armed and having some resources. I'll have 100 rounds, which won't last long in a firefight, but it might get me through a short shoot. Now, I'm in civilian clothes but I have a helmet. I can go either way.

Aldo slipped the helmet on his head, shouldered the backpacks and picked up the MP-40.

Now to examine the rest of this train.

He moved slowly along the cars, opening each door and looking inside. There were weapons, rockets, boxes of equipment, supplies. Then several crates that held "property", which he now understood what that meant. Making a note of those cars he moved along to the remainder.

In the next to the last car, Aldo found more art. Lots of big heavy crates jammed full.

Too bad there's no way to transport those, and where would I go anyway?

Moving to the last car he hadn't checked, Aldo glanced quickly at his wristwatch. Then he thought of his pocket watch.

I'll have to get used to having that. Either way, time is getting short and I can't carry much more.

The last car was again more art, only this time it was different.

There were lots of small boxes and single painting crates, like someone had made one last trip around wherever and picked up a few extras or a few favorites and wrapped them individually. This is promising.

Aldo didn't want to take the time to determine which painting was in each box. He just picked three of his favorites, Renoir, Degas, and Monet.

The criterion is will they fit in the backpack?

He found three that would and loaded them up. Struggling under the weight of the packs and carrying the weapon, Aldo slowly walked toward the opposite open end of the tunnel.

There has to be a town beyond there.

Dee and Friends
Eighth Night

"Well, I'd better get back, Ate will wonder where I'm at. I appreciate you letting me join up for the evening. I feel much better, just a little tired."

"We'll take you," said Angelic. The three women gathered around Anna and rolled her into the stateroom and then down the hall.

The three men remained on the balcony.

"Why do you suppose she wants us to go to the opera?" asked Mike.

"It's a big event. I understand the opera house is huge and very ornate," replied Jamal.

"What's it about?"

"Well, it's Mozart, classical in nature, about the relationship between a man and a woman and all the related complications," said Dee.

"Is she trying to tell us something?" asked Mike.

"Probably just trying to keep us entertained. She figures the women will like it," replied Jamal.

"You sure that's all?" said Mike.

"What makes you think there's more?" asked Dee.

"Back when I was in business, in construction, people were often terrible about telling you what they wanted, what they really thought or felt. You had to keep digging at them. Something about her gives me that feeling."

Dee looked at him for a moment. Mike was from a family that had been in the construction business for several generations. They were successful. He was the oldest son and one day would have been the senior partner in the business. He had good instincts but then he took a cruise where he met Dee and the others, and his life changed, if not forever, certainly for now. But, he had a point.

"I guess we try to keep her talking. Maybe something will come out."

"Here come the women," added Jamal.

Back in their own room, Dee asked Gina, "What do you think Anna's story is really about?"

Gina was in the middle of unzipping her dress, and she paused. "I don't know. I've been wondering that myself. Angelic and Keno too."

Aldo's Adventure

Aldo slowly made his way out of the tunnel. He clung to the sidewalls, which weren't very far from the tracks.

If they blow this tunnel up, it won't take so much to do it or dig it out later. I see no sign of any sentries. We're deep in the fatherland or one of their vassals. I guess they feel safe.

Emerging into the light, Aldo followed the tracks. They didn't go far before he hit the main line.

Right or left?

Aldo slipped out of the packs and sat them against the butt of a tree. Then he worked his way up the branches until he was over twenty feet in the air. Clutching the trunk, he circled his way around the tree.

There it is, a village, or at least it's one I can see. Go left, and to think I'd probably gone right.

Aldo slipped back into the packs and adjusted them on his shoulders.

It's a good thing I saw the village and that it's not far. I couldn't go a long ways like this.

Then he started down the main track to the left, walking slowly. There was a slight grade and then a drop into a small valley.

At some point, I'll want to get off the track and stash this stuff until I can figure out where I am.

Aldo started down the grade. When he got approximately halfway, he veered from the tracks and wandered into the forest. After a short distance, he found a cluster of trees growing closely together. The conflux of the trunks made a small shelf that he piled the backpacks on. He angled them such that they didn't appear visible from a few feet away. Then he walked back to the tracks.

Stopping where he came out of the woods, Aldo built a small pile of stones with two sticks on top laid out in an "x".

Marks the spot, he thought, smiling to himself.

Moving toward the village, Aldo stayed on the edge of the railroad right of way, where he could easily slip into the forest if needed. He held the MP-40 at low ready. He had an extra magazine in his belt.

It will have to be enough until I figure out where I am.

Aldo moved along the track, taking his time.

Wherever I am, this is likely where I'll have to stay for a while. I just have to be careful and find a way to survive and a way to travel.

The grade flattened out and Aldo knew he was getting close to the edge of the village. Then he saw the sign, "Pilsen".

I'm in Czechoslovakia. It could be worse.

Aldo made a decision. He hung the MP-40 on a low branch so that the weapon was just off the ground on the forest side. He ditched the helmet, hiked out onto the tracks, and walked into town.

It wasn't very busy, and he moved along as if he knew what he was doing. Coming upon a small café just beyond the switch yard, he ducked inside.

Look for the pretty waitress, I can make this work.

The woman behind the counter was big and bent and gray and old. She had several teeth missing. Aldo smiled at her and she looked at him blankly.

"Signora?" he said.

Her eyes got a little wider.

"Pranzo?" he continued.

Her face was still blank.

He saw a menu and pointed toward it. She smiled and handed it to him.

I can't read this. Maybe I can gesture.

Aldo laid the menu down and held both hands out about a foot apart. "Grande panino."

She nodded. "Schnitzel?"

"Ja," was the best he could do.

She turned and called off something rapidly to the cook. Aldo went and sat down at the nearest table.

A few minutes later he had a big sandwich.

I could probably eat a couple of these. Now I need to find a place to stay, away from any soldiers.

Finishing his sandwich and paying with the Reichsmarks he had collected, Aldo carefully walked the side and back streets of Pilsen looking for a certain sign. He wanted a place to rent, a small hotel or a "Pension", a boardinghouse, would be even better.

I will always be curious about what happened to Anna but I will probably never know. It seems best that I ride the war out here and then think of returning home. I don't think it can last too much longer, either way, and there's more at stake now. I can no longer afford to run. It has been a long journey, but a worthy one I think.

Dee and Friends
Ninth Day & Night

They got off the longship as a group in Budapest. Taking a taxi downtown, they located the opera house and obtained times and tickets. Then they took a quick tour. It was immense and unbelievably ornate. The dress code was formal.

"We don't have formal clothes," said Angelic.

"Riverboat classic will not do it," added Jamal.

"Where can we find something?" asked Keno.

"I don't think we have time to purchase and have it altered for tonight," said Dee.

"Not likely," added Mike.

"Not to worry," said Gina. "Anna gave me the name of a formal wear rental downtown. They'll fix us up and we can return everything right after the performance. They specialize in river tour tourists."

"Very insightful of her," said Dee.

"She said most tourists don't travel with high end formal wear, whether or not they can afford it. This shop caters to that crowd, who often want to see the opera or the ballet."

"Let's go check it out," said Keno. "I'll do hair and makeup." Keno had been a salon owner before the adventures began. She had been a cheerleader at the school where Mike had played football. They had gotten married. Having Hawaiian ancestry, she had wanted to take a cruise through the Pacific, where they met Dee and the others and became friends.

"I've got the address right here," replied Gina.

———

Later that evening, suitably attired, they made their way to the Hungarian State Opera House. They had great, really expensive seats and were totally mesmerized by the performance, the surroundings, and the atmosphere of the event.

Riding back to the longship, their formal clothing returned, questions emerged.

"How many times do you think Anna has seen the performance?" asked Angelic.

"She said several, I don't know how many specifically," replied Gina.

"Are we sure she didn't marry that wealthy banker?" asked Mike. "That was no small ticket item."

"We'll see what else she tells us, but she said she didn't," replied Gina.

They tumbled out of the cab, boarded the longship and went up to the top deck bar. Dee ordered everyone a round.

"So, what are we supposed to take from that performance?" asked Mike.

"It was amazingly sensual," added Keno.

"Yes, the costumes, the music, the formality of the crowd, the opera house itself, they all positively oozed sensuality. I'm still tingling," said Angelic, who then laughed and fanned her face with her fingers.

"I agree, but what was it really about?" asked Gina.

"It was a quest for wisdom and enlightenment," replied Dee.

"A journey of good versus evil," added Jamal.

"I thought it was a love story," said Mike.

"It was all those things," said Angelic.

"And more?" said Gina.

"What do you mean?" asked Keno.

"Did Anna just send us to have a good time and enjoy the show, or is she trying to tell us more about herself?"

"Providing us backstory or framework?" said Dee.

"Adding texture and suspense to what she has remaining to tell us," said Angelic.

"I just thought it was good," said Keno.

"It was," added Mike. "And I enjoyed it as well, but I think she's telling us something."

"What?" asked Gina.

"We just have to keep listening," replied Dee.

**Dee and Friends
Tenth Day**

As they gathered for breakfast the next morning Gina announced, "Anna will join us on the sundeck after we eat."

"Not for breakfast?" asked Mike.

"She said she had some medication she needed to take and always likes to rest a little afterward, just a few minutes. She wants to hear what we thought of the opera."

"Seriously?" asked Jamal.

"Yes, she has taken quite the interest in us."

"I wonder what she'll share today," added Dee.

————

They were all seated under a couple of umbrellas on the sundeck.

"How did you enjoy the opera?" asked Anna.

"We thought it was amazing," replied Angelic.

"It has so much texture, such depth. I always enjoy revisiting it. I love the element of 3s."

"3s?" asked Dee.

"Yes, Mozart seemed fascinated with 3s. Three muses, three slaves, three chords in the music, and it seemed to be engraved in his senses."

"I suppose it was. He had quite an innate sensitivity," replied Dee.

Anna smiled at him and nodded.

————

"Was today Bratislava?" asked Jamal.

"Yes," replied Anna. "There are things to see but I never

spent much time there, too close to Vienna, which I've always thought of as one of my homes."

"Really, I didn't think you liked it," said Keno.

"It wasn't that I didn't like it, I was just in a hurry when I first got there. I learned to appreciate it. The city provided me great opportunities. It was Lorenz's home, and we went back and forth between Paris and Vienna routinely."

"So, you stayed with him for a time?" asked Gina.

"In retrospect it doesn't seem that long, but yes, it was several years."

"I thought he wanted to get married," said Keno.

"He did, and I eventually accepted his proposal. We were engaged for several years."

"How did that work?" asked Gina.

Anna smiled and winked at her. "Lorenz was quite busy with his opportunities, which gave me some time to return to my family home outside of the city. Fortunately, it wasn't destroyed and my Picasso was still intact. Had I returned any later that might not have been so but my neighbors kept an eye on the place after I disappeared."

"Anyway, when Lorenz wasn't busy, he pestered me endlessly about marriage. So, I finally accepted his proposal. While I believe he wanted to marry me, you can imagine what he was really after. I knew I needed time, to let things settle down, to sort things out, to get some idea of Aldo and Rene, to check on my daughter. I compromised."

"And?" said Gina.

"And, I'd been married, had a lover, and a child. So I told him I was a virgin, and he believed me. He seemed to relish that fact. Lorenz wasn't that passionate or that skilled but he got what he wanted and thereafter wasn't in such a big hurry to get married.

"We were one of new Paris, post-war Paris's, biggest and brightest socialite couples. We went to parties, balls, openings, whatever was happening. It wasn't that grand. Most people were still suffering badly, there was no money, and the locals were broke and resented us. Lorenz made a lot of money, bought up a lot of property, and bankrolled many new startups. He had numerous business partners. It was quite the time and place to be an entrepreneur. He got very involved, which left me time to pursue my own interests."

"What did he think of your painting?" asked Angelic.

"I never told him about it, or the house or farm. I'd simply tell him I was going to visit with old friends or neighbors. He paid little attention when he had a deal going on and often was gone for days."

"But something happened," said Dee.

"Finally, I was bored out of my mind, actually considered taking on a lover, but I didn't want to be that decadent. I still had hope. And one day out of the blue my prayers were answered."

"How?" asked Keno

"Lorenz would often ask me questions about deals he was considering. I don't know if he ever took my advice, but he asked often so I assumed it had some value to him. I don't think he was smart enough to have just been flattering me, not with knowledge. He liked things, material things. One morning he sat down at the breakfast table and after we'd been served, he started to talk."

———

"I have a deal I'm looking into with some Czechs and some Italians. It's a consortium of some sort run by a fellow who is Italian but lives part-time in Czechoslovakia. He has partners in both countries. He wants to build an industrial area at the edge of the city, then possibly housing for the workers the industry will employ. "

"Why Paris? Why not somewhere in Italy? I suppose Prague is out of the question with the Communists. In fact, is he a Communist?"

"No, there's no indication. He supposedly fought in the war and somehow kept or made his money there or shortly after. He has extensive holdings in Venice which I have checked into and they appear legitimate."

"So he's the Italian version of you?"

"Possibly, I'm curious to find out. "

"What's his name?"

"Aldo Buio, he goes by 'AB'."

An alarm went off in my head.

———

"Seriously, why would you think it was him?" asked Dee.

"I didn't for sure. There was just something odd about it, the name, and I was curious."

Anna glanced at her watch, it looked chunky on her arm and Dee realized it was a man's gold wristwatch, a Phillipe Patek. "I'd better get out of the sun. I'm afraid I've talked your ear off." She went to roll back.

Mike stood up. "Let me."

Anna nodded at him and smiled.

Aldo's Aftermath

Aldo rode out the balance of the war in Pilsen. There were the paintings to consider along with the Germans and the aftermath of the war, the trials and accusations. It was a good place to hide. He tried to be seen around town, to blend in, without becoming too involved with anyone. Once the Allies invaded Germany, it was only a matter of time, but the Russians were coming from the east and he didn't want to be trapped in a Communist-bloc country.

There was the big pile of Reichsmarks he had collected, but they would soon enough be worthless. He tried to use them to pay his way until the Nazis surrendered.

Two things happened that made Aldo's life much simpler, in fact they turned his world around. When he had inspected the train with the property crates, aside from loading his pockets with the gold fillings, he'd also wrapped several pounds of them in the extra shirt and tied it up in a bundle. They were one reason he hadn't been able to travel far. Between the weight of the paintings and the gold, it was all he could do to carry them to Pilsen.

In those closing moments of the war, Aldo got a job at the Skoda Works. They produced armaments for the Nazis and were under tremendous pressure for output in those last few months. They were just looking for able bodies. Aldo spoke English, French, and Italian, but got a job anyway. In a short time, he picked up some German and some Czech. *I'm good with languages.*

The second thing that happened was the Czechs realized the Germans were going to lose and began some local resistance—tearing down Nazi flags, toppling monuments, defacing buildings and cars. The Nazis had a swift response and harassed, shot, and killed citizens.

At the community meetings at Skoda, Aldo pushed hard

for disruption of the Nazis. He didn't participate in the open riots but conducted some small acts of sabotage, which endeared him to the locals, and heartily encouraged the others.

I'll never know for sure but perhaps because of those actions, Pilsen was liberated in May, 1945 by the Allies, specifically General George S. Patton and the 3rd Army. And they stayed for six months. Had it been the Russians who liberated the rest of the country, I'd have had to flee again.

In the aftermath of the Allied arrival, the Skoda Works dropped all armament production and scrambled for viable projects. Because many employees left, were frightened, or fled the Communists, Aldo worked in many different areas, one of which was smelting.

It gave him an opportunity to melt many of the gold fillings into small ingots so that they would become tradeable, and suddenly much more valuable while removing him from any Nazi association.

One other thing that happened, a new manager came to the plant. He was a Czech but his mother was Italian and he spoke the language. Aldo heard the rumor and went to meet him.

His name was Dante Bartik. The mother's family was from Venice and he still had ties there. Spoke the language well.

But then he asked Aldo, "Perche sei qui?"

Aldo replied, "I work here."

"No, non é questo che intendevo."

So Aldo told him, "I came up from Italy, Milan, and got trapped. I utilized the circumstances, learned French, German, and now Czech. I've been working here for the last few months."

Dante smiled, took me by the shoulders, and said in English, "I can use a man like you."

Dee and Friends
Eleventh Day

They got together in the hallway outside the staterooms and then went to breakfast. Anna was already there and waiting on them.

"Good morning."

"Good morning to you," replied Angelic as Gina and Keno stepped around Anna. The men nodded and took their seats.

"Up early?" asked Dee.

"I always find this part of the trip invigorating. Whatever you do, if you don't leave the ship the rest of the cruise, you need to go ashore today. Vienna waits for you."

"Are you going?" asked Keno.

"Oh no, it's too strenuous. I've already spent so much time there. But, I'll probably sit up on the sundeck and enjoy the view and my memories for as long as I can stay outside."

"What should we see?" asked Gina.

"There's art museums, palaces, opera and government buildings, the zoo—most of the buildings and sights relate to Austrian royalty and their history. If you go to the old city, there's something on every corner."

"Anything specific we should be sure to see?" asked Dee.

"Be sure to stop and eat at the 'Demel', the 'Hofzuckerbäckerei Demel'. It's a café and bakery that dates back to the 1700s; Lorenz and I ate there all the time. The pastry is to die for. If you're near the Opera House on Riverstrasse, the boulevard that runs around the inner city, you can see where Lorenz's family home was located. It was destroyed by bombing during the war, as was the opera house. They rebuilt the opera in the 1950s, but there's no longer anything in the immediate vicinity. You might also see the 'Imperial Vienna' hotel. That's where Lorenz was living during the war, after the bombing."

"That's where you met him," said Gina.

Anna nodded. "We lived there after the war as well. Housing in the inner city was largely destroyed. After the liberation from the Nazis, the Russians used the hotel as their headquarters, although I never cared for the Communists and avoided them as much as possible. I think Lorenz had a few dealings with them."

"Are there churches?" asked Jamal.

"Oh yes, go see St. Stephen's Cathedral. It was bombed and then rebuilt completely in its original form several years after the war. When we were first together in Vienna, Lorenz used to chase me through the rubble of the church and then when he caught me we'd count the bomb craters. They were everywhere."

"I'm sure it's a beautiful city," said Angelic.

"It is. Everything has a different look now, after all the rebuilding, even though much of it was recreated. When Lorenz and I were here the first time, there was rubble everywhere, dust, dirt, filth of all kinds, broken and defeated people. It's changed a lot over time, yet it remains the same."

"I'm sure it's a city full of dreams," said Gina.

"Yes, dream on, but don't imagine they'll all come true."

Aldo's Aftermath

Pilsen was lucky. With the Allies there, and their staying for a time, a certain normalcy followed them. The war was over but nobody knew what was coming next. It was an uneasy state of mind.

Dante became Aldo's mentor in business. He was looking for opportunities. In post-war Europe there were lots of them, with a failed regime, allies fighting over the spoils, people hungry, tired, and poor. His family in Venice had position and money. He was already building wharf space and warehouses. He'd have access to all of war-torn Europe, if he got there first.

Dante offered Aldo the chance to work with him and he took it, long hours and lots of decisions, but always guided by the principal, make the money work for you. There was one thing that made it easier for Aldo but more difficult or uncomfortable for Dante.

Upon his arrival in Pilsen, Dante had rented a large beautiful home from a local family that needed the money. He prepaid. When the Allies arrived, they took command of the home and evicted Dante who ended up at the hostel with Aldo. When they left, the Communists took over the estate. They ended up working together side by side at the hostel.

After a few months of this, and the very fortunate fact that the country looked like it might avoid the immediate capitulation to the Communists, there was a small window. They had to act fast. That's when Aldo had an epiphany—Paris.

He took Dante the idea, and he shrugged, until Aldo dropped two gold bars on the table. Suddenly Aldo had his attention.

"So tell me what you're thinking?"

"Paris can be the inland hub for our western European

empire, goods shipped through Venice, transported to Paris for collection and distribution. We cover the whole continent from one location or the other."

Dante put out his hand. Aldo took it and slowly shook his fingers. "I'll introduce you to the family."

Dee and Friends
Twelfth & Thirteenth Day

They spent two days in Vienna, touring the city extensively day and night, looking at everything. It left them exhausted and overcome by a feeling that the past and the present just kept circling around them, from one moment to the next. It felt like a dog chasing its tail but not knowing whose it was.

They gathered late in the afternoon of the thirteenth day on the sundeck of the longship. Looking at the skyline they felt they knew the city, but realized it was only a shadow they had seen, a shadow that would soon disappear.

"Do you think we saw what it was she wanted us to see?" asked Jamal.

"I think we just ought to ask her," added Mike.

"She'd never tell us. It's a game. We have to keep playing," replied Dee.

"What are you guys pontificating about?" asked Angelic.

"It's just noise," replied Keno.

"I think there's more to her story and I think she'll tell us in her own good time," said Gina.

The others turned to look at her.

"Do you know something we don't?" asked Dee.

"Nothing she has told me. It's just a sense I get from her. She's dishing this out in small pieces so we can absorb it."

"So we don't rush to judgement?" asked Jamal.

"Maybe something like that."

"Or maybe she just wants to space it out over the cruise so she'll have something to talk about," added Angelic.

"That makes sense," said Keno.

"Or maybe they're all clues, and we have to piece it together to solve the riddle or the equation," said Dee.

"I like the sound of that," said Anna who had rolled up on them without being noticed.

Aldo's Aftermath

The country stayed in independent hands for almost three years. In early 1948, the coalition government had fallen apart and the Czech Communists were taking control. Then in the late summer, 165,000 troops and 4600 tanks from the Soviet Union, Poland, Bulgaria, and Hungary crossed the border into Czechoslovakia and clamped down.

Dante had anticipated this eventuality and, during the interim years, had contacted the local Czech Communist party and negotiated certain benefits for Skoda and his auxiliary businesses. In fact, several of the local leaders were minority partners with him and Aldo.

'Follow the money' was serving them well. Aldo was a full partner in the Czech operations and a minority partner in Venice. He'd met the family and gotten along well. Dante's mother liked Aldo, so did his sister, an attractive dark-haired and dark-eyed beauty. Aldo had largely forgotten the war.

The appeal of Paris was still there, as Aldo always enjoyed the city and the opportunities it might hold. He was expecting to be the executive director of the Parisian operation and to become quite wealthy.

Then one day there was an occurrence. Aldo didn't notice it so much at the time but it became clearer as the operation progressed.

Dante had met an Austrian financier who was doing a lot of work in Paris. Rather than compete with him, Dante felt it best to combine, perhaps consolidate with the gentleman, one Lorenz Muster.

Dee and Friends
Fourteenth Day

"I thought this was called the Four Rivers tour?" asked Mike.

"It is," replied Dee.

"We left Vienna last night, so it's soon that we change rivers?" asked Jamal.

"We stop in Austria again, later today, then two days in Germany and we make the turn from the Danube."

"What river?" asked Mike.

"Actually, it's the 'Main-Danube Canal' that will take us to the Main River."

"So, not really a river, or four rivers, just three rivers and a canal," said Jamal.

"Nothing is ever what it seems, is it?" replied Dee.

They were standing on the deck outside their staterooms, waiting on the women.

"When do you suppose we'll hear from Anna again?" asked Mike.

"Gina said she needed to rest for a day or so, that Anna sees Vienna as the midpoint. Even though we have a little less than two weeks to Amsterdam and we've already been onboard for two weeks."

"I guess it's the emotional center for her, maybe?" said Jamal.

"What?" asked Mike.

"She sees Vienna as the midpoint of her journey, whatever that may be."

"Whatever what may be?" asked Keno as she walked up with Gina and Angelic closely behind her.

"The journey we're on, when we change rivers," replied Dee.

"Soon?" asked Keno.

"Couple of days and then we'll be in Germany for most of the rest of the trip until we're almost to Amsterdam."

Anna's Aftermath

Lorenz mentioned it again at breakfast a week later.

"I met AB a few days ago and he has some interesting plans. He speaks French well, almost like a native."

Anna looked at him blankly.

"AB, Aldo Buio, the gentleman I told you about last week, the Italian with the development plans."

"Oh!" She leaned back in her chair.

Lorenz didn't seem to notice and kept talking. "He had some good ideas for placement of the structures he wants to build and seems to know the city well."

"Did you ask him about that?"

"I did in fact and he said he had been here before the war and shortly thereafter."

"'Thereafter' as in after the war ended or shortly after it began?"

Lorenz paused for a moment. "I'm really not clear, but it seems inconsequential. His knowledge will be immensely helpful. Would you like to meet him?"

I paused and took a bite of breakfast, my mind scrambling to process, too many coincidences, or overactive imagination. "Perhaps later, after you two have seen how the project progresses."

"Excellent idea, I do so love how your mind works."

I bet you do.

Aldo's Aftermath

Aldo met Lorenz, who insisted Aldo call him by his first name, a few weeks after Dante first mentioned doing business with him. Aldo traveled to Paris, for the first time since Anna, Rene, and he had caught a ride on the Nazi steam trains. *That seems so long ago. It's good to be back. I enjoyed my life here and the time with my friends.* He wondered about Anna for the first time in a long time.

Lorenz had mentioned his fiancé, also named Anna, the second time they had talked. He seemed quite proud of her. *Perhaps we'll meet one day.*

Lorenz was quite the showman and the talker. He had grand visions, but mostly he was a financier. That was good for Aldo and Dante. He wouldn't be too nosy as long as they were turning a profit, and he was prospering from the arrangement. He wasn't a details man; he'd be easy to fool. Aldo listened to Lorenz talk as Lorenz paraded him around Paris and looked for his weaknesses. Just something to know and to have for a rainy day, should one arise in their relationship.

The time passed quickly, and Aldo had been in Paris for several weeks. Lorenz had located some property and already owned other parcels that would be suitable. Dante and Aldo were planning on manufacturing of some type, plus warehousing, and possibly construction. Aldo got the building project underway with Lorenz and left for Venice.

———

Dante and Aldo spent several days planning and then a day with his family. Aldo invited Dante's mother and sister, Aurora and Alessandra Uberti Bartik, to Paris. They were most excited about the visit.

He reserved a suite at Le Meurice, the luxury hotel in Paris. The Nazis had commandeered it during the war and the rooms had remained in good order. There had been some resistance and fighting when the Allies took the city in August 1944 but the bulk of the hotel and the suites had survived intact. By the time Aldo arrived in 1948, everything was once again fully operational. He knew they'd enjoy the location and the luxury.

Anna's Aftermath

Anna made numerous visits to the country and to the farm. She had spoken with all her neighbors and even the former Resistance leaders, secretly of course, as no one would admit to their war-time activities. They knew nothing of Rene or Aldo.

She visited Rene's family several times and felt great sadness for them not knowing his fate. She had never meet Aldo's family. He said he was from the south of Paris, but she didn't remember him being specific. Rene and Anna had met him through the local Resistance group. It seems odd in hindsight that she didn't know. *I never thought about it then.*

She presumed they were both dead, which brought a chill to her, as if part of her own soul had passed away. *I keep telling myself that if they had lived, they'd be back in Paris by now. They'd be looking for each other, like I was. While I feel great joy for the Allied victory and for the freedom of my country and the return to my homeland, I also feel a great sadness for what I failed to achieve in my efforts, and for my fallen friends.* It weighed heavily, and she felt ashamed for the things she'd done to survive.

Aldo's Aftermath

The project was going well. Lorenz had connected Aldo with building crews, and they were raising the structures quickly. Aldo spent most of his time with Aurora and Alessandra. He was charming, and they smiled and laughed a lot. He could see Aurora sizing Alessandra and him up as a couple. They seemed to meet her approval. It's amazing what a little push in the correct direction can accomplish.

Aurora began to leave them alone for longer periods of time. Aldo felt it was his duty to charm and entertain Alessandra to the best of his abilities. It wasn't long and she was clinging to him. *Dante and I might yet be brothers-in-law.*

Aldo saw them off to Venice not long afterwards and returned to Pilsen to work with Dante. They were attempting to determine how to best utilize the Skoda Works to further their goals. The company had been subjected to nationalization efforts beginning in 1945 and by 1948 they were primarily a producer of heavy machinery for eastern bloc countries.

But, they had the personnel, the knowledge, the heavy equipment to manufacture various products—locomotives, reactors, freight and passenger vehicles, aircraft, ships, machine tools and an assortment of other products. *Almost anything we want if we could easily access the personnel and equipment.*

That's when they began to have problems. The Russian Communists were leaning on our Czech Communist partners for a piece of the action, or face shutdown, ouster, or death. It was an easy choice for the Czechs and they had new Russian partners, who liked to give orders.

Their first directive as new partners was that Dante and Aldo accompany them to the top of St. Bartholomew's tower, 335 feet in the air, with the cobbled streets of Pilsen below. It was an impressive view.

There was a delegation of them led by a gentleman named Sergei Chesnokov.

"It is a nice view up here, yes?"

"Quite," replied Dante.

"You can see all of Pilsen from here. Access is a wonderful thing as long as you have it."

Dante glanced around in three directions. "Agreed."

"But if you should find yourself down there," Sergei pointed to the street below, "not much of a view, no access, quite hazardous actually."

Dante and Aldo both took a quick look over the side. It was a long way down and a hard fall when you landed.

"I think we understand each other," answered Dante.

"That is good." Then Sergei and his delegation departed, leaving Dante and Aldo alone on the tower.

Anna's Aftermath

Lorenz was really excited now. Many of his projects were coming together. He'd bankrolled everything from butchers, bakers, bankers, and bars. But what got him going was the partnership with the Italian, Aldo Buio.

"He's putting his buildings up quickly. If he can get manufacturing underway, with all the new hires, there'll be a huge demand for housing."

"I thought he was doing construction as well?"

"Oh he is, but it's mostly apartments. I plan to build houses, townhomes, garden places—bigger, more elaborate, the high end of the market. I can reshape Paris's downtown."

"That's impressive."

"Isn't it! By the way, one of my crews was stripping the interior of one of the old buildings I purchased near the Hotel Meurice, where AB lives by the way, and where the Nazis headquartered when they ruled Paris, and you won't believe what they found?"

"I'll believe it. I just have no idea what it might be."

"An entire floor of boxed methamphetamine."

I shrugged my shoulders. "What?"

"It's a drug the Nazis synthesized in the late 1930s. There were always rumors they fed it to their soldiers. It amped them up, kept them going when they would have been too tired otherwise, or too hungry, or too stubborn. It stimulated them and made them cooperative and high-strung."

"Those are the side effects, weren't there others?"

"It's supposedly very addictive, highest highs, lowest lows, heart issues, depression and paranoia."

"Sounds dreadful. What are you going to do with it?"

"Don't know. Perhaps there's a market."

Dee and Friends
Sixteenth Day

It had been a couple of days since they'd seen Anna. The men were seated on the sundeck, waiting on the women and lunch.

"I think she must have tired of telling us stories, probably made them all up," said Mike.

"Or maybe she just got tired. It can't be easy being ninety plus years old and keeping all those details straight," replied Jamal.

"At that age I'm not sure if time passes quickly or drags out into infinity. Maybe I'll ask her," said Dee.

Gina strolled up and sat next to Dee. "Angelic and Keno are bringing Anna up. She texted me this morning and said she'd like to join us if we didn't mind."

"She texted you?" asked Mike.

"Yeah," replied Gina. "Her mind is still sharp, even if her body seems to be failing her."

"What's that about?" asked Dee.

"She had to rest for a couple of days. Said she wasn't feeling well and needed to get her energy back."

Angelic and Keno approached, slowly rolling Anna along. They parked her at the head of the table under one of the big sun umbrellas.

"So good to see you all again. I have to apologize for my disappearance. My health seems to be flagging a bit. My body just needs more rest."

"It's good to see you, glad you're feeling better," said Jamal.

"Happy you could join us for lunch," added Dee.

Mike smiled at her, and she nodded to him.

They ordered and sat quietly in the sun for few moments.

"We should be coming up on the canal," said Anna.

"We're just about to change rivers. I do so love the Danube, but perhaps it's time to be getting home."

"How's the dog?" asked Mike.

"He's good, never a problem."

Another moment of silence followed.

"Alright, I can't stand it," said Gina. "Will you tell us some more of your story, if you're up to it?"

"We'd really like to hear," added Keno.

"Well, let's eat and I'll see what I can remember."

They finished, and the dishes were cleared away. Anna sat for a moment studying the countryside.

"The canal is only about a hundred miles. We won't be on it that long. Then we're on the Main River."

"A couple of days there and then we're onto the Rhine?" asked Dee.

"That sounds about right, the last river."

"Maybe the third or the fourth, but definitely the last one."

Anna smiled and nodded at Dee. Then she spoke. "So, Lorenz and I were in Paris. Several months passed, and I forgot about this new Aldo, or AB as Lorenz called him. Then one day Lorenz sent a messenger to ask me to meet him for lunch. We did this frequently, keeping up appearances and all that. I thought little of it."

"I went to meet Lorenz at a café near the Hotel Meurice. When I walked in, there was a man sitting across from him. The man turned as I approached the table and I stopped short. He was older, a little thicker, and in a nice suit, but it was Aldo.

"My mouth dropped open so fast I put my hand up to cover it, while the man hopped to his feet. Lorenz had been so busy talking, he hadn't noticed.

"Lorenz stood when he saw me. Gesturing with his hand in my direction, 'This is my lovely fiancée, Anna.'

"Aldo dipped his head and then quicker than I could imagine took my hand and kissed my fingers. Releasing my hand and rising to look me in the eye, he said, 'Mademoiselle, I've heard so much about you. I am glad that at last we finally meet.'"

The truth is in his eyes; the eyes don't lie, and his are full of remembrance.

I had to turn away, to Lorenz. "Darling, why didn't you tell me?"

"I thought a surprise might be nice."

"Nice is hardly the word."

The waiter arrived, and we paused to take our seats."

"He didn't know you?" asked Keno.

"Of course he did, but he didn't want Lorenz to know and he gambled I wouldn't want Lorenz to know either."

"What happened?" asked Gina.

"Lorenz rambled on and Aldo and I nodded to him occasionally and watched each other from the corners of our eyes."

"That must have been difficult," said Jamal.

"Actually, I was so shocked not a lot registered at first. Here he was. I'd been chasing all over the countryside looking and Lorenz had been working with him for months."

"Was it possible he thought you were dead, and the name was just a coincidence?" asked Dee.

"Perhaps, but he'd made no inquiries of my neighbors or our friends in the surrounding area. I suspected he had moved on to other things or was up to something. Either of those was fine by me, it was just a shock to see him."

"So, you're going to meet him later?" asked Mike.

Anna turned to look at him, "The voice of experience?"

Mike shook his head and held his hands up while glancing to Keno.

"No, it just seemed like a logical choice."

"Indeed. Lorenz excused himself to speak briefly to a gentleman who was leaving the café and Aldo slipped me a business card while Lorenz had his back to us. I palmed it quickly and Lorenz returned to the table. The meal ended, everyone said goodbye. Aldo left and Lorenz whispered in my ear, 'What do you think' to which I replied, 'Of what?'"

"Was Lorenz that clever?" asked Angelic.

"He was clever in business, but never perceptive in life. I think he was just enamored of Aldo, who was perceptive enough to see that and use it to his advantage."

"So what are you thinking of during all this?" asked Dee.

"I'm thinking Aldo wasn't what he seemed, not now and probably not then. I was always a little suspicious of how he acted but, in the whims of a foolish young girl, I put it down to him sparring with Rene over my affections."

"I think that was part of it," said Gina.

Anna turned and looked at her. "Perhaps, a part, but I assigned it greater value at the time."

"There wasn't any way you could have known, you were just a young girl," replied Angelic.

"Not that young, I'd been married, widowed, and was fighting in a war. I was just, if not foolish, certainly naïve."

"That's a hard thing to avoid when you're young, or even sometimes when you're not," said Dee.

Aldo's Aftermath

Things were progressing nicely with Alessandra. Aldo felt more confident each passing day that she would accept his marriage proposal. Integrated into their family, he would have many more options.

He had kept the paintings a secret from her and Dante. Aldo wanted to surprise them at the time of the wedding, perhaps gift one of them, as long as it stayed in the family.

Lorenz began wanting to spend more time with Aldo, which Aldo was not comfortable with. Aldo allowed him to hang around in Paris but did not want Lorenz accompanying him to Pilsen. Then Lorenz mentioned Vienna and how he'd met Anna there. He wasn't specific, something about staying at the same hotel. This roused Aldo's curiosity.

They'd met one morning to look over a nearly completed warehouse close to the Hotel Meurice and Aldo had a thought.

"Why don't we get some lunch and invite your lovely fiancée?"

"That's a splendid idea. I'll send a messenger to tell her to meet us."

It was that simple. I had the feeling for a while that it might be the same Anna and I wanted to know. She'd make a splendid mistress.

They met. It was her. She nearly fell over. Aldo played it low key and then so did she. He sensed her interest and slipped her a business card. His world was coming full circle.

The following day Lorenz mentioned leaving for Vienna to follow up on a project he was developing there.

"Anything we'd be interested in participating with you?"

"Apartment buildings, so yes, possibly."

"Perhaps I could accompany you?"

"Ideal, we could make a trip of it."

"I'm sure Anna will miss you."

"Of course not, she's going with me. We'll all go together."

Anna's Aftermath

Lorenz came home in a fizz. It seems we're going to Vienna and Aldo is going with us. Lorenz is so excited. We leave in two days.

Not knowing what else to do, Anna sent Aldo a note at the Hotel Meurice. It said, 'Looking forward to the Vienna trip. Perhaps we can talk, get to know one another. It's so nice of you to come along.'

There it was, perfectly deniable if ever read by anyone else.

Aldo's Aftermath

Aldo put Aurora and Alessandra on the overnight train for Venice. They would arrive in the morning.

"I'll be a couple of days in Vienna on a joint project and then come to see you. I have a surprise that I hope you'll like."

Both of the women beamed at him. *I couldn't ask for more.*

The trip to Vienna would be several hours longer than the trip to Venice. Aldo, Anna, and Lorenz would leave on a similar overnight schedule and arrive mid-morning the following day.

Lorenz booked them into adjacent sleepers and made reservations for a late dinner. *There won't likely be an opportunity to talk to Anna on the train, but I'll make sure we have the chance when we get to Vienna.*

The train ride was uneventful but dinner was excellent. Anna dressed very seductively. *I can't wait to talk to her.*

Anna's Aftermath

The train ride was tedious, and dinner was average. Since the war ended, Anna had gained a few pounds and rounded out a bit more than necessary. She wore a simple dress with a bit of a lower neckline and Lorenz and Aldo couldn't take their eyes away. It was embarrassing. Lorenz even made a pass at her when they got back to the sleeper car. Anna hit him with a hatbox.

Aldo's Aftermath

They arrived in Vienna and checked into the Imperial. Lorenz and Anna maintained a suite there and Lorenz had messaged ahead and arranged a comparable suite for Aldo down the hall.

The next morning Lorenz and Aldo inspected the properties he was reviewing for apartments. They looked good, and the price was right. Aldo offered his and Dante's participation. Lorenz was excited.

Lorenz then told Aldo he needed to check on some of his other partnerships the following day. Aldo nodded to him and suggested that he'd tour the city.

"Let Anna guide you, she's very knowledgeable."

See how simple that was. "That would be wonderful."

They started in the morning, and Anna actually showed Aldo around the city. Midday they stopped for lunch at Demel. It was one of her favorites.

"I think you'll like it here. The food is quite good, and the pastry is to die for. Lorenz and I eat here frequently."

"Will we see anyone you know here?"

"Perhaps?"

"Is that appropriate?"

"Most definitely, anyone thinking anything will realize we are in one of Lorenz and I's favorite places. There couldn't possibly be anything wrong with that."

"You seem quite confident."

"I am."

Anna and Aldo sat near one of the main windows at the front of the café with a view of the surrounding streets. They ate and watched people pass by. Little else was said. Aldo tried the pastry, and it was delicious.

"You were right, these things are exceptional. I'll need to find a reason to stop by each day we are here."

Anna smiled at him in return.

Finished eating, they took a five-minute walk to the Volksgarten, the people's garden, a nearby public park in the heart of the city.

They strolled for a few minutes and Anna looked at Aldo expectantly, without speaking.

"How did you get to Vienna? Is that where the train took you?" Aldo asked.

"We went to the art castle and from there to somewhere in the Bavarian Forest, Germany or Austria, then to Vienna, until the war was over. I've been checking the old neighborhood, the surrounding farms, for any sign of Rene or you. No one has heard from you."

"This is my first time back to Paris. My train went to the art castle as well, then to Czechoslovakia, the town of Pilsen. I stayed there until the war was over and since then."

"Do you know what happened to Rene?"

Aldo shrugged.

"I think he would have returned if he had lived."

Nodding. "Yes, I expect he would have."

They continued walking, strolling the grounds like any ordinary couple. Anna didn't speak again.

I admit I am eager to reestablish our friendship. "What are you thinking?"

"Just curious about Rene, wondering what might have happened to him, how it happened."

Looking away for a moment, Aldo then turned back. "Before my train went to the art castle, we passed through the underground factory in Mittelwerk."

Anna stopped walking and looked at him closely. "The big plant—rockets, bombs, tanks, everything the Nazis were working on?"

Nodding. "Rene's train was there as well. We saw one another on adjacent tracks and tried to escape. Rene was killed, and I was captured. I later escaped and caught another train, which went to the art castle."

"What happened, I mean how?"

"We were between the trains, soldiers saw us and approached. We tried to run. They shot him. Could have been me. I surrendered."

"That's terrible, to watch your friend die."

"Yes, it was difficult."

They started walking again.

"I hoped that somehow he had survived."

"I'm sorry for him it ended that way."

Anna paused and then looked closely at Aldo for a moment.

"I didn't know that you spoke Italian, or that you were from Italy. We all thought you were French."

Aldo looked away before speaking, "I immigrated at one point. I wanted to help with the war effort."

Anna moved around to look Aldo in the eye.

"For whom? Why would you fight for the French if you were Italian? What aren't you telling me?"

Dee and Friends
Sixteenth Day

Anna looked at each of the group and then nodded slowly.

"There aren't that many of us left from World War II. Soon, when we die, the stories will die with us, like they never happened."

"That will be a sad day. We'd love to hear the rest of your story," said Angelic.

"Let's get something cold to drink, wet my whistle, if I'm going to keep talking." Anna waved to a waiter. "We need to order some drinks here. Everyone tell him what you'd like."

They sipped the drinks and watched the scenery for a short time.

"I've never been that comfortable in Germany. I just never got over the whole thing, I guess. I've always loved Paris, and Vienna, and for the last few years, Amsterdam. I moved there on a whim, a change of pace from Paris. I visited, I liked it, and I stayed. You'll enjoy it, very open-minded."

"Just a whim that took you there?" asked Keno.

"Time," replied Anna. "Time was the healer that rescued me. Paris was becoming overwhelming, unbearable, and I had to leave. Too many things from my past were coming back to haunt me wherever I turned. The place I lived, memories of Lorenz, places I'd go, images from the war, thoughts of my daughter. The older I got, the more Paris seemed to amplify all of that. I could never rest. I needed someplace different, someplace new to me, where I could start again, or at least survive."

"Would you tell us?" asked Gina.

Anna sat her drink down and looked out over the water.

"Aldo and I spent an afternoon in Vienna together. We walked in the park and talked. He told me Rene was dead, had been killed by the Germans. I had felt that was the case for a long time, but it hurt when I heard it. It was like a secret or an idle thought in my mind that I had tried to contain or suppress but had always known it was there, that it was true. I was really quite devastated. Rene was the one I was most worried about. I knew Aldo would survive. While seeing him for the first time was surprising, it wasn't unexpected, I knew he was alive. I just didn't know his story."

"Aldo left for Venice the next day on an early train. Lorenz and I left for Paris that evening on the overnight."

"I was glad to be away from him. There was much more I wanted to know, but I needed time to think."

Aldo's Aftermath

Aldo took the early train, so he'd have all day to think. Leaving in the morning he'd arrive in time for a late dinner. *There are many opportunities available to me now—Alessandra, Anna, Paris, Vienna, Pilsen, and I want to capitalize on all of them.*

Agreement between the Allies and the Axis spared Venice, the city, any bombing during the war. On the other hand, the harbor and the surrounding area were leveled by the Allies when they retook Venice. But, the city itself was still magnificent.

Aldo made arrangements for dinner at 8pm at 'Poste Vecie', Venice's oldest and finest restaurant, for just the three of them, Aurora, Alessandra, and himself.

He had a plan. A jeweler Aldo made the acquaintance of in Paris had removed the two carat stone from the pinky ring he'd taken from the train and mounted it in an engagement setting from the 1800s. Aldo felt confident both women would love it. He had the jeweler replace the diamond in the pinky ring with a sarcolite crystal, a pale, colorless stone that only comes from one location on Mount Vesuvius in Naples. Aldo had the signet ring on one hand and the crystal ring on the other. The Vacheron Constantin pocket watch was on a gold chain in his vest pocket.

If Alessandra accepts my proposal, and I feel confident she will, how long before we marry? That will impact my relationship with Dante. How will he react? Surely his mother and sister had spoken to him of the development.

I ponder on this question and others—how to deal with Anna, as I would like her in my life, the Communists in Pilsen—how will they require to be treated. There was also Lorenz and the opportunities in Vienna, aside from my plans in Paris.

Whiling away the day with these thoughts, time passed

quickly, and Aldo realized he needed to prepare himself for the upcoming dinner.

He took a taxi from the train station and picked up the women at their home in the San Marco district. The taxi dropped them at the Grand Canal and they rode a gondola the short distance to the restaurant.

It was a beautiful night, the air full of the fragrance of flowers, the stars twinkling above and the night lamps highlighting the buildings and the canal. They disembarked and crossed the short bridge to the red door of the restaurant. *My moment is at hand.*

Anna's Aftermath

When Lorenz and Anna arrived back in Paris, he immediately went to work on his projects. When Aldo had been in town, Lorenz had hung around a little more, looking for opportunities to mingle. With Aldo gone, Lorenz was busy. Anna found this to be perfect.

She went to the farm. Walking the house, she found herself in the bedroom studying the Picasso. *I suppose I looked like that at that age, a young girl in a woman's body. I suspect Pablo embellished a touch, which was nice of him. He was rumored to be working in ceramics in the south of France at the present time. A man of many talents, it was like watching a shooting star.*

Getting in the car, she drove a short distance to the home of Henri Moreau, the local resistance leader she had reported to during her time in service.

Henri himself answered the door when she knocked. He stepped outside and pulled the door behind him. They walked toward his barn.

"You only come to see me when you want to talk about the war. It's over; you need to get on with it. We can't change things now."

"I don't want to change it, although I would if I could, I just want some answers."

"Some questions cannot be answered."

"I agree, but I think you can help me with this one, and I promise I'll leave you alone."

Henri looked up in surprise. "What question could I answer that would cause you to consider such a thing? I know how you are. You were one of my most tenacious agents. I feared for you all the time."

Anna smiled at him, probably for the first time since she'd been seeing him again. "Just tell me about Aldo?"

He looked at her, his face expectant.

"He's alive. I've met and talked to him. His train took him to Czechoslovakia, to Pilsen. He rode out the war there. Recently he came to Paris to work with my fiancé, totally by chance, or so it seems."

Henri smiled. "Aldo never ceased to amaze me. I was never quite confident of him. He just showed up one day and said he wanted to help."

"You trusted him?"

"Of course not, I'm not that crazy, but times were desperate. I gave him several small tasks, on his own, things that could easily have gotten him killed. He came through every time. About the third job, he brought back a cable he'd taken off a Nazi officer about an Italian offensive. I forwarded the information along. It turned out to be true, and we were successful in destroying an Italian fortification.

"After that I sent him out with a few of the other men. He put himself in the line of fire to save one of them and killed several enemy while retreating."

"Unbelievable."

"Yeah, kind of, after that I put him in charge of you and Rene, rookies, or so I thought. He completed most of the tasks given but there were occasional misses or changes of direction he made while in the field. I was never completely comfortable with him. That's part of the reason I isolated him with you two."

"Threw us to the lions, did you?"

"You were the youngest, the least experienced. Plus, you kept him occupied, and we didn't share other maneuvers we were involved with."

"Were you ever going to tell me that?"

"Not unless you asked. The war's over."

"Just the aftermath remains."

Henri nodded. "So he ended up in Czechoslovakia and you were in Austria?"

"Yes, he said the trains were bound for Berlin. Did you tell him that?"

"No, we didn't know where the trains were bound. We guessed Germany. We thought they were full of confiscated property, maybe the art castle."

"Why did you send us?"

"I didn't. Aldo volunteered you. He must have known or heard something. Then he laid it off on me, on the Resistance. What happened to Rene?"

"Both Aldo's and Rene's trains initially stopped at the Mittelwerk."

"The underground bomb factory?"

"Yes. Aldo says that he and Rene were discovered and that the Germans killed Rene. He surrendered and then later escaped and caught another train."

"Unbelievable."

"That's kind of what I think. Why would he volunteer us for that?"

"I wasn't sure, then or now, other than disrupting one of the trains could have been helpful."

"One of the trains?"

"Yeah, he said the three of you would board one of them and attempt to disrupt it. I was going to ask how you ended up on three different trains."

"He told us we were each to take one, that those were the instructions."

"Not from me."

"What could he have had in mind?"

"He must have had some idea what was on the trains, maybe where they were going."

"That makes no sense."

"Many of the things he did never did."

Aldo's Aftermath

The evening was a great success. *I don't know who was more excited, Aurora or Alessandra. Their eyes were almost as big as the diamond when I pulled it out.* They returned home and requested Aldo stay in one of the guest rooms. While he'd stayed in the house in one of the guest rooms before, when Dante was present, Aldo had expected to return to the hotel this evening.

"You're practically family now, you must stay here," said Aurora.

With Mom's blessing, I knew I was good to stay.

"If you insist. I think perhaps I should turn in; it's been a long and exciting day."

Alessandra took my hand and kissed my fingers. "I agree. I feel almost faint."

"It's settled then. We'll all retire and Alessandra and I will begin planning tomorrow. I expect you both will want to proceed quickly from here."

They hugged all around and proceeded to their rooms.

Aldo planned to stay another day and then return to Paris. Aurora advised him in the morning that she had received a telegram from Dante and that he would arrive the following day. He had asked that Aldo stay so that they might celebrate and talk additional business. *I have to admit; I am excited.*

Dee and Friends
Nuremberg
Seventeenth Day

Anna met them for breakfast.

"What are your plans today?" she asked.

"We haven't decided so far. There seem to be some interesting things in Nuremburg," replied Jamal.

"The Tribunal?"

"That was one of them," said Dee.

"It's fascinating, I saw it once. I've never wanted to see it again. Many people said the Allies were imposing retroactive justice upon the Germans. But they committed so many heinous crimes during the war, yet only eleven of them were put to death. There was no accountability for the thousands of members of the Nazi regime and the silent bystanders who allowed the Nazi atrocities."

"Many of the officers were hunted down over time," added Dee.

"Rightly so, you can't just blindly say yes to murderous orders. That was one of the Nuremburg principals that came from the trials. 'Someone has to stand up and speak for the truth.'"

"So, we should go see it?" asked Gina.

"If you like. It's a monument to looking the other way when things go wrong."

"What do you suggest?" asked Keno.

"We're only about halfway through the canal but we'll dock here for the day, then travel to Bamberg and the Main River tomorrow. I can tell you more of my story if you want to meet up on the sundeck this afternoon."

The group glanced around at one another. "That sounds like a plan, a fascinating plan," said Dee.

Aldo's Aftermath

Dante arrived the following day, and they had a great celebration with the women—dinner, and a night on the town with many toasts and many promises.

Late the next day Dante and Aldo talked business. He planned to return to Pilsen to try and appease the Communists. Their demands continued to grow. Dante was worried.

Aldo returned to Paris to try and accelerate their plans there. And, of course he wanted to see Anna.

———

Anna messaged Aldo before he could her. She wanted to meet at the Eiffel tower.

They met at the base the following day. The lifts had been restored in 1946, just a few years before, and the couple elected to take them to the top, 906 feet above the ground.

Standing near the railing and the coin-operated telescopes, Anna and Aldo gazed over the city and finally talked.

"It was a terrifying time on the trains. I felt sick most of the time."

"Motion sickness?"

"Something like that."

"You stayed on the same train the whole time?"

"Yes, all the way. I was going to ask, when you mentioned changing trains, where did your train end up?"

"Outside Pilsen."

"In a tunnel?"

Aldo was surprised. "Yes."

"Mine too. I've always wondered what happened to that train. It was full of art but we didn't stay at the art castle, passed through it, like we picked up more work. When we finally stopped, it was in the mountains right across the Austrian border. I left the area for Vienna a couple of days later and never went back there."

"That's odd. I abandoned the last train, also full of art, in a tunnel outside Pilsen. I thought maybe it would be destroyed also….." He stopped abruptly.

"Destroyed also, like what exactly?"

He thought for a minute. *How much should I tell her? What would it hurt?*

"After I escaped the Mittelwerk, I caught a passenger train that took me into a small town. At that rail station was one of the Nazi steam trains. I jumped on it, going east. When it stopped, somewhere in the Bavarian Forest—still in Germany as best I could tell, the engineers parked it in a tunnel on a spur line. Because I didn't want to be left there, I jumped another train in the tunnel that was on the main line."

"What happened?"

"As that train pulled out of the tunnel, a flatcar full of soldiers jumped off, blew up a portion of the tunnel, pulled up the rails, then were shot down by a couple of sergeants."

"What was going on?"

"Best I could tell the Nazis were hiding things—art, supplies, personal property, treasure, for some time later."

"You saw all of this? They buried trains in a tunnel?"

"Yes, and killed almost everyone who knew about it."

"So, maybe, that's what happened to my train. It was the only one in the tunnel, on a spur line. I walked out into the night."

"Sounds lucky."

"Yeah, maybe, it led me to Vienna."

"And Lorenz?"

"Eventually. What about you?"

It was a fascinating story she was telling, so I decided to share, to impress her with my exploits.

"I rode the train into a tunnel outside Pilsen. On the train there was art, personal property, supplies, a laboratory, and whatever else. After it sat there for a while, I got out and examined the area. Everyone was gone. I found gold, some small paintings and guns. I helped myself. The Nazis didn't need all of it and I didn't know if they were coming back or going to blow the tunnel."

"So there were three trains or three tunnels, which we know of. But that's why you stayed in Pilsen. You had no way to move all the items you collected."

"The war was nearly over, Italy had already surrendered. I needed to look out for myself."

"That's right. Italy had already surrendered, and you were Italian, weren't you?"

Aldo looked away. Anna moved closer.

"You were one of Il Duce's stooges, a Mussolini minion, a traitor to our cause, a spy. You abandoned us, your friends, companions, art, beauty, love—for fascists and Nazis, what purpose did it serve? Why?" Anna banged his chest with her fist.

"Only at first did I ...."

"And at the end."

He nodded his head, no arguing that one. She struck him again.

"Did you even escape Mittelwerk? What really happened to Rene? You turned him in didn't you?"

Aldo couldn't look at her.

"You killed him, didn't you?"

She pushed him against the rail, far above the ground.

"You did it!" She looked him hard in the eyes.

Aldo turned to look at the city below and felt the pressure of Anna leaning against him.

Suddenly, she took a step back. "How could you?" Her voice was pleading.

He looked up and into her eyes. "It was about staying alive, to see you again."

She sighed and looked down at her hands. "You have the paintings?"

He smiled. "They are in my room at the hotel. Would you like to see them?"

Anna's Aftermath

When they returned to the hotel, Anna followed Aldo to his suite. In a single wooden crate with a hasp and a lock, he had three paintings. She watched as he drug the crate from under the bed and stood it upright on the floor.

"Do you really think they're safe here?"

"If you'd seen the floor under the bed, nobody has touched it in a long, long time, probably since the Nazis."

He pulled the first painting out, draped in several layers of protective cloth. It was a Monet, one of the water lily series. Then he unwrapped a Renoir floral arrangement, and finally a Degas ballerina.

"That's an interesting set of choices you made."

"Actually, I just grabbed a box that had the artists' names on it. I didn't have time to see what was inside."

**Dee and Friends
Nuremberg
Seventeenth Day**

They met Anna on the sundeck after lunch. She seemed energetic; her eyes bright. After speaking with her that morning, they'd stayed aboard to meet with her rather than going ashore.

"Did you have a good lunch?" she asked.

"It was very good," replied Angelic.

"How about you?" asked Keno.

"I had a quick bite in my room."

"We're eager to hear more of your story," said Gina.

"I hoped you would still be interested. I've carried it for a long time and I appreciate you listening to it."

Dee and Jamal shared a quick glance.

"We'd love to hear it, please continue," added Angelic.

"After Lorenz and I returned to Paris, I had suspicions about Aldo. His story didn't feel right."

"How do you mean?" asked Gina.

"It wasn't anything really tangible, just a feeling I had about him. The time we'd been apart made me more suspicious, more of a realist, and I just didn't believe him."

Aldo's Aftermath
Paris

That could have gone a lot worse with Anna. I think she liked the paintings. Perhaps I can involve her with them in some fashion.

But I received a telegram from Venice. Aurora and Alessandra had planned the wedding, even faster than I expected.

There was also a telegram from Dante in Pilsen. Apparently the women were keeping him informed. He indicated we would meet in ten days in Venice for the festivities. He also added his regrets that Alessandra and I might not take an immediate honeymoon as the Communists were pushing him harder for more control of Skoda and our external plans and output of products.

Aldo was elated.

I'll wait a couple of days, let Anna settle down, and then tell Lorenz that I must be in Pilsen for a couple of weeks. Perhaps when I return I can follow up with Anna.

Aldo's Aftermath
Venice & Pilsen

Aldo worked tirelessly for the next few days, wanting to establish his presence in Paris. Concerns about Pilsen flooded his thoughts and the beginnings of a plan took shape.

A few days before leaving for Venice, he prepared for the trip. Aldo thought to take a painting, but then decided the one-year anniversary might be a better time. He wanted it to go to Aurora, and he wasn't sure that would happen at the present moment. Dante was a lover of fine art as well.

Aldo had a suit tailored especially for the wedding and selected suitable gifts for all the family. There couldn't be any mistakes.

While traveling to Venice he had time to think. *It's becoming increasingly important to me. I have bounced around for much of my life, making opportunities where and when I could find them. But this time I need a plan. This was long term and had to be handled properly.*

Aldo arrived and was greeted at the rail station by Aurora and Alessandra, who informed him that Dante would arrive later that day.

He had given some thought to flying down but commercial airline travel was still somewhat unpredictable, although looking at the industry Aldo could tell it was going to take off. Air France the largest airline in Paris was growing exponentially. *I want to invest but the airline is primarily state-owned and I'm leery of tying up my money with government regulation. However, there will be a time in the future when it would be wise to include some legitimate, recognized business holdings.*

Nearly 100% of Italians are Catholic and Aldo had received some instruction in his youth. While he had neglected that training for many years, Alessandra's family was solidly practicing. While the largest and most famous church in the city is the San Marco Basilica, they were to be married in San Giacomo, the oldest basilica in the city. It was none the less elaborate. The family had been parishioners there for generations.

There was a huge crowd, although Aldo knew no one outside the family. The service was lengthy and registered little with him, but then it was over. *I'm part of the family.* Dante gave them two days and then he and Aldo departed for Pilsen. Alessandra stayed in Venice. The couple would have a wing of the house as their own. *She wanted me to impregnate her immediately, and I gave it my best effort.*

Dante and Aldo talked while traveling by train.

"The Communists continue to want more control and more profit."

"Hard for them to have both, isn't it? I mean they don't know what they're doing and impacting that causes less profit."

"Agreed, but I think they want control more than anything and they're trying to push us out or anger us so that they can claim we aren't cooperating and expel us, nationalize the plant."

"We can't let that happen."

"Agreed again, but we'll need to work out some kind of arrangement with them. I have a couple of ideas. See what you can come up with. I expect they will want to meet shortly after they realize we have returned. They watch the train station all the time, so it won't be long."

They discussed several options as the miles passed, and developed a plan of possibilities. It would all depend on how hard and for what issues the Communists pushed on them.

———

Dante was right. They heard from Sergei and his fellow Communists within an hour of arriving. Sergei wanted to meet at the bell tower again. It seemed to be the Communists' favorite place, a representation of their overall power.

Dante and Aldo took one of the plant vehicles and met them on the ground level. Sergei wanted to ascend to the top of the tower.

Standing together as a group, they looked out over the city. The plant stood a short distance to the west. It was a stunning view, all light and airy, until they took a closer look- Sergei and four of his men and Dante and Aldo.

"You need to keep us better advised as to your plans and your profits," said Sergei.

"We meet weekly and discuss those things with you," replied Dante. "What would you like?"

"We, the comrades and I, feel like there should be someone onsite, one of us, at all times. Just so the state feels comfortable that our interests are being protected."

Aldo started to say 'protected from what' but Dante held up a hand and nodded at him.

"That can be arranged. Your man can work the same hours we do."

"I'm afraid that won't be adequate. We demand a man there at all times and another one who has access to all the financial information and planning."

"That's not possible. We stay very busy; decisions are made in real time. It would be difficult for a third party to keep up and also they'd be in the way."

"It's not an option. The state has decided. Our man will be onsite or you will no longer be onsite."

"What does that mean?"

"It means the state has your best interests at heart, your future, your longevity."

Sergei and two of his men had edged closer to Dante, pinning him against the low rail of the balcony. The third man was standing near Aldo.

Sergei continued, "It would be tragic if you had to be removed, but the state comes first and you must realize that." He pressed closer to Dante, whose knees buckled against the rail. Sergei leaned closer.

The man between Dante and Aldo took a step sideways and suddenly there was a small open gap between Dante and Aldo. Taking a quick step, Aldo moved toward him. *On the train we had worked out option A and option B, now suddenly I see an option C.* Aldo pressed his hand firmly in Dante's chest and pushed while stepping across in front of him, as if to protect him. Dante stumbled backwards and his weight took him over the rail. The group on top heard him scream just before there was a thud when he hit the cobblestones, several hundred feet below.

Aldo looked at Sergei. "I would love to have one of your men on hand and another in the office with me. Send them over in the morning and we'll get started. I need to look after him." Aldo pointed over his shoulder to the street below.

Sergei looked at Aldo, his eyes suspicious, but then he broke into a smile. "I see you understand your position."

"Quite clearly. I am at the state's disposal."

Later at the plant, Aldo gathered a few things he needed and prepared to leave. *I didn't want to do that to Dante. But they were about to kill us both and I couldn't let that happen. I liked him and I feel bad about it but now is not the time if I'm to escape. The*

Communists will be here in the morning and I probably won't survive the day once I show them everything. It's time to go.

Aldo took a different company truck and left the plant. The rail station was under surveillance so he knew not to go there. It was a little less than four hours to Linz, Austria. *I'll drive there, abandon the truck, and catch a train to Venice. I'll need to explain the new circumstances to Aurora and Alessandra, and finish consummating my honeymoon.*

Anna's Aftermath
Paris

Aldo was back in Paris and he had Lorenz following him around like a puppy. Anna saw little of him and didn't hear from him. Aldo seemed to work extremely hard. Lorenz rarely got home until late in the evening. It became a recurring thing. *I wonder what is going on with Aldo. I felt certain the day we looked at the paintings that he wanted to see me again.*

Anna was content for the moment to observe and to wait for his next move, expecting that it wouldn't be all that long.

Aldo's Aftermath
Venice & Paris

When Aldo arrived in Venice, Aurora and Alessandra greeted him. *It's almost like I married them both.* He stayed for several days after breaking the terrible news of Dante's death and his escape.

Aurora was nearly destroyed. I comforted her as best I could. Aldo planned to leave Alessandra to look after her but Aurora insisted that if he needed to be in Paris to look after their mutual interests, since they'd lost Pilsen, his wife should go with him.

Aldo advised Alessandra that he still lived in the hotel and that she might need to limit her traveling cases, but she insisted upon taking over a dozen, just so she could look her best for him.

It wasn't long, perhaps a few days, and Aurora telegrammed that she was on her way to Paris to stay with them. It seems she was lost without her daughter.

Upon returning to Paris, Aldo did his best to keep Lorenz from finding out about Alessandra. However, she was not a low profile woman. She liked to make grand entrances and exits.

One morning Lorenz popped in to the hotel lobby as Aldo was leaving and Alessandra came trooping down behind him. Lorenz was quite taken with her and ran straight home to tell Anna.

Anna's Aftermath
Paris

Lorenz came running in one morning and Anna knew he had something to tell her.

"Anna, Anna, you'll never guess who I just met."

"You're right, so why don't you just tell me."

"Aldo, it's Aldo's wife, a fine looking Italian named Alessandra. She was the sister of his late partner Dante."

"Sister of his late partner?" Anna was scrambling for possibilities in her head.

"Apparently the Communists killed Dante in Pilsen and Aldo escaped."

I've heard that one before. "What's her name?"

"Alessandra. Her mother's here as well."

"I'm happy for them, aren't you? Nothing like a wife and a mother-in-law for motivation. Surely your joint deals will be successful now." *I see Lorenz thinking about that. He is easy to distract.* "Hadn't you better be checking on your end of things? Perhaps this is why Aldo has been so busy lately?"

"Yes, I'm sure you are correct." Lorenz looked at his watch, 18K gold Phillipe Patek. "Perhaps I should get to the office."

———

After he was gone, Anna took a few moments and composed herself. *I felt like Aldo was interested in me and I expect he still is. But he married to solidify his business position which meant he was thinking of me as a mistress, even with Lorenz around.* Anna took a few minutes to decide a course of action.

———

Arriving at the Hotel Meurice, Anna inquired as to Aldo's suite. Taking the lift to the top floor, she presented herself at the door.

A beautiful young woman answered.

"I am Anna Simone, a friend, comrade, and former lover of your husband Aldo Anouilh."

She took a step back and raised a hand to her throat. "You must be mistaken. My husband's name is Aldo Buio."

"I'm not mistaken, whatever he calls himself now that was what he called himself then. I have seen him and talked with him. Trust me, it is the same man."

She took another step back and looked at Anna with defiant eyes. An older woman who looked very much like the younger woman appeared from another room.

"Alessandra?"

Anna didn't give them a chance to speak and looked directly at the young woman. "Take your mother and your things and go back where you came from."

"My husband is a good man."

"Obviously you don't know him that well. For your own benefit, keep it that way."

Anna paused, lost in indecision. *While I could have originally described her skin as being white as Italian marble, it certainly is now.*

"Young woman I must ask you to leave," said Aurora.

"Certainly, but know this. Aldo was a spy during the war, he killed his companions, he stole from the dead, he deserted his country, and he is the father of my child, if only biologically. Ask him yourself." Both of their mouths dropped open, and Anna took that as her cue to leave.

Aldo's Aftermath
Paris

Aldo returned from work in the late afternoon. The suite was empty.

"Alessandra? Aurora?"

He moved between the rooms, and no one was there. Turning quickly, Aldo realized there was no luggage either, in any of the bedrooms. They were gone. *What the….?*

Then he saw a note on the drawing-room table. Next to it was Alessandra's wedding ring setting, but the diamond was gone.

'Aldo, I'm afraid I shan't be calling you dearest any longer. Some dreadful woman appeared and told us of your past. Somehow I know it's all true. I feel it in my bones. I'm afraid I can't go on with that lingering over you. I could never love you or be comfortable around you. You have no honor. Alessandra.'

I should have guessed that when Lorenz told Anna she would respond.

Pacing about the drawing room trying to think, Aldo saw another note on the window ledge. Picking it up, he saw this one was from his mother-in-law.

'What a cad you are. Misleading and lying to my beautiful daughter, ruining her life. Stay far away from us, forever. I expect you to manage the holdings here in Paris and in Vienna. Run them well and keep me informed or I will destroy you completely. You are already dead to us now. Aurora.'

Aldo dropped onto the couch, one note in each hand. *What a disaster, my plans ruined. I'm lucky Dante is dead or I'd be completely on the outside. I can still survive; I have the paintings, and there's still Anna. I have time to sort this out.*

Now to talk to Anna.

Anna's Aftermath
Paris

It was 2pm in the afternoon and there was a knock at the door. When Anna opened it, a messenger stood there.

"Anna Simone?"

She nodded. "Yes?"

He handed her a dispatch, turned away, and marched down the steps.

Anna glanced at the message while standing on the front porch, having absolutely no idea who it could be from or what it might say. Lorenz always sent someone from his staff when he had a message. She tore the envelope open, noting that it was stationary from the Hotel Meurice. *No doubt it's Aldo.*

The note was succinct. 'A, Meet me at the base of the Eiffel Tower at 4pm this afternoon. Lorenz will be working on a job I've given him. A.'

Alessandra, and maybe the mother, must have confronted him. I wonder what he'll have to say.

At 3:30pm Anna started for the tower. As her home was in the downtown area, she didn't have far to travel. *I want to be there and have a seat so that I might watch Aldo appear.*

She sat in the small café and watched him approach. *I expected a slouch perhaps, but he strolled along casually as if he didn't have a care in the world.* Anna waited as he neared her table and pulled up a chair.

He sat, and a broad smile appeared on his lips. "Are you happy?"

"About what?"

"You ruined my marriage, my life."

"I told them the truth."

"The truth has many shades."

"It shouldn't."

He smiled again. "It's just as well. I'm free of them now and there are still…opportunities."

Anna smiled at him, actually laughed.

"See I can still make you laugh."

"This time I'm laughing at you and not with you."

"For now." Then he spoke again. "You don't love Lorenz. Why do you stay with him?"

"Maybe I don't and maybe I do. That's between him and me, not you."

"We were in love once. That never really goes away, does it?"

"That was a long time ago. Things have changed."

"Have they? I think you still love me and I want to see you again."

"Don't be ridiculous, there's Lorenz."

Aldo nodded to her and rose from the chair. He leaned forward and, before she could stop him, grabbed her fingers and kissed them. "I'll be seeing you." Then he turned and walked away.

She sat there for several minutes afterward, sipping her tea, seething on the inside but calm on the outside.

Aldo's Aftermath
Paris

Lorenz is getting on my nerves. He wants to hang out all the time whether or not we're working. I keep him as busy as I can, but he persists.

The next day Lorenz was jabbering away, and he told Aldo something that struck a chord. They were talking about the construction or rehab of several of the buildings to be used for housing.

"My men were cleaning out that property over by your hotel…"

"The Hotel Meurice?"

"Yes, the building is just down the street and around the corner, and my men found an entire floor of methamphetamine left by the Nazis."

"How did you know? What did you do with it?"

"It was stamped on the box and fortunately one of my men knew what it was. I have it stored in one of the warehouses."

"What are you going to do with it?"

"I thought perhaps there might be a market. It has to be several years old now. I don't know."

"I know someone who might take it off your hands. Would it be possible to examine it? Get a small sample for testing?"

"Of course, I'd like to get rid of it, at a profit if possible."

————

Lorenz sent a man over to the hotel with an entire box of the stuff. They'd wrapped it in brown paper. Aldo took out several small amounts at a time and crushed it into fine powder, like sugar.

He'd been working on assembling the plant in Paris for production of various machine parts. Fortunately, Aldo had been far enough along that when he fled Pilsen, most of the equipment he needed was in place. *I would have liked to have brought a few of the workers along to get started but that hadn't been possible with my quick departure.* Still having worked with many of them for several years, Aldo contacted a small group of the workers and offered employment if they fled Czechoslovakia. Several of the men had arrived just as some of the housing and apartment units were finished.

Aldo took Lorenz out to celebrate.

"We've done it. The plant's ready. The housing is ready. The workers are arriving. We'll need some local hires but I have the foremen in place. We'll be making money in no time. Let's celebrate."

"Should I send for Anna?"

"No, this is a men's night out to celebrate our work. We'll eat, drink, and be entertained. Let Anna stay home but tell her you'll be late."

"Sounds fun."

"Of course it will be. We deserve it. We'll start with drinks at Harry's."

———

Some hours later, they'd been at Harry's for most of the afternoon consuming Old Fashioneds.

Lorenz was always a talker, and the evening seemed to have loosened his tongue even more. He was constantly babbling away. Aldo listened with one ear and nodded a lot as he scanned the crowd. Always keeping fresh drinks on hand.

"These things are rather bitter aren't they? And a touch smelly," said Lorenz, holding his glass up to the light.

"Nonsense, that's just the taste of good liquor."

He guided the glass to the bar. "I think perhaps I've had enough. Some dinner?" he slurred slightly.

"By all means, let's have one more and we'll go."

Lorenz sighed but chugged down the drink placed in front of him.

Aldo walked and supported Lorenz, as he staggered, out to the curb and they caught a taxi to Maxims. One very large dinner and several more Old Fashioneds later, they emerged to look for another cab.

"I really should get home, Anna will be worried."

"Nonsense, this is a night to celebrate." Aldo squeezed his shoulder.

Lorenz leaned against him. "What do we do next?" he asked.

"I have some entertainment for us."

In the cab Lorenz began that incessant chattering again and seemed suddenly refreshed and full of energy.

That's good, he'll need it.

The cab dropped them off, and Aldo escorted Lorenz inside and to the lift. They departed on the third floor. Aldo knocked on door #7. A young girl answered and, upon seeing them, opened the door wide. With his arm around Lorenz's shoulders, Aldo propelled him inside. Lorenz needed little help.

There were eight scantily clad young women who jumped from their seats and clustered around Lorenz. He babbled away.

Aldo slipped out the door and back to the lift. *I'm sure he'll have a night that he'll never forget.*

Anna's Aftermath
Paris

Anna got the call in the early morning, just before dawn. She looked across the room and saw no sign of Lorenz. Sitting up in bed, she listened more intently.

"Yes, I'm Anna Simone. Where did you get my name?"

She listened for a moment.

"Lorenz Muster, you're speaking about Lorenz Muster?"

She listened again.

"You're where? I'll be right there."

Anna got ready quickly and kept looking around the room for Lorenz. *This can't be possible.* She called one of the cab companies, not trusting herself to drive.

"Take me to Notre Dame Cathedral."

"To the church?" asked the driver.

"No, to the morgue behind the church."

When she arrived, there was no one at the door so Anna entered and walked down a long dark hallway toward a distant light. When she reached it there was another door. Anna entered and found herself in a long room with many drawers along the walls. *I've never been in a morgue.*

An older man, thin, in a white smock and wireless glasses approached.

"May I help you?"

"You or someone just called me, Anna Simone, about my fiancé, Lorenz Muster?"

The man nodded and motioned for her to follow him. "Come this way."

Anna walked along a few feet behind until the man turned to a drawer in the wall and pulled it out. He lifted the sheet. It was Lorenz. Anna's hand went toward his face but stopped only inches away.

"Is he…how?"

"Yes, he's quite dead. Heart attack I imagine. The police will want an autopsy but they wanted positive identification."

He replaced the sheet over Lorenz's face and slid the drawer back.

She turned to him. "How did…what happened?"

"I don't really know yet. The details from the police indicate that someone called in there was a man passed out in the hallway of an apartment building. That there was a bunch of noise and then quiet. The police found him and called me. He was dead when they found him. They will conduct an investigation later this morning. Probably going on now."

"I don't understand?"

"Did he have medical issues of any kind, any problems?"

"No, he was in good health. He was a businessman, well to do."

"Yes, I recognized the name."

"He called early yesterday evening and said he would be working late. That was the last thing I heard from him."

"Give the police a little time, they'll figure it out. You'll probably want to go home and rest. I need to get to work."

Anna rode home in a daze. *My world has irrevocably changed.*

For two days there was no news. Then someone, police, morgue, someone, leaked the information, and the newspaper ran a small story, really more of a caption, on the lower half of the front page. 'Prominent local financier Lorenz Muster found dead'.

For the next two days Anna's phone rang, her doorbell rang, she received telegrams and wires. Lorenz had many partners in business. The most commonly asked question was, "What do I do now that Lorenz is dead?"

Her response was simple. "Keep doing what you are doing. You're responsible now. Make it work. If you owe money, pay it back. If you are a partner, share the profits according to the partnership agreement."

In all that time, Anna never heard from Aldo. *I could contact Aldo but I want more facts, if there are any. Since I haven't heard from him, I suspect he knows more than I. Maybe the how, the why, the where. I will talk to him soon.*

———

Then the police came to see her, a man in a suit and a man in a uniform. Anna invited them inside.

"Ms. Simone, you were Mr. Muster's fiancée, is that right?"

"Yes."

"We've tried to locate any next of kin but there don't seem to be any."

"That's correct. Lorenz was from Vienna but all of his family has passed, except for me."

"That's just it. While you are his fiancée, you aren't technically family."

She held up her hand with the two carat engagement ring. "We've been together for over five years. Most of Paris knows us or have heard of us. Lorenz was close friends with your chief of police."

"Yes, ma'am we realize that and our chief asked us to speak with you, which we are here to do. We just wanted to make you aware, in case you have any legal issues or problems surrounding Lorenz or his businesses."

"I appreciate your concern. I've spoken to many of his partners already. Now, what did the police have to say?"

The two men looked at each other and shrugged. "It's not all good news."

"Well of course not, he's dead."

"That's not what I meant. Look, the police dug around in the building where your fiancé was found in the hallway. He was just a couple of doors down from a young woman who has been run in for prostitution on a couple of occasions. Under repeated questioning, the young woman admitted first that she had called the police and later that the man had been in her apartment with her and several of her friends. She claimed they were just drinking and dancing and he seized up and started gurgling and staggered into the hallway. She claims there was no sexual activity."

"I expect not, Lorenz wasn't all that passionate."

They both looked at her.

"He wasn't a skirt chaser. It was too strenuous for him. He liked to observe, to possess things."

The man in the suit swallowed hard. "Well that may be, the coroner said he had no traces of sexual activity…"

"Told you."

"But, he had an excessive amount of methamphetamine in his system. Was he a druggie?"

"What?"

"He had a lot in his system. It's probably what brought on his heart attack. That stuff doesn't normally kill you but it's really addictive and can make you crazy. He had no history of using it?"

"Lorenz was a very calm, sedate man. The only thing that ever got him excited was money or talking about money."

The men shook their heads. "We can only tell you what the coroner found."

———

After they were gone, Anna sat in the drawing room and pondered the situation. *They're right. Lorenz and I weren't married. I'll probably lose access to the money in the banks, some properties, if mortgaged. The house he owned outright—so I'll have a place to live. Some businesses will continue to pay for a while. To counter that, I'll need lawyers, time, and money. Difficult to come by. I don't really care about any of it other than time. Time to find the answers I'm looking for, now including what happened to Lorenz. I need to talk to Aldo.*

Aldo's Aftermath
Paris

Lorenz's funeral was scheduled for a few days later. That was a surprise, not that it was a few days later, but that there was a funeral. *I hadn't intended to kill him, not really. I didn't know he had a weak heart. I just knew he had all those Nazi drugs, and I thought a fun night out with the girls might do him some good, loosen him up. We still had a lot of work to do together.*

I need to talk to Anna. We'll have to secure some of those properties. Others will try to move in or just pretend like they don't owe Lorenz anything. I'll have to be strong with them. The banks could be a problem. We need the cash flow while still in start-up. I have one gold bar left, and it's my backup in case I need to run.

At the funeral Aldo kept his distance but made sure he was in Anna's line of sight. She looked quite dignified all in black. *I still don't think she loved him.*

Aldo caught her eye, and she nodded. After the service he lingered until all the others were gone. He'd taken a cab to the gravesite. Walking slowly toward the cemetery gates, sitting alone along the tarmac was a 1948 Citroen Traction Avant. It was a magnificent looking car. It had belonged to Lorenz, and Aldo had always admired it.

Approaching the car, Aldo saw Anna sitting alone in the back seat. As he reached the window, she rolled it down.

"You drive," and she rolled the window back up.

He got into the driver's seat, engaged the motor, and pulled away.

It was quiet for several minutes. They were both waiting.

"I can help you," Aldo said.

"Like you helped Lorenz?"

"I didn't know he had a weak heart. It was just supposed to be a fun evening."

"Lorenz wasn't really a 'fun' kind of guy."

"Yeah, I realize that now."

"You drugged him."

Aldo didn't answer.

"So, what kind of help do you think I need?"

"With the bankers, the business partners, the lenders, anyone that was in a deal with him will try to take advantage of you."

"Really."

"Of course, but I'm a partner in several of his dealings and I'll speak for both of us. Set them straight. I'm not afraid. You don't want to be cheated."

"How noble of you."

"I'm just that kind of guy."

———

Aldo drove to the Hotel Meurice and parked the car. He turned toward her.

"Do you want to come up? We can strategize."

"Not this evening. I'm afraid I'm not up to any strategizing. We'll talk later."

He handed her the keys, and she drove away.

Standing there watching her go, I feel like things are turning my way again. She'll be mine before she realizes it.

Aldo strode into the hotel and up to his room.

Anna's Aftermath
Paris & Vienna

That was the thing about Aldo, everything was always so convenient. Nothing was ever really blatant with him. He admitted to killing Rene, but the others, I don't know for sure. I suspect he killed Dante, his business partner, and probably Lorenz, whether or not he meant to. He wasn't sad or guilty about any of it.

Unfortunately, I need to work with him, for my own survival. I just hope that it won't be too messy.

Aldo was true to his word and met with bankers, business partners, and officials. Anna retained access to everything. Of course Aldo immediately needed access to funding for the warehouse and apartments he and Lorenz had been building. Anna didn't let on that she knew more about the projects and the finances than what Aldo thought. Lorenz had shared most details with her. He didn't have anyone else, and he liked to talk.

They spent the next few weeks getting things underway; hiring workers for the factory, renting out the apartments, keeping up with Lorenz's many other business partners.

I keep Aldo at arm's length. I want him anxious, and I want some time to pass.

———

Then Anna suggested they go to Vienna, check on the properties there. She'd received several telegrams and a couple of calls. There were properties and businesses to be dealt with.

Aldo was happy with the idea.

They traveled by train. He wanted to fly, especially after Anna told him she'd booked separate sleeper cars.

Arriving in Vienna, they checked into the Imperial. As

Lorenz and Anna had a suite there, she allowed Aldo to stay in the spare bedroom. *I want to get his hopes up, just a little.*

They checked on businesses and properties the first few days. There were no problems. *I have to admit Aldo is good at that, problem solving, in whatever fashion.*

Anna suggested they have dinner one evening.

"Let's eat light so we can get a pastry from Demel."

"Those were amazing. Let's skip dinner and have a couple of them instead."

"Perfect."

———

When I'd been in Paris cleaning out the house, I'd run across a box of methamphetamine that Lorenz had brought home to show me and to have on hand if some opportunity arose.

I opened the box, disassembled the tablets, and ground them into a very fine powder. It didn't smell very strong, but it was a little unpleasant. The taste was about like the smell. So, I mixed a little powdered sugar and cinnamon with it. Just enough to cover the smell and taste.

———

This time Anna and Aldo started in the public gardens and again they strolled, talking about the old days—the early days of their missions, about going to the beach in Marseille —and then business in Vienna which was good. Anna let Aldo take her arm. They smiled and laughed. Then they went to Demel for pastry.

They had a tart with sugar and other glazes on top.

"Don't those look lovely. Let's try them," Anna said.

Aldo nodded and smiled, "Yes, let's do."

"Find us a seat and I'll bring them over."

He turned to go, and she ordered four. Balancing them, Anna walked to the table and sat them and herself.

"Oh, I forgot my tea. Would you mind?"

Aldo hopped up and made his way across the café. Anna arranged the pastries and waited for his return.

He sat the cup of tea down, and she smiled brightly at him. *I can see the tension melt out of his shoulders.*

He slid into the seat opposite her, their knees touching.

They ate the pastry with great relish.

"Those were so good," Anna said, wiping her lips.

"Yes, they were. A little sweeter than I remembered and a touch more cinnamon, perhaps."

"Let's sit and talk for a while," Anna suggested. She noticed Aldo had begun to flex his shoulders a bit and twist in his seat. He fidgeted with his teacup. His eyes darted around the room.

He nodded. "What do you want to talk about?"

Aldo's Aftermath
Paris & Vienna

Things in Paris were a little slow with Anna. Aldo focused on making sure she retained Lorenz's property. A few weeks into that she suggested they go to Vienna. *I know she loved it there, and I feel like I'm making some progress.*

They got to Vienna, and Aldo stayed with Anna at the Imperial. He took that as a good sign. Aldo ran through the local properties and the businesses and got them in order. Anna asked him to dinner. *Things were looking better.*

She took him to Demel. They ordered two pastries each. Aldo was hungry and wolfed them down. Then Anna wanted to talk. *Why not. I feel a little fidgety but, hey, I am proud of what I've accomplished so far. I'm making things right with her.*

"What do you want to talk about?"

"So you were Aldo Anouilh when I knew you and now you're Aldo Buio, what's that about?"

"It was just a name, a fresh start. Who knows, maybe next time I'll be Aldo Cella, that has a ring to it."

"It was unfortunate about Pilsen, losing it to the Communists."

"Yeah it was. Dante tried to argue. They were going to kill us both…"

"But you pushed him from the tower didn't you? Just like you killed Rene?"

"Hey, it was that, or we both died." *Why am I telling her this?*

"And you overdosed Lorenz as well, didn't you? Not just for a night out and a good time but to kill him."

"No, I didn't know he had a bad heart, kind of funny though." *What am I saying? I keep squirming in my seat, but I feel great.*

"So you think we can be together? That we can be happy?"

"Yeah, of course, why not? We were happy before." Aldo stood up quickly. "Let's get out of here. I need some air."

They walked back to the Imperial. Aldo held her hand. *When we get to the lobby, I want to kiss her but I don't feel well. I am sweating profusely.* She held a hand to his face.

"Let's go to the room. You don't look well."

They took the elevator up, and that's the last thing Aldo remembered.

Anna's Aftermath
Vienna

Aldo passed out in the elevator on the way to the room. *I think they call it 'crashing'.* Anna had poured the powder on both his pastries, and he had wolfed them down. *I didn't intend to kill him. I just want to know the truth. I've lost a great deal in my life —my daughter, my fiancé, my one true friend, my innocence, although that one wasn't strictly Aldo's doing, but he played a role in every one of those events, and to what purpose? Yet, he is still here pursuing me.*

Aldo slept through the night and early the next morning, when Anna opened the curtains in his room, she heard him groan.

"How are you feeling?"

He moaned again. "I don't know what happened, my stomach…"

"Could it have been something you ate?"

"I don't know. We had the same pastries, maybe earlier in the day."

"Some breakfast?"

He waved a hand. "Just coffee."

She watched him for a few moments, sitting there looking confused. Aldo was not a man who liked to lose control.

"I have an idea," she said to him.

He looked up at her, his face quizzical.

"You've been an enormous help with everything. Kept you and I both in a position to control our situations."

He nodded and looked away. She was losing him.

"What do you think of taking a few days off? Everything seems in good order now. Maybe take the train to Belgrade. It runs along the river, relax for a few days." She had his attention again.

"That sounds like fun," he murmured.

"Rest up and I'll make the arrangements."

Aldo's Aftermath
Vienna

I really don't feel well. But the good news is Anna is finally coming to her senses. There's just her and I left now. We have plenty of resources for a good life. Everything has worked out after all.

Aldo cleaned up while she was gone and got his things together. This trip to Belgrade would be a new beginning. His mind went to work immediately. *Since there's just the two of us and we each have access to all the assets now, if we don't get along, we can go our separate ways. Who knows what is possible.*

Aldo met her with open arms when she returned, and they embraced. *I forgot how good she feels in my arms, how good she smells. This trip is going to be fun. Then we'll go back to business.*

Anna's Aftermath
Vienna & Belgrade

Anna purchased the tickets for Belgrade. *If we leave in the morning, it's an eight-hour trip and we'll arrive in the evening. I won't have to be concerned about a sleeper car. We'll stay in our separate rooms here in the suite tonight. It's been a long road.*

They checked out early the next morning. Aldo clung to Anna like glue. She smiled. They looked the happy couple. The train ride was beautiful along the Danube. Anna really enjoyed the river. Aldo was unusually quiet, occasionally pointing to something or whispering in her ear. He could be charming. The sun was shining, and she felt at peace at last. This was a new beginning.

They ate supper in the dining car, by candlelight, a nice steak and a good wine. It was the perfect meal. Finishing they returned to their car with perhaps an hour to arrival.

"Have you ever been to the Belgrade Fortress?" she asked him.

He shook his head. "No, but I've heard of it. Should we have a look?"

"I think so. It's near the station and on our way into town. It will be beautiful at sunset."

"Let's do it."

She smiled and leaned back in her seat.

In only a few minutes, the train was pulling into the station. They gathered their luggage, and Anna commissioned a porter to have it delivered.

"I made reservations for us at the Hotel Moskva, in downtown. It's Belgrade's oldest and finest."

"I like it. We are going to have a good time."

She squeezed his hand. "Yes, we are. Now, let's go see the fortress."

They strolled up the mound from the train station.

Sunset was approaching as they reached the top of the ridge and walked along the embankment. Pausing as the sun set, they gazed down upon the conflux of the Sava and Danube rivers. It was a beautiful sight as the night sky filled with stars and the light reflected and danced off the waters.

Anna felt Aldo move closer to her and shivered as a slight breeze picked up. He slid out of his jacket and draped it across her shoulders. Taking his hand in hers, they started down the path.

"Let's go look at the catacombs and we'll rekindle some history."

He smiled and squeezed her hand.

She led him along the path and they descended into the lower regions of the Fortress. There are many things below, prison cells, storage rooms, bunkers, tunnels, it's a maze. *But I want the catacombs, built by the Romans so long ago.*

As they got closer, she let him lead the way. Aldo was pulling Anna by one hand. With her free hand, Anna reached inside the pocket of the vest she was wearing, feeling the coolness of the cloth and then the little wooden handle as she shook it free.

They had reached the catacombs. Aldo stopped. Anna motioned with her head to move a little further on.

"Let's look over there. I think you can see down to even lower levels."

Aldo stepped across and Anna followed, free from his grasp.

When he looked down, she whipped the garrote from her pocket and slung the wire around in front of him, securing the other handle as it came about. At the same time, Anna placed her knee in the middle of his back and pulled the garrote with both hands.

Aldo gasped and tried to grab her hands. Anna kept

applying pressure to his back, bending him and keeping his hands from her.

"Why?" he gasped.

"You were our leader, and you abandoned us. Killed some and abused others. You weren't just a traitor to the cause, you were a traitor to your friends."

"But we were a couple. We were in love."

"Don't flatter yourself. I never loved you, not then and not now."

She pulled hard with both hands.

Aldo gasped and gurgled and sank to his knees. His neck collapsed to one side and his body leaned to the other as Anna removed the wire and pushed him through the opening in the floor. Anna could look down into the tomb below and see Aldo sprawled across the floor.

She took his jacket off her shoulders and cleaned the wire of the garrote before rolling it back up and placing it in her vest pocket. Anna dropped Aldo's jacket over his head and turned to walk to the road.

I have a hot shower and a clean, soft bed at the Hotel Moskva waiting on me.

PART III

————

DEE & FRIENDS

Dee and Friends
Seventeenth Day
Nuremberg

They'd broken up that afternoon when Anna said she needed to rest. But she was quick to add that she'd like to see them after dinner in her stateroom.

After finishing dinner, the group made their way to her cabin. Dee knocked softly in the event Anna was still resting. But the door opened quickly and Anna breathlessly invited them inside.

"Let's go out to the balcony. I made sure there would be enough chairs and I have some wine."

Everyone got seated and, after admiring how pleasant the night was and the view along the Nuremberg dock, the river, and the skyline of the city, Anna cleared her throat.

"I really do appreciate your interest in my story. You have been so nice to me. It seems the older I become the more invisible I am to most people. It is sad to grow old, to have gained some wisdom and lost the energy to do anything with it. As I said, when I finish the story you may have a different opinion of me, but think what you will."

"I'm sure you did what needed to be done, no one can find fault with that," said Dee.

"Perhaps. Some days you do what you want to do and some days you do what you have to do. The trick is knowing which is which."

"Please tell us," said Angelic.

Anna cleared her throat and shifted in her chair in an attempt to be more comfortable.

"As I said I didn't trust Aldo's story. I was back in Paris so I went to see my former Resistance team leader. I had questions about Aldo. Turns out he knew nothing about the trains, that boarding them was Aldo's idea."

"Why would he have done that?" asked Gina

"I never learned for sure but Henri, my team leader, and I suspected Aldo was just looking for an opportunity. Italy had surrendered, and the Nazis were losing. The war was going to be over soon. Aldo was playing for the wrong team, but he had a cover-up. He was just looking for a way out. Aldo must have known something about the trains. He split the three of us up, which was something he hadn't told Henri, like he was shaking off Rene and me."

"How could he have known what was on the trains?" asked Dee.

"I don't know, maybe he just took a chance. In hindsight, he did that a lot. But I had questions for him. Armed with the information from Henri I contacted Aldo when he came back to Paris. What I found out later was that he had been in Venice getting married to his business partner's sister."

"That sounds shaky," said Keno.

Anna smiled at her. "We'll get to that soon enough. I

confronted him at the Eiffel Tower. We talked about the trains we were on. This was the fascinating part. The Nazis were hiding trains in various mountain tunnels and blowing up the tunnels and removing the tracks."

"What for?" asked Mike.

"They were hiding things for the future or to keep them out of Allied hands."

"What kind of things?" asked Keno.

"Much of the art they stole, gold, weapons, supplies, rolling laboratories and materials. Anything they might need in a reversal of fortune."

"Two trains?" asked Dee.

"I was on one and Aldo was on two, so at least three that we examined, plus we both saw several more in the tunnels. Don't know how many total there may have been."

"Where were they?" asked Jamal

"My train was in Austria, Aldo's were in Germany and Czechoslovakia. My train led me to Vienna and Lorenz. Aldo's led him to Pilsen along with four paintings and several pounds of gold fillings he took."

"Gold fillings?" asked Keno

"Barrels full of them, from people's teeth."

"That's grisly," said Mike.

Anna nodded at him. "Yes, I thought so as well. When I confronted him on the observation deck of the Eiffel Tower, Aldo admitted he was a spy for Italy, and that he had killed Rene to save himself. At that point I was truly afraid of him. I'd taken him up the tower and pinned him against the rail to scare him but then I feared for my own life so I took a different strategy. I asked about the paintings."

"You distracted him," said Gina.

"He wanted to show them to me, so I let him. There was a Renoir, a Degas, and a Monet. They were outstanding pieces of art. I found out later that he also had a Picasso, an abstract of a woman. It had the name Anna painted on the back. I recognized it immediately. Pablo had painted it of me when I was a child. I had told Aldo about it and he recognized the painting."

"How did he find that?" asked Jamal.

"Just by chance he said. There was a box on one of the trains, holding a single painting, and was stamped Picasso. Aldo knew the Germans didn't generally care for Picasso, so he was curious; there it was."

Dee looked at his watch.

Anna saw him. "It is getting late and I'm afraid I've kept you too long."

"Not at all," said Gina.

"Really, I need to rest if you don't mind. Perhaps we can continue tomorrow or the next day."

"We'd like that," said Angelic.

"Tomorrow we will be in Bamberg and on the Main River. We're getting close now and I'll be home in Amsterdam."

Dee and Friends
Eighteenth Day
Bamberg

They met for breakfast and went up on the sundeck afterwards.

"Do you think she'll want to talk today?" asked Jamal.

"We were going to let her contact us," replied Angelic.

"If she doesn't by this afternoon, we might check on her," added Gina.

"What do you think the purpose of her story is? Why is she telling us this?" asked Mike.

"I think she's just an elderly woman with no friends and she's happy to have someone to share with," replied Angelic.

"I think it's important to her, and she wants to share it with someone," added Gina.

"It's an incredible story," said Keno.

"I think she's trying to tell us something, and perhaps not sure how to do so, or if we're interested in knowing," said Dee.

"You mean like there's something still undone, or that needs to be uncovered, or revealed in some way?" said Jamal.

"I told you there was more to it," added Mike.

"I think you're right. We just have to keep listening," replied Dee.

"Clues," said Angelic. "You guys are so crazy. She just wants to share."

———

They took a short tour in the morning. Bamberg had been spared heavy bombing during World War Two and most of its medieval buildings and cobblestoned streets survived intact.

The group assembled on the sundeck after lunch.

"That was picturesque," said Angelic.

"For once it looked just like the brochures," added Keno.

"It was nice that it was smaller and we could feel like we were actually visiting and not part of some large tour," said Gina.

"Amazing architecturally," added Jamal.

"Will we hear from Anna today?" asked Dee.

"I checked on her right after we got back and she was still resting. She had me feed the dog. Maybe tomorrow."

"What do we have left travel wise?" asked Mike.

"Two more days on the Main and then three days on the Rhine, fourth day into Amsterdam," replied Dee.

"Almost over," said Keno.

"We've been out about three weeks?" asked Angelic.

"Just about with a little less than a week to go," answered Dee. "Do you think we'll get to hear the whole story from Anna?"

The women looked at each other. "I think so. I think that's why she is resting so much so she can tell it all to us before the trip is over," said Gina.

"Still think there's more to it?" asked Angelic.

Dee and Friends
Nineteenth & Twentieth Days
Wurzburg & Miltenberg

Dee and Gina were sitting in their cabin. They had finished dinner with the others and broken up to their separate staterooms. The cruise had gotten lengthy. The group was getting tired, and they had only received texts from Anna the past two days.

"I'm going to go by and check on her," said Gina.

"I thought you got a text from her this afternoon?" replied Dee.

"I did, but it's been a couple of days. I just want to make sure."

"Want me to go with you?"

"No, I don't think so, may be better one on one."

"Text me if you need me."

———

Gina knocked softly on the door and waited for a minute. She was about to knock again when the door slowly opened. Anna's back was to her, but she called out, "Do come in, I'm just going to lay back down."

Gina followed her into the bedroom and sat in a chair beside Anna, who was now resting against the headboard.

"I just wanted to check and see if you needed anything," said Gina.

Anna leaned out and took her hand. "Thank you so much. I'm sorry I've been absent the last couple of days. I think we're about on the Rhine aren't we?"

"Yes, I think so. You've told us such a wonderful story. I'm amazed at your life and your experiences."

"There are a couple of key events that I still haven't shared. Then we'll see what you think."

"You've done so many unusual things, I'm envious."

"Don't be, all you can do is learn how to be you, same as I did."

Gina paused.

"I'll see the group up on the sundeck after breakfast and try to wrap the story up, if you think that works?"

"Absolutely, we'll see you then."

Dee and Friends
Twenty-First Day
Koblenz

Anna met them on the sundeck after breakfast. It was beginning to feel like they'd spent the entire cruise there. But after the ocean cruises, it was a small ship.

"Good morning everyone."

"Morning Anna," murmured several of the group.

"I'm sorry to have been unavailable for the past couple of days. Sometimes I just feel so tired. Thank you for being patient with me."

"I think we're all a little tired. It's been a lengthy cruise," said Dee.

"It's almost over."

"Amsterdam awaits," said Jamal.

Anna smiled at him. "Indeed, it does." She shifted positions in her chair. "To continue the story, after Aldo showed me the paintings, he and Lorenz stayed busy with their projects. At some point Aldo went to Venice and married his partner Dante's sister." Anna looked at Keno. "I told you I'd come back to it. Apparently the wife and her mother came to Paris to stay or at least visit. Lorenz came running into the house one morning telling me he'd met the wife. I wasn't really surprised. Aldo was an opportunist, but I felt he still wanted to be involved with me. Well, I didn't care for that. So, I went to see the wife and mother-in-law."

"Oh, my gosh. What did you say? What did they say?" asked Gina.

"I told them the truth, about everything, and they believed me."

"How did you know?" asked Jamal.

"I saw Aldo the next day. He confirmed it. They had left

and told him never to come around them again. Then he made a pass at me."

"Seriously?" asked Keno.

"Oh yes. He was always looking for the next opportunity."

"What did you do?" asked Angelic.

"I waited. I was sure I'd hear from him again. In hindsight, that may have been a mistake. It cost Lorenz his life."

"How?" asked Mike.

"I don't know that it was deliberate, as in specifically intended, but Aldo obtained some methamphetamine that Lorenz's workers had found in one of their buildings, something the Nazis had left behind. He crushed it up in a fine powder and put it in Lorenz's drinks on a night they went out together to celebrate completion of one of their projects. Once he had Lorenz high, he dropped him off at a cathouse."

"A what?" asked Keno.

"Prostitute or maybe a house full of them," answered Gina.

"In this case an apartment. But the methamphetamine in Lorenz's system caused his heart to race, and he had a fatal heart attack. Aldo later admitted to it as well as killing his business partner in Pilsen."

"Why did he do that?" asked Dee.

"He said the Communists wanted control of their company. That they took Aldo and Dante to the top of a bell tower and were threatening them with their lives. Aldo said he pushed Dante over to save himself, similar to what he'd done to Rene."

"And the Communists let him go?" asked Jamal.

"Apparently he agreed to their terms and bought himself enough time to escape."

"He's despicable," said Angelic.

"Yes, but he was a survivor. After Lorenz's funeral, the police came to me and suggested that I might have legal issues since we weren't married. I had to agree with their assessment. But Aldo stepped in and secured the money, the properties, and the business arrangements. I had to give him credit for that. It kept us going, and it gave me time to think. I decided it best to work with him for the moment."

"That must have been difficult," said Gina.

"Yes, and no. I was frustrated with Aldo, disappointed in Lorenz's death, and not sure how I was going to survive, or answer the questions I still had. We got everything in order in Paris and I suggested we go to Vienna, to do the same. Aldo readily agreed."

"I bet he did. He thought you were giving in to him," said Keno.

"I imagine he did think that, but I kept him at arm's length."

"Was that difficult?" asked Gina.

"I was careful and lucky. Aldo had proven that he could be a brutal man, but mostly when he was forced. He'd never been rough or difficult with me. I had to rely on that and hope that his patience didn't run out."

"You took a big chance," said Angelic.

"Yes, but it was really the only one I had. We got to Vienna and straightened everything out there. Then I asked him to Demel, the pastry shop. We'd been there before and he loved the desserts."

"Were you fattening him up?" asked Jamal.

"In a manner. I'd located some of the methamphetamine at my house in Paris. I crushed it up very fine and mixed it with sugar and cinnamon. We bought two pastries each, and I laced his with the mixture. I wasn't trying to kill him, I just wanted the truth. The answers to the rest of my questions.

He killed Rene, he killed Dante, he killed Lorenz, and he wasn't the least bit sorry or even unhappy. Plus, he'd made me pregnant with a child I'd had to leave behind. That part wasn't all his fault, but I knew he didn't want to be a father and I never told him about our daughter. The meth made him very talky and very antsy. He squirmed for the rest of the evening, until he came down, in the elevator on the way to our suite."

"That was fortunate," said Dee.

"It was. I wasn't sure how long it might take him to wind down and I knew I'd have to keep him occupied until he did."

"What did you do then?" asked Gina.

"I made my decision. I invited him to take the train to Belgrade for a few days of holiday."

"After all that?" asked Keno.

Anna smiled at her.

"We traveled by train through the day. I suggested to him that when we arrived, we visit the Belgrade Fortress and view the sunset."

"The same fortress you sent us to," said Jamal.

"Yes, I believe I said it was full of intrigue."

"You did," added Mike.

"And so it was. We watched a beautiful sunset and then I led us down into the catacombs."

"The burial site of Attila the Hun," said Dee.

"That's right. I led him down the path and when he stopped to look through an opening to the tombs below, Aldo had a terrible fall."

"Did he die?" asked Angelic.

"Yes, he was quite dead."

"Lucky for you or he might have pushed you over," said Gina.

"Yes, he might have."

"Unbelievable," said Mike.

"So it would seem. I felt I needed to tell someone."

Dee and Friends
Twenty-Second Day
Cologne

The group gathered for breakfast the following morning.

"Anyone heard from Anna?" asked Jamal. There was no response. "That was quite a story."

"Yeah, it was amazing," added Mike.

"Sad," said Keno.

"So incredible that it must be true," said Gina.

"How could you trust a man named Aldo?" said Keno.

"I think there's more," said Dee.

"What else could there be?" asked Jamal.

"I don't know, but I think we need to ask her."

———

The group took a morning tour of the Cologne Cathedral and the Museum Ludwig before hustling back to the ship. They didn't hear from Anna that morning or during lunch. They broke up to rest in the afternoon before considering going back into the city for some nightlife.

Dee and Gina were in their cabin, one resting in a chair and the other on the sofa.

"I'm worried about Anna."

"Why is that?"

"Just a feeling. She seems so weak, like she's really fighting to hang on."

"She is ninety-something."

"Don't be cruel."

"I'm not, I just mean she's lived a long life. That's a lot of mileage. Most people never get close to that age. She's bound to be tired."

"I'm going to check on her."

"I'm going with you. I agree with your instincts."

———

They reached Anna's room and Gina knocked softly. There was no response. Dee knocked a little louder. Still no response but then they heard the dog barking and then a bit of a gurgle. Dee tried the door, and it opened. Gina pushed him aside and hurried into the suite.

"Come in." It was faint and coming from the bedroom.

They hurried toward the sound. Anna was lying in the bed, her head resting on a pillow. She smiled at them. "I'm glad you came by. I left my phone in the drawing room and didn't have the energy to get it."

"Are you all right?" asked Gina.

Anna nodded. "Just weak, tired, and old, nothing to be concerned about."

"That's not true. We've been missing you."

Anna raised a hand from the cover and touched Gina on the arm. "Thank you." She nodded her head toward the room. "Have a seat, let's talk."

Gina pulled up a chair and she and Anna held hands. Dee stood to the side, looking down upon both of them. There was silence for a few moments.

"You never told us what happened to your daughter," said Dee.

Anna looked up at him for a moment.

"You're persistent," she said and then chuckled. "Some years after Aldo's demise, probably around 1960 I contacted the family in Austria. My daughter would have been about sixteen years old."

"Why did you wait so long?" asked Dee.

"I actually checked on her not long after Belgrade, when I returned to Paris. She was about five at the time and her parents said she was very happy and integrated into the family with her brother and sister. I didn't want to ruin that. She didn't know me and wouldn't remember me. I thought it best to leave her alone. I didn't ask at the time if they'd told her she was adopted or wasn't theirs. I didn't think it mattered."

"That must have been difficult," said Gina.

"Yes, it was. I was very much alone, had no faith in men. It's when I got my first dog. They've kept me company ever since. But as time passed, I wanted to know more. So in 1960 I reached out to the family again. They welcomed me and invited me to come and visit. I was surprised to say the least. They introduced me as a cousin of the wife. I had short hair and wore glasses by that time which was a good thing. When I saw my daughter she looked just like I had at that age, just like the realism painting by Picasso. I almost cried. It was like looking back in time before all those things happened."

"Did you tell her?" exclaimed Gina.

"No, I couldn't and it was for the best. An attraction had developed between my daughter and her brother. The parents wanted them both to be happy and were concerned about telling her she wasn't theirs, so that the relationship might proceed. They wanted my approval, which I gave them."

"What happened then?" asked Gina.

"They told her she was dropped off during the night and that they decided to care for her and to raise her. That she and her brother, Grigor, were not actually related."

"Did they get together?" asked Dee.

"Not immediately, but in time. There was a moment while I was there that Elise caught me by surprise and looked me directly in the eyes. It was like looking into a mirror. I think she recognized it then too. She reached out to me some years later. But, before that she and Grigor got involved and then engaged. While the parents had done well with the farm and were successful and affluent, the father's family back in Sophia, in Bulgaria, was exceedingly wealthy. Grigor wanted to go and work for his uncle, who was childless. After the marriage they returned to Bulgaria, began work and a family. Some years later she contacted me. Grigor had succeeded his uncle; they had three children, my grandchildren, and were very wealthy. She asked me to tell her our story. We met in Bucharest and shared the past. Thereafter it's always been a special place for me, and we meet there every year."

"That's who you were visiting, before the cruise," said Dee.

"Is he always this perceptive?" Anna asked Gina.

"He thinks he is." She winked at Anna. "But we know better."

"Let me show you something and I'd better rest."

"It can wait I'm sure," replied Gina.

"No, let me show you." She looked up to Dee. "In that closet there's a large upright trunk. Would you bring it over here?"

"Certainly." Dee moved to the closet and opened the door. Reaching inside he pulled out a trunk that was four feet high, four feet wide and three feet deep. He slid it across to the bed.

"That thing is heavy."

"Yes, for a reason."

Then he went to unlatch it.

"It's locked. Flip open the plate below the handle. Press it and let it pop out."

Dee pushed below the handle and a six by four-inch plate popped open. Inside were two key entries and a combination dial.

"The keys are over there on the counter on that ring of keys. The combination is 581945."

"VE day, victory in Europe."

Anna looked at Gina and said, "He is perceptive." Then she looked at Dee and winked.

Dee grabbed the keys and opened the two locks then turned the combination as she had told him. The top of the trunk popped open.

"Look inside. There are five items, extract each of them carefully."

Dee looked into the case. There were five slots and inside each one he could see a frame.

"I'm thinking I might know what these are, at least some of them."

"Why don't you have a look and see."

Dee extracted each one carefully and unwrapped the light coating surrounding it.

There was a Renoir landscape, a Monet water lily, and a Degas dancer. But there were two more—an abstract and a portrait, both by Picasso, both of Anna.

"I take them with me everywhere I go. I don't feel complete without them."

"Does anyone know you have them?" asked Dee.

"Only you two."

———

Dee had put the paintings away, and they had left Anna to rest. Gina and he sat in their stateroom.

"I can't believe she carries those around with her," said Dee.

"She's lost almost everything important to her in her life. That's what's left."

"That and the dog."

"So it would seem. What are we going to do?"

"We'd better try to get contact information for the daughter."

"I'll ask her in the morning. What should we tell the others?"

"Everything but the fact that she has the paintings with her. The fewer people that know that the better. They could put her in real danger. Who knows what they're worth?"

"Could we ask Diego or Eva?"

"Probably but it might raise questions."

"You're right. She's seen so much danger already in her life. How much longer can she live?"

"She looks really frail. We need that contact information."

———

They met the others for dinner and shared what they had learned. By the time the story finished, it was too late to go ashore, and they all retired for the evening.

Dee and Friends
Twenty-Third Day
Kinderdijk

"We've crossed out of Germany and we're in Netherlands," said Jamal.

"One day from Amsterdam. I am so ready," said Keno.

The group had met for breakfast, for perhaps the last time.

"I'm for checking out as soon as we can tomorrow and finding something different," said Angelic. "The food was good but we've been eating it a really long time."

"Maybe we keep it shorter next time," added Dee.

"Amen to that," said Mike.

"There's a windmill tour that might be fun," said Gina.

"Anything to get off the boat for a while," said Keno.

They assembled shortly afterward to disembark for the tour.

Dee held up a hand as they moved toward the gangway. "My stomach is churning. Must have been something from breakfast. I think I'll stay nearby."

Gina turned toward him. "I'll stay too."

Dee turned her back around. "No, you go on. So you can tell me about it. I'll be okay." He nodded at her and she nodded back.

She turned to the others and said, "Let's go."

They trooped off for the tour and Dee watched them board the bus and offered a final wave.

———

A short time later, Dee knocked on Anna's door. He heard the dog and a sound. Trying the handle he found it unlocked and walked inside. He called from the stateroom, "Anna?"

"Back here, do come in."

Dee entered the bedroom. "How are you doing today?"

"Not much change, still tired." She paused. "I thought you might come back alone, persistent little man aren't you. I like that."

"There's a lot of substance to your story but a lot of unanswered questions, to me."

"What is it you want to know? But be careful what you wish for."

"Did you ever go back and find the location of the trains?"

"That's right; you are a treasure hunter aren't you?"

"I'm not interested in treasure. I'm wealthy enough."

"Is there ever such a thing?"

"It seems like there was for you."

"Touché."

"I just wonder about the tunnels and all those things left behind. Sure the art's valuable and could possibly be returned to its original owners, but you mentioned weapons, labs and supplies. The Nazis were developing many things."

"I see. You have an interest in history, in mankind."

"If those things are still out there, they could be hazardous in their own right or especially if they fell into the wrong hands. That's why I asked if you knew where the tunnels were located or if they'd been unearthed."

Anna paused for a moment as if recapturing the past in her mind.

"After I resettled in Paris and determined my daughter was well, I looked for the tunnels. I knew exactly where the one I rode into was located. I could have found it in my sleep. I had to work a little harder with Aldo's two. Finding the Pilsen tunnel wasn't too difficult, but the other one, with the large switching station and arguably the most trains and potential problems was more difficult. I knew from Aldo that it was somewhere along or near the German-Czech border in the Bavarian Forest. I looked a while for that one."

"And?"

She smiled, her face brittle and her lips dry, but light in her eyes. "And they were all still sealed when I located them. Most of the Nazis had fled, they had the Allies on the west and the Russians on the east, and there was no time and no desire to stage a comeback. They all wanted Hitler dead. They ran like rats in the bright light."

"Did you tell anyone?"

"No, there was no need."

"So they're still out there?"

"It was years ago, I haven't checked."

"The Nazis were doing a lot of research—atomic, biological, chemical, space exploration, and many other areas. There might be something in there that would be helpful to the world."

"Or harmful. It's better to let it rest in peace. Besides, you ever hear of Operation Paperclip?"

"Yes, where the Allies kept a bunch of the German scientists who ended up developing atomic energy and the space program."

"That's right. But the Russians carried off numerous German scientists, engineers and technicians as well. They don't teach that in school and people don't remember but it was common knowledge, widely reported, the Russians took over 2200 people while the Allies only got 1600. The Russians took the biological and chemical groups. There were some nasty things the Nazis were working on at the time, air-borne viruses, chemical additives and contaminants, diseases from all their blood work. "

"What about all the art? Shouldn't it be returned to the rightful owners?"

"I thought about that a lot. The problem was you

couldn't just pull out the art. You open Pandora's Box, you get all the contents. Besides, I figured the governments of the respective countries would just appropriate everything and it would never get back to the original owners. Like I said, the world's a better place without all that stuff, let it stay buried."

"I don't know that I agree, but it's your decision."

"Thank you. You're a smart guy with a beautiful and kind wife. Don't make your life more difficult than it has to be." She hesitated for a moment. "The past is never where we left it. The world changes, but sometimes we don't."

Dee nodded. *What's she telling me?*

"I think I'd better rest now. But I'd like to see that lovely wife of yours, maybe this afternoon."

"They went to see the windmills."

"To watch them tilt?"

"Something like that, I'll tell her to come by."

"Tell her to just come inside."

———

Dee was waiting on the sundeck when they returned. They came dragging along, laughing and cutting up.

"Man, half this country is underwater," said Mike.

"A few well-placed explosives and Paris would be ocean side," added Jamal.

"Shut up, it was beautiful," said Keno.

"You can't take them anywhere," said Angelic.

"It was fun," added Gina. "Wish you'd been there. Feeling better?"

"Yeah, just needed to hang out a bit, let it pass."

"Dawg, you're getting old," said Jamal.

"Yeah, I'm six months younger than you," replied Dee.

"Age is just a number, and it's yours not mine," replied Jamal.

"Did you hear from Anna?" asked Angelic.

"She's resting, still tired. Trying to get her energy up for getting home, getting off the ship."

"Let's grab some lunch, I'm hungry," said Mike.

They all started toward the grill.

―――

"Meet back on the sundeck in a couple of hours?" said Jamal to the group. Everyone nodded and broke up for their respective staterooms.

Back in their suite Gina sat next to Dee on the couch. "You talked to her didn't you?"

"Yeah, had a few questions I wanted to get answered and we're running out of time. We'll dock tomorrow."

"Was she helpful?"

"Yes and no, informative I guess you'd say but I still think there's something more. There's something that bothers her."

"What could it be?"

"Don't know yet, but she asked to see you this afternoon."

"You think I should go now, before we get together with the others?"

"Yes, I don't think she has the energy for a large group anymore."

―――

Gina exited her stateroom and slipped down the hall to Anna's. She opened the door quietly and slipped inside. Making her way to the bedroom, she saw Ate laying at the foot of the bed and Anna sleeping peacefully.

Gina quietly pulled up a chair and sat beside the bed. In

only a few moments, Anna turned her head and spoke in a groggy fashion. "I thought I heard something or maybe it was my dream. I'm glad you came by."

"I didn't want to wake you."

"Nonsense, I've been waiting on you. It's just that sometimes when I wait, my eyes close."

"Mine too."

Ate had crawled up the bed near Gina and she reached out and petted him.

"See how much he likes you. He didn't even bark."

Gina smiled at them both.

"Can I ask you a favor?"

"Of course, anything?"

"This sounds rather gloomy but should anything happen to me would you take care of my dog, would you take care of Ate? Unless my great-granddaughter should want him, which would also make a nice home."

Gina was taken aback. She raised her hand from the dog, who whined, toward her face, but then reached out and squeezed Anna's arm. "Nothing bad is going to happen to you. But yes, I'd be happy to take care of Ate if the need should arise."

"Thank you. I just want to know that he'll be in good hands."

Gina leaned forward and petted Ate again. He curled up to her fingers. She looked up at Anna. "How did you pick us to help you?"

"I saw your group standing on the rail watching me as I traveled across the dock when we first boarded back in Romania. You all had such curious and expectant faces. I thought I'd say hello and see if we got along. You looked interesting. I thought we might share stories."

"It's been amazing, so many things you've told us."

"Do you remember the play in Budapest?"

"Mozart, the Magic Flute."

"Yes, I told you that things in the play came in threes—three trials, three ladies, three children, three doors. To that I can add three people, three trains, three destinations, all wound together, c'est la vie."

Gina wasn't sure how to reply, then had a thought. "But we're on the four rivers cruise."

Anna smiled and squeezed Gina's hand. "It's really three rivers and a canal, things are never what they seem. But you are right about the four rivers. There are four rivers in your life-the one you are born on, the one you travel, the one you dream of, and the one you die on. I am on the 4th river. Do you know where you are?"

"I…. I'm not…."

Anna patted her arm. "Would you tell that perceptive husband of yours that I'd like to see him? Maybe this evening? I need to rest now." She closed her eyes and leaned into the pillow.

———

"She wants to see you."

"Why? When? What did she tell you?"

"Not sure, tonight, she wants me to take care of her dog, if she can't."

Dee looked at her with an odd expression on his face.

"She scared me. I don't know what to think. Just go see her."

———

Dee slipped quietly into Anna's room. Ate came running out of the bedroom, his tail wagging.

"Hey boy, where's your mistress?"

A voice rang out, "She's in here. Why don't you come in, let's talk."

Dee went into the bedroom and sat in the chair Gina had left behind.

"Actually, I'll talk and you listen. Save your questions until the end."

Dee nodded his understanding.

"I've made some arrangements and I need to know that you will see them through. Nod your head."

He did.

"Good. This is what I want.

"I've lived alone with my dogs and my memories for the last sixty years. Lorenz left me money and property but sixty years is a long time. I lived well. There is a little money and the house in Amsterdam. There's no need to leave it to my daughter or her family. They're insanely wealthy and wouldn't even notice it. I was never really a part of their lives, just an occasional guest. They won't miss me.

"I'd like the two Picassos to go to my great-granddaughter Tatiana who wants to be a prima ballerina with the National Ballet in Sophia. When I last saw her in Bucharest, she was the spitting image of my daughter, and me. I'm giving you the other paintings, the personal property, the house. The keys to everything are on the ring. I've notified my banker and my Advocaat (lawyer); they'll accept you as my proxy. Cremate my body and spread the ashes on the Danube around Vienna. If you'll take care of those things as you see fit, I'd greatly appreciate it. When I'm gone, the decisions are yours. Do what you think is right. I see you as a man of honor, a man I can trust."

It took Dee a second to respond. "I'd be honored to do those things for you. It would be a privilege."

"I need to rest now. But I think everything will be alright.

I was worried how it would end." She reached out and squeezed Dee's hand.

He sat there, holding her hand, and watched her for a long time.

———

When he got back to his suite Dee asked Gina to text the others and have them come over. When everyone had arrived and was seated Dee held up a hand.

"I have something I want to share with you. I just watched Anna die. I didn't realize it at the time but then it started and there was nothing I could do to stop it. I don't think she really wanted to go. Her legs twitched and her head flopped from one side to the other, then her eyes rolled back like she could see the end of the world and it was waiting for her. She went quiet and then she was gone."

"What did you do? What do we do?" asked Jamal.

Dee looked around the room and Gina, Angelic, and Keno were dabbing their eyes and crying quietly.

"She gave me some instructions and asked if I'd follow them, which I told her I would."

Dee looked around the room to each of them. "I'd like to ask if each of you would help me."

There were nods all around.

"Man plans and God laughs," added Jamal.

Dee and Friends
Twenty-Fourth Day
Amsterdam

Dee had gone to see the captain to make arrangements after Anna passed. To no one's surprise, the ship had a holding facility for the recently deceased. The captain advised Dee that it happened at least every other trip.

"I have a name and a number for a crematorium that the deceased requested," said Dee.

"I'll have the Guest Care Team see to it," replied the captain. "Do you need other assistance?"

"No, there are several of us. I think we'll be fine. Thank you for your help."

"I'm sorry for your loss. Ms. Simone was one of our favorite passengers; she made this cruise many times. I'm glad you could be here for her."

"So are we. Thank you again."

———

Back in their stateroom Gina was packing.

"I'm going to go down and try to pack Anna's room and feed the dog. I need to find any paperwork she may have had plus prep him for departure."

"You want me to go with you?"

"No, go ahead and pack up. I'll text you if anything happens."

Dee went the couple of doors to Anna's suite and entered through the living room. "Ate, you in here? Ate?" Dee stepped into the bedroom and saw Ate on a mat in a crate in the corner.

At least he knows where he stays; let me find some food and water.

After Dee got the dog cared for, he went to the closet and

checked to see that the trunk with the paintings was still intact. It was. The ring of keys was still on the counter and he pocketed those. Pulling the other suitcases from her closet, Dee began to gather and pack Anna's personal items from about the cabin.

Dee was slipping some clothing in one case when he saw an envelope sticking out from one of the interior pockets. He couldn't help it. Slipping the envelope out, he opened the flap. The envelope was lumpy so Dee palmed it and turned the envelope upside down and shook it. An object wrapped in flannel landed in his palm. He pulled the material away and was left with two bamboo handles and a wire. There was also a piece of paper in the envelope. He pulled the paper out and opened it.

Scrawled across the page were the following words, 'the last thing he saw before he drew his final breath'. Dee laid the note down and separated the bamboo handles. He realized it unrolled so he did so. It took a second, a garrote. *This must have been what she used on Aldo in the catacombs, right before he fell. Not sure I want to share that.*

Dee rolled the garrote back up and put it in the envelope. He placed the envelope in his pocket.

Finishing up the packing, Dee checked the paintings once more. *I'll take pictures and send them to my friend Diego, director of the National Gallery in Seville Spain, to see if he can get specific title information. Maybe from there we can get some idea of who the original owners might have been.* Finding the right keys and entering the combination, he opened the trunk and pulled out the first painting. It was the Degas dancer. Dee unwrapped it and studied the work briefly. It was beautiful. He'd seen a few pictures of Degas' art, but they didn't do the work justice. *Somebody will claim it.* He turned the picture over for no reason other than he could and there was nothing on the back of the canvas. Then he noticed it. Stuck in the frame at the bottom of the work was a piece of cardboard. Dee reached with one hand and tugged on the item. It popped out and wasn't cardboard, but a postcard. It was a picture of a tree-covered mountain range and it said 'Bavarian Forest'. He flipped the card over and there were two sets of numbers printed on the back. There were six digits in pairs of twos in each listing. *What in the world…* and then it hit him, longitude and latitude. *That might be a wishful guess but it could be.*

He sat the Degas against the bed and pulled out the second painting. It was the Renoir. He turned it around and there in the same place tucked against the back of the frame was another postcard. Dee pulled the card out, and it also had two sets of numbers, six digits each, in pairs of twos. He set the Renoir down and compared the numbers. They were different. Then he turned the postcard over. 'Austrian Mountains' it read. *This was Anna's train.*

He laid the postcards on the bed and reached for the third painting. It was the Monet, and it too had a postcard with numbers. The picture on this one said, "Greetings from Pilsen". *That was Aldo's last train.*

Setting the third postcard down he quickly pulled out the two Picassos. Neither of them had anything in the back frame. *Three works of art, three trains, and three postcards. What was that Anna said about threes? C'est la vie.*

Dee quickly re-wrapped the paintings and put them back in the trunk. He pocketed the postcards.

Several hours later they disembarked and took a taxi to the address of her home. It was located off the Keizergracht canal.

Standing outside the home while Dee fiddled with the

keys, Jamal remarked, "This is a nice neighborhood, central Amsterdam, off the main canal. And she left this to us?"

"She was a generous lady," said Gina.

"There wasn't anyone else she wanted to leave it to or who needed it. She liked us. She thought we were kind to her," said Dee.

"I guess we were," said Keno.

"We listened to her story," added Mike.

"Maybe nobody else would," said Dee.

Once inside, they found a roomy and pleasant home, nicely and comfortably decorated. There was a large kitchen and a sitting area on the first floor along with a single bedroom and bath. On the second floor, there were two bedrooms, and a shared bath. On the third floor, there was storage.

"It looks like it's big enough for all of us," said Mike.

"A lot of space for one woman and a dog," added Jamal.

"I expect she bought it some years ago, and this is how it came," said Dee.

"She did a nice job decorating," added Angelic.

"We should all be comfortable here," said Gina.

"Are we going to keep it?" asked Keno.

"For now," replied Dee. "Let's go back down to the kitchen and sitting area. We can decide who is staying in which room and talk about Anna's requests."

———

They'd split up the rooms, deciding who would stay where and then gone to unpack. Angelic and Gina had gone to the market for food and they were all preparing lunch.

"This is the biggest kitchen I've ever seen," said Jamal.

"How much time you ever spend in the kitchen?" asked Mike.

"More than you," replied Jamal.

"Boys," said Angelic. "Let's eat."

After finishing up, Dee stood before the group. "Anna left us this house and whatever money she had on hand. I'll go to the bank and to the attorney tomorrow and try to get all that squared away. In the meantime I want to know what you think about this idea." He took the three postcards from his shirt pocket.

"On the back of each of the three paintings Anna took from Aldo there was a postcard. Each one has a photograph of a general area and some numbers on the back. I think they are longitude and latitude. Once again, she has left us clues, just like in her stories."

"The numbers are for the trains?" asked Jamal.

"The pictures match the general locations Anna told us about."

"What are you thinking you want us to do?" asked Mike.

"I don't know if we do anything. She said the tunnels were all still sealed the last time she looked. She also said the things in the tunnel were best left buried, the bad and the good."

"What do you think?" asked Gina.

"I think we should go and look and see if they're still buried."

"Just to make sure?" asked Angelic.

"To answer a question that I'd never stop wondering about."

"Why does this always happen? We can never just go on vacation," said Keno.

"What fun would that be?" said Gina.

"Let's do it," said Jamal.

"I'm in," added Mike.

"You guys are the best."

"Just don't push your luck," added Angelic.

Dee and Friends
Twenty-Fifth Day
Amsterdam

The following morning Dee took off for the bank and the attorney. He took the big ring of keys. Presenting himself at the bank, he was led to the offices of one Hendrik Bakker. Dee observed that Mr. Bakker was an older gentleman in an expensive suit.

"Mr. Bakker, I'm Dee Sanders, a friend of Anna Simone."

"Ah yes, Ms. Simone, Anna, contacted me last week and indicated that I should expect you. I'm very sorry to hear of her demise. She'd been a customer for a long time. I'll miss her. In these last few years, I went to her home whenever she needed something."

"I'm sure she appreciated that. She was very gracious."

"Indeed, she was quite rare in this day and time. Not a surprise, her passing, at her age. I'm glad you could be there for her."

"Yes, thank you."

"I assume you'll want to see the contents of her safe deposit box, while all the other paperwork is being prepared?"

"That would be satisfactory."

The two men rose and left the office. Starting down the hall, Mr. Bakker spoke again.

"Anna only kept a little of her money liquid. There won't be a huge amount in the account. She always kept everything in safe deposit although I tried to get her to invest over the years."

"I guess she just felt more comfortable, coming from the time period she experienced."

"I expect you are correct."

They had arrived in the safe deposit area of the vault. Dee picked out the one key on the ring that resembled his perception of a safe deposit key. Mr. Bakker nodded and opened the box. Dee withdrew it and was pointed to a small office with a door where he could examine the contents.

"I'll check back with you in a few minutes," said Mr. Bakker as he went back down the hall toward his office.

Dee sat looking at the box for a few seconds. *I have no idea what I'll find in here.* He slowly opened the top, and a smile broke across his face. The box was stuffed full of currency. As Dee pulled it out on the table and stacked it, he noted several different countries. He began a stack for each country. After sorting it all he looked into the bottom of the box. There was a gold-colored bar. He reached inside and pulled it out. It was an ingot, a gold brick, which had been poorly cast at some point. It had to be Aldo's. It must have been his last one, his exit strategy if he had to run. Anna had found it or perhaps he'd told her where it was, although that seemed unlikely. Dee held it up and weighted it in one hand, must have been ten or twelve pounds. *That was a lot of dental filings. Gold is over $20K dollars per pound. This thing is probably worth a quarter of a million dollars.*

Dee laid it down on the table and looked in the box again. There were two rings and a pocket watch—a gold signet ring, a pinky ring with a clear stone, and a Vacheron Constantin pocket watch. Looking again all that remained were two photographs. He reached in and pulled them out. The older one was in black and white and of a young girl that might be Anna. Dee turned the photograph over and it said 'Elise-1960', *that was her daughter as a young girl. Maybe the first time Anna realized how much they favored one another.* The other picture was a group shot; Dee didn't see Anna in it but an older version of the girl looked to be present along with several children and a man, *the daughter's family.* The box was empty. *That's all she had of her life, that and memories.*

There was a knock on the door. Dee put the pictures, the gold bar, the jewelry, and an envelope, into the box and closed it. "Come in."

The door opened, and Mr. Bakker strode inside. "Questions or anything I can assist with?"

"Yes, there seem to be several currencies here, could I get this converted to something I'll understand, perhaps dollars?"

"Of course, let me call a teller back and we'll count it out with you."

When Dee returned to the house, the others were grouped in the sitting room.

"Hey dude, you look tired," said Mike to Dee as he walked inside.

"Yeah, those two, the banker and the lawyer, wore me out."

"I told you that you were old," said Jamal.

Dee just nodded.

"We've been busy too," continued Jamal. "These numbers, on the postcards, are in fact longitude and latitude. I've located all three, pretty much where the picture on the postcard indicates. There's one each in Germany, Austria, and the Czech Republic, formerly Czechoslovakia. I got the best Google earth pictures I could. These are heavily forested areas that still aren't widely populated seventy-five years later. We should be able to get to the closest town and go from there."

"Good work. Next time you can go see the banker and lawyer and I'll look up the sites."

"So, what did you find?"

"At the bank there was about $30,000 in the checking account but the safe deposit box was interesting."

"And?" said Mike

"There were two photographs, one of her daughter at about sixteen, and then a later picture of the daughter and her family. That was it."

"She had a safe deposit box for two pictures?" asked Angela.

"Well, there were a couple of other things, about six different currencies totaling three quarters of a million dollars, and a gold ingot about ten to twelve pounds, worth another quarter of a million dollars, and some very expensive men's jewelry."

There were shocked looks on their faces.

"I thought Anna told you she was about out of money," said Gina.

"That's what she said."

"Makes you wonder how much money she started with? Lorenz must have been quite wealthy," said Angelic.

"I suspect she collected Lorenz's and Aldo's money. Also the gold bar, which would have been Aldo's getaway money if he'd had to run, and his jewelry."

"The stuff he took from the train," said Jamal

"Must have been a lot of money if she never cashed the bar in," said Keno.

"I have a feeling she looked at the gold bar and the jewelry as artifacts, like the paintings, her revenge over Aldo for his actions and his schemes."

"Unbelievable," said Gina.

"Yes, the attorney was pretty normal. I signed some initial paperwork, and he's sending the rest over. We'll all own the house in joint custody."

"So we are keeping it?" said Keno.

"It'll make a good base of operations for now. Then we can decide later."

———

They met after dinner to talk about plans.

"Do we want to check all three locations in one trip or go out and back for each one?" asked Jamal.

"Do we all need to go?" asked Keno. "I like it here and while I want to know what's going on, does it take all of us?"

"I'll need to look after Ate. I don't know about traveling with him. Although I'd kind of like to go," said Gina.

"I think the women stay here, look after the house, wait on the papers from the attorney, make plans for later, let you guys run out and check. Hopefully, all the tunnels are still sealed up and we can move on," said Angelic.

"So just the three of us," said Jamal.

"Probably quickest," added Mike.

"I'm okay with it as long as the women are comfortable," said Dee.

"We'll be fine," said Gina. "Just don't fiddle around and be gone too long."

———

Dee got online and booked them flights to Salzburg, Austria. They'd rent a car and drive from there.

"What do we need?" asked Mike.

"Sturdy clothes, hiking boots, our phones, we'll use Google maps once we get on the ground," replied Dee.

"Maybe small backpacks, water, hats, sunglasses, flashlights might all be helpful," added Jamal.

"Just like back in the Boy Scouts, huh Dee," said Mike.

"You always got to be prepared."

**Dee and Friends
Twenty-Sixth & Twenty-Seventh Day
Amsterdam & Salzburg**

They flew out the next morning; it was nonstop and lasted a little over an hour and a half. They arrived midday and rented a car.

"We've got some time, let's try to find this place," said Dee.

They threw everything they had in the rented BMW and took off. Jamal drove, Dee rode shotgun, and Mike sat in the back.

"We take highway A8, which heads toward the German border. We're looking for a little town called Kufstein. Somewhere in the surrounding area," said Dee.

"How far or how long?" asked Mike.

"Little over an hour, about 70 miles."

———

They got to Kufstein, and the GPS kept them going. They turned off the A8 onto smaller roads and wound back into the mountains. A couple of miles later they had moved beyond the location.

"Hold up, circle back, we're past it," said Dee.

Jamal turned the car around and started back the way they had come.

"Stop, we're moving away again."

The road was empty so Jamal backed up a hundred yards.

"There." And Dee pointed up the mountain. "It's up there."

"This is the part where we break in our new hiking boots," said Jamal.

"And our feet," added Mike.

"Let's go," said Dee.

They climbed a steep pitch for about a hundred yards. Then they broke the crest of a small rise. There was the track.

"Left or right?" asked Jamal.

Dee was turning the phone trying to orient himself.

"You got a fifty-fifty chance," said Mike.

"Left, we go left," said Dee.

They walked another fifty yards and rounded a bend. Jamal saw it first.

"Up there, looks like a branch line." He pointed.

They sped up and made their way to the side rail. Standing at the fork, they looked down the track and in less than one hundred yards the rails disappeared into a tunnel.

They turned and looked at each other.

"You sure you got the coordinates right?" asked Jamal.

"That's not supposed to be there," said Mike.

"Let's go take a look," said Dee.

They scrambled up the grade until they were at the mouth of the tunnel. Walking inside a few feet, they didn't have much clearance.

"I'd like to walk to the other end but I'd be afraid if a train came through. There's so little clearance and the rails seem shiny as if this gets used frequently," said Dee.

"Do you think we're even in the right place?" asked Jamal.

"Let's go back outside."

They stepped into the sunlight and stood several feet away from the track. Dee dug in his backpack and extracted the postcards. Finding the right one, he matched the numbers to the GPS coordinates. He held the card up.

"Assuming the numbers on the card are correct, this is the correct place."

They walked slowly back to the main line and then along the rail until they reached the spot where they had ascended. Working their way slowly down the grade toward the car, Dee made a suggestion.

"Let's stay the night and see if we can find the rail office or someone who knows the history."

"Maybe the librarian at the reference desk," joked Mike.

"Or a talky barber?" added Jamal.

"Somebody."

———

They reached the car and drove into Kufstein to find lodging and dinner. Early the next morning, they grabbed some breakfast and asked the desk clerk if and where there was a local rail office. He gave them directions that were only a few blocks away.

After parking in the small lot, they headed inside the rail office three abreast.

"I hope he doesn't think this is a robbery," said Mike.

"I don't think the trains carry money any more, only freight," replied Jamal.

"I have no idea," said Dee.

They stopped a few feet away, and Dee approached the man behind the counter.

"Good morning, English?" asked Dee.

"Rather well, actually," replied the clerk.

"Sorry about that."

"Happens a lot, we're not really a tourist town. How can I help you?"

"We're," Dee pointed to Jamal and Mike, "railroad enthusiasts and…"

"You want to know about the Nazi trains and the tunnel," replied the clerk.

"Yes," answered Dee in a surprised tone.

"We don't get that question as much as we used to, but it still pops up occasionally." The clerk was writing something on a card. He handed it to Dee.

"I'm too young to know anything about it firsthand, but the Russians came through sometime in the 1980s and excavated. Hans Mueller can tell you about it. Call him and offer him dinner and a stein and he'll answer all your questions. He loves to talk."

"Thank you."

"Not a problem, enjoy your stay."

————

Back in the car they discussed the options.

"Just call him," said Jamal.

"What can it hurt?" added Mike.

"He may work so it'll probably be this evening or tomorrow. We'd better let the women know."

"I'll take care of that," said Jamal. "You call Hans."

It turned out to be easy. Hans said he'd be happy to talk to them over dinner.

————

Hans said he'd meet them at the hotel restaurant, the Auracher Lochl, where they'd spent the night. Dee told the others, "Hans said, 'we'll take a seat and look out over the mountains and I'll tell you everything you want to know about the tunnel'."

He showed up promptly at 7:30pm looking fresh and in a suit, no tie.

They saw him walk in and he looked up and around, the dining room was about half full, and headed straight towards them. He held out a hand. "Hans Muller, at your service."

Dee introduced himself and the other two. Everyone shook hands and took a seat. Hans held up a finger and waved at the bartender who started their way.

"What would you like to know? Excuse me. That was rude. I am Hans Mueller, as I said. I have worked for the railroad since I was a teenager. First as a laborer, then in the offices, then on the trains, then engineer, now inspector. I'll retire soon if all goes well. What part of the story would you like?"

"We read an article about trains being parked and hidden by the Nazis and that this was one of the locations."

"Read an article, huh? Well, I'm not sure about that," he winked at them, "but it doesn't matter. Let me tell you."

The bartender arrived and dropped off a liter stein for each of them.

Hans hoisted his in the air. "Salute."

They all toasted.

"Okay, when I was a boy, before I started for the railroad, I was maybe 12 or 14. This was in the early 1980s, maybe 1982, before the fall of the USSR, the Soviets came to town and they had these detailed maps of where a tunnel line had been during the war. I'd heard stories from my grandfather and some of the older men that there had once been a tunnel through the mountain. But it was a branch line that connected some unused track on the other side. No one came looking for it after the war and it was forgotten over time until the Soviets arrived. They were very secretive, as Soviets or Russians will be, but they hired several local boys, including me to be laborers, to clear rock, carry water, whatever they wanted. They worked for about two weeks clearing each end of the tunnel. They paid good money, it was what eventually led me to my railroad job. Anyway, I was friendly with one young officer. I would bring him water, and biscuits from my mom when I could get them. He let me closer to the railcars than most of the others. I saw into several cars. There were crates, many of them with artists' names stenciled on them, Monet, Manet, Murillo, even Rembrandt. Some expensive paintings I would imagine, I never saw any of them. There were also crates marked property. I never saw what was in them."

"How many trains were there?" asked Dee.

"Three, one on each end of the spur line inside the tunnel and one on the main track in the tunnel."

"Did you see in the other two trains?"

"Only in one of them briefly, art and property, the same as the first train."

"What did they do with everything?" asked Jamal.

"They loaded it up on a train of their own that was parked on the main line, blocked freight traffic the whole time they were here."

"Did you see what was on that train?" asked Dee.

"It was heavily guarded, and they kept us away from it. They would send us home at dark and continue to work into the night with portable lights."

"What happened then?" asked Mike.

"When they finished they took the trains with them once they got them running. I heard my officer say they would be dropped off somewhere along the way. They tore out the interior spur line and filled it in with the rubble they cleared from each end of the tunnel."

"What did the local train operators do?" asked Dee.

"Nothing until the Soviets were gone. Filling in the spur line gave them an idea. The engineers were afraid of the condition of the tracks and the tunnel. They talked the railroad into putting the branch line tracks back down connecting the tunnel and filling the space around the tracks so that it was a tight fit and would discourage anyone else from trying to enter the tunnel. They put up 'Narrow Tunnel-Danger' signs on each end of the branch line. The tracks on the other side got connected to one of the other lines and the tunnel got used all the time for several decades."

"They filled it in, just like that?"

"Yeah, I think they were afraid and didn't want the Soviets coming back. I've ridden through the tunnel dozens of times. You can reach out and touch the wall from end to end. If there was anything back there it's gone now or the Russians took it."

"Back in the 1980s?" said Mike.

"Long time ago, most people outside the railroad don't even remember. That's why I didn't really believe your story about reading an article. But it doesn't matter. It's all gone. It was over a long time ago. What are you, treasure hunters?"

"No, we had a friend that was on one of the trains. She told us about them."

"That's quite a story."

"Only one I've got. She was quite elderly and thought the art should go back to the original owners."

"It probably should but the Russians have it now." He paused. "One other thing you might appreciate."

He reached in his pocket and pulled out a small knife, like a penknife. He unfolded the blade and handed it over. There was a German swastika with the eagle above it stamped into the handle.

"The Soviet officer I helped gave me that right before he left. Said he found it in one of the rail cars as they were emptying it out."

"Might be worth some money," said Mike.

"Maybe to the right collector. If my pension doesn't work out, I'll put it on the market." Then he grinned.

"Let's have another round," said Dee.

Hans, Gregoriy, Ekaterina, and Adrik
Twenty-Eighth Day
Kufstein & Moscow

He heard the phone ring several times. It was bright and early the following morning and had been a few months since they had last spoken.

Gregoriy was a busy man. A high ranking official in the Russian government and a billionaire, Gregoriy Orlov still liked to keep in touch with old friends. One never knew when a useful piece of information might come up. With that in mind, he walked toward the ringing private line that sat upon a library table on the top floor of a downtown Moscow high rise. "Da?"

"Gregoriy, Hans," said the man on the other end of the line. "I had some curious visitors yesterday evening." There was silence, so Hans continued. "They were American tourists, looking for the tunnels and the trains. They were quite well informed."

"Continue."

"I told them the basic story of the Soviet retrieval and the subsequent filling in of the tunnel. They seemed to accept it. They'd had contact with someone who knew about the Nazi art trains. I didn't press them on what else they knew or planned to do. But, there was something about them, they weren't just treasure hunters. They were on some kind of mission and they were tight lipped about it. I thought perhaps you might like to know."

"But of course, do you have a name?"

"Dee Sanders and friends."

———

Gregoriy hung up the phone and walked across the spacious office to his main desk. He paused to glance at the far wall where his favorite artwork, Degas' *Five Dancing Women*, hung in lighted, glass-encased splendor. It took his breath every time he looked at it and thought of its beauty and its history. He pressed the intercom, "Ekaterina, send in Adrik."

A few moments later a tall, dark-haired, muscular young man entered Gregoriy's office. "Yes?"

Gregoriy looked up from his desk. "Find out everything you can about an American named Dee Sanders and anyone traveling with him. They were in Kufstein yesterday. If he's still in Europe make plans to pay him a visit."

"Long-term?"

"One night only."

Adrik nodded and left the office. Gregoriy returned to his work.

Dee and Friends
Twenty-Eighth Day
Salzburg & Amsterdam

They drove back to Salzburg the next morning. There was an afternoon flight to Amsterdam.

Kicking around the airport, they ate, then sat and waited.

"That kind of lets the air out of your balloon, don't it?" said Mike.

"Wonder how the Soviets found out?" asked Jamal.

"They took a couple thousand scientists, engineers, and technicians, same as the Allies. Somebody must have known about it and the Russians finally got around to checking," said Dee.

"I thought Anna said she checked," said Mike.

"She did, but it was probably in the 1950s or no later than 1960. Twenty years later you probably wouldn't think much about it."

"It's still an amazing story. You think the women will believe it?" said Jamal.

"I told Gina last night. I guess we'll know when we get there."

Adrik
Twenty-Eighth Day
Moscow

Adrik had gone to the security center in Gregoriy's building and run information and background requests on Dee Sanders. He was mildly surprised. There was so much information on the internet, plus what he could access through his country's internal security systems.

Sanders was a former television executive that had been lost on a deserted island for a month. He had found gold, guns, a group of friends, and trouble in the form of Antoine Debaucher, a known global gun runner and human trafficker. *I'm impressed Sanders is still alive.*

There had been a reward, Sanders and his friends seemed to spend their time traveling now. There was a gold bell in Mexico and an Egyptian artifact in North Africa, *look like treasure hunters to me. This shouldn't be difficult.*

Adrik found evidence of tickets from Amsterdam, where the group appeared to be headquartered, to Munich. There were several tunnels in the area. Since they'd already been to Kufstein, the one near the Czech border, Viechtach, was a good bet. Adrik booked his own flight to Munich and reserved a BMW XM SUV. *I'll fly down, maybe ask them a few questions, or just punch their tickets, and be back in time for Sacha's party this weekend.*

Adrik had been seeing Ekaterina on the side. He called her Sasha. Gregoriy didn't know it and didn't need to. Ekaterina was a busy girl. Adrik filed a brief report with Gregoriy updating his findings and left for his apartment to pack for the quick trip he expected to make.

Dee and Friends
Twenty-Ninth & Thirtieth Day
Amsterdam

Arriving back in Amsterdam, the men made their way to the house off the Keizergracht Canal.

They entered and saw the women were seated in the open area beyond the kitchen, having just finished a late breakfast.

"The great explorers return," said Angelic. "Empty-handed I see."

"No treasure," said Keno.

"No treasure and no train," said Dee. "We were about forty years too late."

"I thought Anna said the tunnels were sealed?" said Gina.

"I expect they were when she checked them. But a lot of time has passed. The Soviets cleaned out the tunnel in the early 1980s. We met a man named Hans Mueller who worked for the railroad. He assisted the Soviets. They filled the tunnel partially in and the locals followed suit, it's just barely big enough to get the train through. No visible evidence that it ever existed."

"What do you think that means for the other two?" asked Angelic.

"Don't have any idea. If the Soviets had maps and details on that tunnel, they may have them all. We'll just have to go look."

"There was potentially nasty stuff on some of those trains, what if it's all gone?" said Jamal.

"There's not much we can do except go see."

"You guys look worn out, rest for a day before you go," said Gina.

"Good idea, that was disheartening," added Mike.

"We got the paperwork from the attorney, on the house," said Keno.

"Good, we can all sign before we take off again. Diego texted me and said he had an idea on the titles of the paintings. He suggested holding an exhibit at his gallery and promoting it as 'lost Nazi art' to see what turns up and who might have a claim."

"A little promotion for the National Gallery?" asked Jamal.

"Yeah, he said he'd help but you know that usually means he'll help himself too."

"An exhibit probably is the easiest way to make their existence known," said Angelic.

"I agree it is efficient. I just get a kick out of how Diego always makes it work for himself."

"He's a clever guy," added Mike.

Dee and Friends
Thirty-first Day
Amsterdam & Munich

They rested a day at the house and made reservations and plans for Munich, much the way they had for Salzburg.

Arriving in Munich a little less than two hours after leaving Amsterdam, they again had the balance of the day to find their location.

"The drive may be a little further this time, but we should get there okay," said Jamal.

"Munich was the easiest place to get into," replied Dee.

"Traffic will be worse," added Mike. "We take the A92 headed toward the Czech Republic. The coordinates look like they're very near the border."

"That would make sense if the second train Aldo caught took him to Pilsen, Czechoslovakia, which became the Czech Republic in 1992."

"They were following a line of tunnels along the mountains," added Jamal.

"Amazing that it was nearly forty years before one of them was found," added Dee.

"As far as we know," replied Jamal. "We're looking for a little town called Viechtach, should be near there. Looks like about 2 hours."

———

Pulling into town, they noticed the tracks ran right along the highway until they turned off the main road and started up into the mountains.

They eased around one of the many curves in the road as it ascended, and then heard a loud rumble behind them. A big, black BMW SUV came screaming around the curve and only swerved at the last minute to avoid rear-ending them. There was no oncoming traffic and the vehicle deftly pivoted into the other lane, roared up the mountain and out of sight.

"What was that about?" asked Jamal.

"Must have thought he was still on the Autobahn," replied Dee.

"Or he was just plain crazy," said Mike.

They resumed the climb up the mountain, with Dee watching the GPS. Only a few seconds later and they heard the loud rumble again. This time the SUV was in their lane and coming straight down the mountain at them.

"What is this guy's problem?" asked Jamal.

"Now's probably not the time to ask," replied Dee, holding steady to the wheel. "Let's see if he pulls another quick maneuver."

The tension in the car was palpable as Mike and Jamal both leaned forward and in toward Dee, who was closely watching the oncoming vehicle.

At less than a car length away, Dee jerked hard to the left and went onto the shoulder and the ground beyond. The SUV continued straight and the lack of space between the two vehicles created a loud whooshing sound and a heavy vibration as they nearly collided. The SUV rounded a turn and disappeared from sight. Dee swerved back onto the road and floored the accelerator.

"Let's get away from that madman," shouted Mike.

Jamal turned to Dee. "That doesn't make any sense. The first time maybe it's a fluke, but he came directly at us. That's no accident. Who is he?"

"I don't know," replied Dee. "Maybe someone doesn't want us looking for the trains."

"Or maybe he's from our past. That crazy guy on the island threatened us, you remember?" said Mike.

"Why now?" asked Jamal.

"Maybe he just got out of jail," replied Mike.

"I think it's the trains," said Dee. "Let's see what we find on these last two."

They heard a distant rumble and Mike looked back. "Here he comes again."

Dee punched the accelerator to the floor and the big BMW sedan leapt forward. The handling was good but Dee still slid from one side of the road to the other as he rounded the turns.

"He's gaining on us," called Mike.

"We're coming up on the top of the hill with the train track. The lights are flashing, the sign's coming down. You'll never beat it," exclaimed Jamal.

"Maybe I won't have to," replied Dee.

Mike and Jamal were both staring at him. Dee barreled toward the train. The SUV was now on their bumper and beginning to bounce them forward.

Two car lengths from the train, as it passed them at high speed from left to right, Dee let off the accelerator for just a second, bumping the SUV back slightly, and then punched it back to the floor as he jerked the steering wheel hard left and pulled the emergency brake as firmly as he could. The car swerved, buckled, and bounced as the back end flipped around and they were facing down the mountain. Simultaneously, since the other SUV wasn't able to swerve to the right in time, it crashed into the passing train, where it was pulled down the track until being sheared off by a large stand of trees and bursting into flames.

"That was nasty," said Jamal, glancing toward the fireball.

"Who was that guy?" asked Mike, also looking at the fire.

"Don't know, but he's toast now," replied Dee as the train finished flashing past them. It hadn't even slowed.

"Should we call '911'?" asked Mike.

"Yeah, but I think it's '112' in Germany. Give it a try," said Dee.

————

"Where did you learn to drive like that?" asked Jamal.

"Yeah, that was scary, thought we were going to die," added Mike.

Dee sighed before speaking. "When I was at the TV station, we had a weekend special with a bunch of NASCAR drivers. After it was over, they all sat around talking about how they race, tricks they use—knowing the car, the weather, the track, and any other elements that come into play. Then they mentioned a driving school. Turns out there was one near Nashville. I went and took a weekend course."

"A weekend course?" asked Jamal.

"It was a long weekend," replied Dee.

"How did you know any of that stuff they mentioned, about our circumstances?" asked Mike.

"I didn't. I took a chance, there was no other choice."

————

On top of the mountain, the road circled along with the tracks until the familiar "you have reached your destination" sounded on the GPS.

They pulled off the road and stopped the car.

"It doesn't look like we're very far away," said Dee.

A short distance ahead they could see a branch line take off to the right. Walking toward it there was some expectation.

"What do you think we'll find this time?" asked Mike

"Surely different from last time," replied Jamal.

"I don't have a clue," said Dee.

They started down the branch line, looked up at the mountain and saw the mouth of the tunnel.

"The branch line tracks give it away every time. There really shouldn't be any track if the tunnel was still sealed," said Dee.

Walking closer, they saw there was a small park surrounding the mouth of the tunnel. If they'd driven a little further around the road, they'd have come to the entrance. There was a large sign, like in a national park. They approached it slowly and stopped.

The sign read, "Viechtach Tunnel Park-In late 1944 and early 1945 the Nazis parked trains in this tunnel and then sealed it at both ends for future retrieval. As that never happened, the German government, in cooperation with the Soviets, in 1983, reopened the tunnel and removed the Nazi contraband. There were six trains which were removed for the public's safety. An example locomotive and car are on display for public viewing at the switching station inside the tunnel. Please stay on the footpath if you elect to visit. Enjoy your stay in Viechtach and in Germany. City of Viechtach 1983."

They looked at one another in something near disbelief.

"Shall we?" said Dee.

They followed the sign which took them onto a wooden walkway with chains on both sides which served both as a handrail and a barrier. Inside the tunnel there were overhead lights and it was a lengthy walk back to the engine and car they could see.

As they followed the boardwalk toward the engine, there were occasional photographs on the wall of the tunnel. It appeared to be a sequence of the tunnel being uncovered. There were no captions, but photographs of the tunnel before being reopened, the clearing process, and the final one before they reached the display engine showing the six trains inside the tunnel. In a couple of pictures, German and Soviet uniforms were visible. The pictures and the story appeared to match.

They looked out across the rails, prevented by the chain from getting closer; there were in fact six total tracks.

"They left it completely alone," said Jamal.

"Just took the trains," added Mike.

"Guess that was all they came for," said Dee.

They reached the engine and the car and walked quickly around them.

"Just an engine and a boxcar, from much later in time it would appear," said Jamal.

"Probably from around the time of the reopening," said Mike.

"Nothing here to see. Let's go."

Walking back toward the tunnel entrance Jamal asked, "What was on those trains?"

"Anna said that Aldo told her there was art, property, and supplies, maybe a car set up to be a lab, but nothing going on in it."

"No way to know what or if the Russians, or Soviets, were looking for something specific," said Jamal.

"They could have just been looking because someone told them the trains were there. I mean wouldn't curiosity cause you to go see," said Mike.

"Like us you mean?" said Dee.

Mike grinned at him.

"I agree with you, but it also seems that maybe you might go looking if there was something specific that had been identified to you. Take whatever you find, but be alert for something particular."

"Nothing is ever what it seems," added Jamal.

"Anna said that too."

"How far are we from Pilsen, why don't we go on?" said Mike.

"You in a hurry to get this done?" asked Jamal.

"No, I just want to find something," replied Mike. "I don't enjoy coming up empty-handed."

Gregoriy, Ekaterina, Boris, and Olga
Thirty-First Day
Moscow

Ekaterina stepped to the door and knocked. She could have used the intercom but she thought Gregoriy should hear this. She wanted to see his reaction and compare it to her own. It didn't seem possible.

"Yes."

She opened the door and stuck her head inside. "Adrik's monitor went flat line a few minutes ago."

Gregoriy looked up from his desk and directly at her. "What? Get in here."

Ekaterina swallowed hard and stepped inside. "The trackers on Adrik's monitor went flat line a minute ago. Security called up and told me."

"Was there a problem with the reception or…."

"Apparently not, one minute it was fine and the next it was flat. It was continuous, not interrupted."

"Did you call him?"

"I tried, straight to voicemail."

"Have security recheck it and run diagnostics."

"Yes sir." Ekaterina turned to leave.

"Contact Boris and get him up here. Tell him to get a team together to travel."

"I didn't think Boris traveled anymore?"

"He does now. You can go."

Ekaterina exited quickly and pulled the door behind her. She was grateful. Gregoriy had thrown things at her in the past. Not because he was mad at her, he saw her three nights a week, but because he was mad at a circumstance. Losing Adrik, his go-to guy, seemed like a situation where he would have reacted strongly. But then calling Boris, who was semi-retired and old, was a strong response.

Gregoriy sat at his desk looking at the Degas, but staring into space.

So, what could have happened to Adrik? It was a bunch of tourists. How difficult could it be? Maybe it was just the monitor, but instinctively I know better. Adrik is dead. Who are these supposed tourists? What are they really after? Who do they work for? Only another professional could have taken out Adrik. Despite any misgivings I have about him, Boris will find out and stay alive.

There was a knock at the door. "Enter," said Gregoriy.

Boris Antonov stepped inside the office. He was an older man, in his early 60s, barrel-chested and stocky, he carried few extra pounds but significant mileage. Boris stepped across to Gregoriy, a slight limp in his step. "You asked for me to assemble a team?" It was both a question and a statement.

"Yes, Adrik is dead."

"I heard that. Do we know what happened?"

"Not the specifics, but he was pursuing an American tourist who has been inquiring and searching for the Nazi art trains."

Boris nodded. "The ones you and I worked on all those years ago?"

"The same."

"And your request?"

"Find them, find out why and who, then end it."

"You want a team for that?"

"Yes, an entire team, and no mistakes. You know what was on those trains."

Boris glanced to the Degas. "That was so long ago, the art has mostly been forgotten by the world at large. The experiments have been culminated, technology has advanced, what do we care?"

"You forget the Chinese and their part in the biological and viral experiments, their research and further experimentation."

"I didn't forget it. I just think too much time has passed. There is no longer a connection."

"I would disagree." Gregoriy glanced at the Degas. "There is still much evidence as to many of the items. The Chinese are thought to be developing viruses for world-wide distribution. Besides, no one needs to be poking around in Russian installations."

"They were Soviet."

"Doesn't matter, it's none of their business. I don't like intruders," Gregoriy spoke again. "Besides that, I want you to send Olga and another team to Amsterdam and contain the women who are in the group, in case we need them."

"You're quite serious about this." Again it was a statement.

"Yes, do it, now!"

———

Boris moved quickly. He hadn't been in the field in several years, but he stayed current, kept up with the missions Gregoriy had ongoing and supervised the results. Some would have seen being sent back out as an insult, but Boris welcomed the opportunity. He was looking forward to crossing swords with whoever had eliminated Adrik.

I need more information. Adrik was quick on the trigger, perhaps he wasn't beaten or killed, just disabled, or maybe he underestimated his opponent, which seemed most likely. I won't make that mistake.

Boris called a team of three other senior operatives together and instructed them to immediately prepare to depart for Munich. Then he called Olga Morozova, another long-term field agent known for her icy demeanor and her composure under stress.

"Olga, Boris, take a team and go to Amsterdam immediately. Adrik is dead, but see his notes on an American named Dee Sanders. There are a group of women traveling with him that are in a house on the Grand Canal. Contain them until further notice."

"I have two other women that work with me. I'll take them. How firm are we to be?"

"Do what's necessary, but keep them alive until you hear from me."

————

Boris grabbed a go-bag that he still kept in his office and rounded up his three fellow travelers. The flight from Moscow to Munich would take a little over three hours. He had arranged for two SUVs from local sources for when they arrived in Munich. These were to be provided by Russian field operatives in the area and would be fully stocked for Boris and his team's needs.

I want to be on the ground quickly and intercept this group before they get any further. Intelligence reports suggest Adrik was killed in a collision with a train. Perhaps it had nothing to do with the tourists. They seem typical from the background reports. My team can grab them and wrap this up. I'm thinking of making arrangements to fly them back to Moscow. We'd have more time and privacy to question them there. Unless there's more to this and they resist.

————

Olga gathered her two comrades and made for the airport. It was a little over three hours to Amsterdam, about the same time as to Munich. She wanted to be on the ground and have the women secure before Boris and his team captured the men. She felt confident in that she knew exactly where to go, and Boris and his team had to locate their prey.

I'll make these women talk while we pass a little time waiting. If one of them happens to drown in the canal, so be it.

**Dee and Friends
Thirty-first Day
Pilsen**

Back at the car Dee pulled up the GPS and the next set of coordinates.

"Pilsen is only seventy miles. It's closer than Munich at this point."

"Let's do it," said Jamal and he put the car in gear.

"When we get back to town, we're looking for the B85, probably an hour and a half with these mountain roads."

"We'll get there about dinner time," said Mike. "Maybe we look first thing in the morning."

Gina, Angelic, and Keno
Thirty-First Day
Amsterdam

Gina and Angelic had walked to the outdoor market near their house in Amsterdam. It was late afternoon and they had strolled along the canals taking in the sights.

"It's so beautiful here, "said Angelic.

"I know. I love it; maybe we can stay for a while. It's so calm and pleasant," replied Gina

"Peaceful even, and I love the house," answered Angelic.

They made their way under the market tents and began to select various items. Gina went one way and Angelic another. They met in the center of the tent, each with a basket of goods. They pointed and looked over some fruit.

"This sounds silly, "said Angelic. "But I think someone's following me."

Gina pointed to another piece of fruit. "Yeah, I thought that too. They move when I move."

"Same here. You'd think they'd be more subtle," said Angelic. "Unless they're trying to scare us," she continued.

"Why?" replied Gina and the women turned slightly to look at each other. "Let's get back to the house."

The women paid for their items and quickly walked back to the house. The women they thought were following them disappeared from sight.

"We must be getting paranoid," said Angelic.

"Agreed," replied Gina.

Angelic reached for the door and it swung inward, but it wasn't Keno standing there. A tall, stocky, but shapely, blonde woman, with short hair and dark eyes, was standing in front of them holding a gun, a pistol.

"Do come in, we've been expecting you," said the woman. She took a small step back and motioned at them with the gun. Angelic and Gina were about to step inside when the two women who had been following them at the market stepped up from behind.

"Move along," said one of them.

"I guess we weren't paranoid," said Angelic.

"Guess not," replied Gina.

"You were because we wanted you to be. I don't think we could have made it any plainer," said the blonde woman as she waved them further inside.

Getting to the kitchen, they saw Keno strapped to a ladder back kitchen chair, a gag over her mouth, her eyes as big as tennis balls. She started bouncing the chair.

The blonde woman turned toward her, pointing the gun in her direction. "Stop that."

Keno immediately sat still. The two women from the market moved around Gina, Angelic, and the blonde. They stepped into the kitchen and grabbed two more of the ladder back chairs.

"I see where this is going," said Angelic.

As the two women moved toward them, Gina asked, "Who are you and what do you want with us? We're just tourists."

"That's it precisely," said the blonde woman. "Nosy, pestering tourists, we really don't have any use for you. Once your men are collected, we'll see about removing you from this beautiful country, this beautiful home."

Gina interrupted, "This is our house."

"Really," said the woman looking around, "quite lovely. But, you won't be here long and it doesn't matter who we are. Now sit down and shut up."

The two women brought the chairs forward and sat them, one on each side of Keno. The blonde with the gun motioned them to sit.

Boris and his Team
Thirty-First Day
Munich

Boris and his men deplaned in Munich and found their SUVs. They took possession and drove out of the airport. Boris led the way. Each man had in an earpiece. As Boris drove he explained the situation.

"Hans called Gregoriy from Kufstein. Adrik pursued them in Viechtach before he died. The last tunnel in the immediate area is Pilsen. They flew into Munich and rented a vehicle. They have not returned it or flown out. We should find them there. We know where the tunnel is and we'll go there and wait. Let them come to us."

Gina, Angelic, Keno, Olga and her Team
Thirty-Second Day
Amsterdam

The next morning the women still found themselves tied to the chairs. They had been escorted to the bathroom once each and given a small piece of bread and some cheese late in the evening. They were gagged during the late evening and through the night. They had been zip-tied to the chairs with their arms behind them and their ankles against the legs. They could rise but it required them to bend double to accommodate the angle of the chair seat. The zip-ties were tight enough to restrain them but not tight enough to cut off circulation.

The blonde woman removed their gags. "When were you expecting the men back?" she asked.

"Don't know, you have our phones," replied Gina.

"Best guess?"

"Tomorrow or the next day, there wasn't a firm date. They have open-ended tickets."

"The sooner they get back, the sooner you get free."

Dee and Friends
Thirty-Second Day
Pilsen

They spent the night in Pilsen at the first hotel they came to and got up early the next morning to get underway. Only a short distance outside of town, Dee zeroed in on the coordinates. They'd driven up out of a small valley as far as they could go.

"Didn't Anna tell us Aldo was loaded down with contraband he'd taken from the train and couldn't go very far," said Jamal.

"I think so," replied Dee.

"The branch line has to be near. A man carrying a bunch of heavy weight wouldn't have made it far," added Mike.

They found the main line at the top of a small rise and began walking. They went for several hundred yards and Dee realized they had passed it.

"Hold up, it's back the other way."

"You sure?" said Jamal.

"There was no branch line," said Mike.

"Let's go back, walk slow, look at the mountains and not the tracks."

They turned and started back toward Pilsen. Walking slowly and seeing nothing. Coming around a small bend, Dee held up a hand.

"Look." He pointed toward the mountain. "The trees there are different. Just in that space. Everything else is old growth evergreen. There's a mixture there, hardwood and some bushes, along with the evergreen. They're shorter as well."

They stopped and looked. It was like a swath of slightly different colors and compositions.

"Let's walk the main track until we get in front of it and

look directly up the mountain. See if we can't tell a difference."

"You figure this out yourself?" asked Jamal.

"Not exactly, the GPS was beeping. It had to be right here somewhere."

"Looks like this one could still be sealed," added Mike.

"Trees wouldn't be shorter would they? I mean that's nearly eighty years ago. Everything would be full growth," said Jamal.

"But he's right about the color and the type of trees," said Mike.

They stopped in front of the cluster of trees and took a few steps back beyond the main line until they began to descend the slope. Stopping there, they looked through the trees and toward the mountain.

"It looks a little different. What do you want to do?" asked Mike.

"GPS says it's right here."

"Let's hike to the mountain," said Jamal.

They started from the main tracks and followed the line of trees toward the mountain face. They noticed quickly that the surface they were walking was flat, while the area to each side inclined.

"We're on a flat surface. Could be part of the reason for the difference in tree height," said Dee.

"I think we're on to it. Maybe this one is still sealed," said Jamal.

"Has to be doesn't it, given these circumstances?" said Mike.

A little over one hundred yards of walking and they reached the mountain face. The sides beyond the path they were walking, maybe twenty yards across, rose sharply up the mountain.

"This has to have been the rail bed," said Dee.

"Looks like it, the way it abruptly runs into the mountain. And the way these rocks are all jumbled. Take a step back and it looks like a little mini landslide, about the size of a tunnel, while the rest of the mountain face is smooth," added Jamal.

"Wonder why the Soviets didn't find this one?" asked Mike.

Both Dee and Jamal turned to look at him.

"That's a really good question," said Dee. "I'm thinking we better check it out."

"Who is going to know at this point in time?" said Jamal.

**Boris & his Team
Thirty-Second Day
Pilsen**

The man stepped out from behind a tree with a PKM machine gun leveled at them. "We know what happened, and while we're sure you would like to, unfortunately it's not going to happen. Hands on your head." Three other men stepped out from behind trees, each of them holding a machine gun. "Catching you was rather simple," said the first man. "You walked right into our trap."

"Who are you? What do you want?" asked Dee.

"We are Russians. That is as much as you need to know. We don't like tourists meddling around our installations."

Dee pointed to the mountain. "It looks like the side of a mountain. What installation are you talking about?"

"You came here looking for the tunnel and the trains."

"We were hiking. This looks like a cliff face. You must be mistaken?"

"Don't be foolish Mr. Sanders." Dee, Jamal, and Mike gave each other a startled look. "Yes, we know who you are. Somehow you escaped Adrik in Viechtach, tell me how that happened."

Dee looked at Jamal and Mike. "We don't know an Adrik. There was somebody behind us in an SUV that hit a train. Looked like he was trying to beat it across the tracks. Have no idea who it was."

The man grinned at Dee. "Adrik was sometimes an idiot. This sounds like one of those times. So you found that tunnel, a public park, but no trains. Why didn't you go home? You might have lived. Look at you now."

"We just came to see if the tunnels were sealed," replied Dee. "That was our only mission."

"Why?"

"We had a friend, dead now, who knew about these tunnels. She said they were sealed the last time she checked."

"Must have been long ago."

"It was. She said there were good and bad things stored on the trains, buried in the tunnels, and it was best that they be left alone. If the tunnels were still sealed, we walked away. In this case they were already reclaimed. We still walked away."

"I know your history. You're treasure hunters."

"Not this time. Too many nasty things on board, likely contamination."

The man looked at them for a moment. "I was on the team that reclaimed these tunnels and trains. Who did you know that was so informed?"

"She was an old woman when we met her, but once she'd been a young girl with a couple of friends who rode three trains from Paris to their final destinations."

"And they knew what was on board?"

"They studied it along the way."

"You say she's dead?"

"They're all dead."

"And soon you will be too."

"Why?"

"You're interfering with Russian autonomy."

"You can't be serious. It was over seventy-five years ago. We were just checking to see if the tunnels were still sealed."

"Bad luck, turn around and face the mountain."

Gina, Angelic, Keno, Olga and her Team, and Hans
Thirty-Second Day
Amsterdam

Later that morning there was a knock on the door. The blonde woman went to answer it. An older, burly-looking man stepped inside. "Olga," he said and wrapped his arms around her.

"Hans," she replied. "You're early."

"But I missed you." He pulled her closer to him and kissed her aggressively. She replied in kind.

"That's embarrassing," whispered Angelic to Gina and Keno.

"Disgusting," said Keno.

"Surprising," said Gina.

The couple finished their embrace with a flourish, the man squeezing the woman on both hips, and turned to the three women.

"Now that you've called me by name," said Olga, "what shall we do with them?"

"What we'd always planned to do, my darling."

"Hans?" said Gina.

He looked at her.

"Hans Mueller?"

He bowed with a flourish. "At your service."

"Dee mentioned you. You were in the town with the first tunnel. You told them about it."

"Yes, I did, most of the details. They seemed to appreciate it."

"What do you want with us?" asked Angelic.

"That depends on how well you cooperate."

"We don't know anything, how can we cooperate?"

"Are you familiar with the canals?" asked Hans.

"Just a little," replied Gina.

"I suspect you'll get more familiar with them. They're not very deep, but they are dark and dank and people drown in them all the time."

"I'm a good swimmer," said Gina. "And I float really well."

Hans glanced at her from top to bottom. "I expect you would, but it doesn't really matter. You know too much and so you have an appointment with them when this is over."

Dee and Friends
Thirty-Second Day
Pilsen

Everything was black and fuzzy. The ground was spinning. Dee struggled to push himself up and felt blood running down the side of his face. He looked over and Jamal and Mike were sprawled on the ground beside him. He felt the spinning again and leaned back, placing a hand on his head to feel the bruise. Dee was facing the mountain. He turned slowly to look around and the men with the machine guns were gone. He crawled over to Jamal and Mike.

"Hey, you okay?" he asked, shaking each of them by the shoulder.

"Whoa," mumbled Jamal.

"What happened?" asked Mike while rubbing his head.

"Apparently they knocked us out," replied Dee.

"I thought they were going to kill us," said Jamal.

"Me too," answered both Dee and Mike.

"Wonder why they didn't?" said Jamal.

"Maybe they thought warning us would be enough, or maybe they got interrupted, which means we should go, either way," replied Dee.

They got up and started walking.

"Do you suppose we should keep looking?" asked Dee.

"I think we should go home, count ourselves as lucky we're alive, forget about it," replied Mike.

"What do you want to do?" Jamal asked Dee.

"I want to know what happened," answered Dee.

"I agree," replied Jamal.

"You're both crazy," added Mike.

They hiked to the car and returned to Pilsen. While eating a late lunch, they inquired about someplace different to stay and if there was a local railroad office. The waitress was happy to oblige with information on both. The rail office was across town and she recommended the Hotel Rango in the historic downtown area.

Driving across the city to the rail office, they decided to try the direct approach again. The three of them entered the small facility and Dee began his spiel.

"We're railroad enthusiasts and we heard there were some old tunnels in the area that we thought might be worth exploring. Could you…"

"I'm afraid not. You must be mistaken or in the wrong area. There is nothing here. Furthermore, we don't like people poking around the tracks and you would likely be arrested. Please keep that in mind and be on your way. I'm quite busy."

Back in the car, there was some confusion, disappointment, and a little fear.

"That was rude," said Mike. "I wonder if he was a Russian too."

"I'm not sure I believed him," said Jamal. "He was almost too adamant. Do you suppose he'll tell the ones that were on the mountain?"

"I don't know, maybe they told him. It's like they had something to hide?" said Dee.

"How bad do we really want to know? I mean we're lucky to be alive. Shouldn't we just leave it alone and go home?" asked Mike.

Neither of the other men responded.

———

They drove into downtown and located the Hotel Rango. Grabbing what little they had and finding the check-in desk took them a few extra minutes as they strode around the hotel facility looking it over.

"Interesting place, I bet the women would like it," said Jamal.

"I know Keno would. She'd love all those arches. Do you think it would be safe to come back," added Mike.

They arrived at the desk and Dee began the check-in process while Jamal and Mike stood beside him.

"Where would we look for the history of the railroad?" asked Jamal.

"Local library?" replied Mike.

"Sir," said the young woman behind the desk.

Dee looked up, and she was a dark-haired, fair-skinned, young girl with dark eyes.

"These are your friends?" She pointed at Mike and Jamal.

"Yes, we're interested in the local railroad and are trying to figure out where to get any information."

"My great-grandfather worked for the railroad. My grandfather, who is in his 80s, knows a lot of the stories. He would probably talk to you, just to have someone to talk to. My grandmother passed away a couple of years ago and he gets lonely. He's outlived most of his friends."

"That would be great. How would we get in touch with him?"

"Let me just double check with him and I can have him contact you if that's alright."

"That would be fabulous. Thank you so much."

Gina, Angelic, Keno, Olga and her Team, and Hans
Thirty-Second Day
Amsterdam

"Have you heard from Boris?" asked Hans as he sat in the kitchen nibbling on some of the items Angelic and Gina had brought from the market.

Olga called to him from the living room where she was standing, looking over Gina, Angelic, and Keno. "He said they'd located the men and were developing a plan."

"What's to plan? I'm sure Gregoriy told him to 'locate and terminate' how difficult is that?"

"Boris and Gregoriy go back a long way. I think there is some rivalry."

"Of course there is. I was there working the trains with them."

"You were just a boy."

"Yes, but it was plain to see. They butted heads over everything."

"But Boris always followed orders didn't he?"

"Ultimately, but he didn't like it. Especially when Gregoriy appropriated the 'property crates' for himself. Then he blew up the back side of the mountain so there could be no access but left an opening at the rear of the tunnel."

"That was for the gold wasn't it, the boxes of ingots?"

"Yes and the basis of his fortune."

"He took all the boxes? There's still boxes on site aren't there?"

"Gregoriy arranged for half a railcar full of the boxes to be offloaded separately. They were one side of a car that had a laboratory on the other side.

"From what I can tell from Gregoriy, he has retrieved about half of them."

"All at once or has he made several trips?"

"One at a time I would imagine as he doesn't take anyone with him and he has to either climb down from the top of the mountain or up from the valley floor to reach the tunnel. A gold bar is approximately twelve inches long, four inches wide, and two inches thick. They weigh roughly twenty-seven pounds. There were eight of them in a box making it weigh a little over two hundred pounds."

"So he'd strap it and carry it on his back?"

"If he took the whole box."

"What is the box worth?"

"Depends on when in time he sold it. Recently it would be worth \$2,150 an ounce, about 35K a bar or 275K a box."

"And he had a half a rail car?"

"Probably fifty boxes, between ten and fifteen million. But then it was forty years ago, late 1980s when we found it, or I should say when he took it."

"Boris knows this?"

"No, I don't think so. He may suspect it. He was curious and asked why Gregoriy blew up the mountain but not all of the backside of the tunnel."

"What'd Gregoriy say?"

"We blew up the mountain, what does it matter? We sealed the tunnel about a third of the way back. No way to get up there now."

"But he has hasn't he?"

"Yes, he admitted as much, but was cagier about how much gold was left."

"So, let's go get it."

"What about the ladies?" He jerked a thumb at the three of them tied to the chairs.

"We'll follow your suggestion and give them a close personal look at the canals."

Boris & his Team
Thirty-Second Day
Pilsen

Boris and his team stayed in a safe house in Pilsen. It was one of the residual benefits of Czechoslovakia being a Soviet satellite for all those years. Even today, in the Czech Republic, there were still remnants of the past.

"Why didn't we kill them? Wasn't that our job?" asked one of the team members.

Boris fired back, "Don't tell me our job. I am the team leader and I make the decisions."

"But Gregoriy…" replied the man.

"We'll deal with him at the proper time and place. Those tourists knew nothing. It was an adventure. Scaring them was probably enough. Three dead bodies will not be well received in Pilsen."

"We throw them over the mountain, no one will ever find them," replied the other man.

"We'll tail them for a day and see what they do. How they react. Then I'll decide their future."

Gina, Angelic, Keno, Olga and her Team, and Hans
Thirty-Second Day
Amsterdam

Hans and Olga were standing apart from the other two agents on Olga's team and the three women. "Do you remember when we met?" asked Hans.

Olga nodded. "You had come to Moscow to spend a few days with Gregoriy. He introduced us at a dinner. We hit it off, been together ever since."

Hans squeezed her hands. "That was when he first mentioned that he had gone back to the train. And that the monies had helped him get started in business. His tongue got a little loose that night. He's said very little since; only that he hadn't recovered it all."

"Let's take care of this here, including my team, and then go get what's left. We'll figure a way to blame it on Boris and walk away clean."

Hans smiled at her and kissed Olga's cheek. "I love how you think."

They moved toward the kitchen where everyone else was gathered.

"Cut their legs loose but leave their hands tied. Put them in a light jacket or long shirt where their hands are hidden. We'll walk them to the canal," said Olga.

Then she turned to Gina, Angelic, and Keno. "We're going to take off the gags but each one of us will have a pistol, with a suppressor, on each one of you. If you scream, the shot will make very little sound and you will die instantly, as will your friends," said Olga.

Each of the three women nodded and their gags were removed.

"Let's go," said Olga. They marched out the front door into the street. Keno, then a guard, Angelic and then a guard, then Gina followed by Olga, and then Hans bringing up the rear and watching the streets.

They marched away from the house and down the street away from the lights of the night. They could see the canal waters, dark and swirling, just beyond. In the distance they heard police sirens moving in their direction. Hans and Olga both glanced quickly toward the sound.

They sped the group up as the sirens drew nearer. Suddenly a man and woman clad in the black and yellow striped uniform of the National Police of Netherlands stepped out from behind a tree along the canal. They were carrying pump-action, tactical shotguns.

"Halt please," said the male officer. "There is an issue ahead. You are not permitted."

"What issue?" snapped Olga harshly.

"There has been a drowning, you will need to reroute. An investigation is underway," replied the female officer.

No one moved. The male officer took a step closer, lifting his shotgun slightly. Both Hans and Olga noted that his finger was not yet on the trigger.

"Move along," said the male officer.

Gina took a step toward the man and began blinking her eyes quickly and wildly. The officer paused for a moment. Angelic and Keno saw what Gina was doing and while not certain why; they began to do the same. The woman officer took a step forward.

It happened quickly; Olga pulled her pistol away from Gina and shot the male officer as he took another step forward. It was a small sound. He discharged the shotgun as he fell and rolled toward the canal, hitting the guard standing near Angelic, who dropped to the ground.

The female officer swung her gun around while pumping the action and sprayed the guard near Keno, who was screaming. The blast hit the guard but the overspray caught Keno in the shoulder and she spun to the ground.

Olga fired again, hitting the female officer in the forehead just as Gina snapped her arms from behind her and pushed Olga into Hans. They stumbled onto the ground leading down to the canal.

While they tumbled, Gina saw Olga's pistol and grabbed it from the ground. Holding it in both hands, she pointed it toward the couple, only a few feet away, and pulled the trigger. She hit the canal.

Olga and Hans both rolled into the water and Gina heard the splash as they submerged.

Angelic was back on her feet and helping Keno up.

"You have a few pellets in the shoulder," said Angelic as she quickly examined the wound. " You'll be okay, but we need to get you cleaned up."

Gina took a step towards them. "Let's get back to the house!"

She and Angelic got on each side of Keno to support her and quickly began to retreat in the opposite direction.

They could hear a lot of commotion and sirens as the shotgun blasts had drawn more attention.

"You still have the gun," said Angelic, pointing toward Gina's hand.

"In case they come back."

Angelic nodded, "Yeah, good idea."

———

Hans and Olga drifted downstream on the far side of the canal, past the investigation. They stayed in the shadows and took only an occasional stroke to keep themselves afloat and moving. Once they were a few hundred meters beyond, they approached a dark set of steps and made their way ashore.

"Should we go back for them?" asked Hans.

"No reason, they'll probably call the police. They don't seem to know anything, probably just treasure hunting tourists," replied Olga. "Let's be on our way to Pilsen. We can catch Boris and check the tunnel."

They eased into the shadows and disappeared.

———

Gina, Angelic, and Keno made it back to the house, entered and locked the door behind them. There had been a lot of confusion along the canal when the two officers that had been shot were found. The women had kept their heads down and kept walking.

Angelic sat Keno in a chair in the kitchen. She pulled off Keno's shirt and checked the wound.

"You're lucky; you just caught a couple of pellets. I can get those out and bandage you up. We can stay away from the hospital for now," said Angelic.

"I thought you were in Oncology," said Gina.

"I was a nurse for a short time before I became a Practitioner and specialized in Oncology," replied Angelic.

"It doesn't look too bad," said Gina, bending to examine the wound more closely.

"You were very lucky," said Angelic to Keno. "We'll draw less suspicion if we stay out of sight. Gina, get on the phone and see when the guys will be back. I don't think we should stay here long. Olga and Hans might come looking for us. When I get Keno cleaned up we can go and stay in a hotel for the night, or however long we need."

Gina called Dee and the phone went to voicemail. "He's not answering."

"Try mine and call Jamal."

Gina repeated the process and got voicemail again. "They must be up to something."

"It's late; you'd think they'd be in bed," said Keno.

"By the way, how did you get free?" Angelic asked Gina.

"Tell us what magic you conjured," said Keno.

Gina smiled. "No magic. There was a slightly raised nail head on the back of my chair. Whenever they weren't looking at us, I was rubbing my binding against it. Didn't think it was ever going to work, but walking along the canal I felt it start to give away. When the shooting started, I pulled as hard as I could and it popped."

"Lucky for us. Gather some things, just for overnight. Get the dog. In case Hans and Olga come back, I don't want it to look like we fled. We can try calling the guys again in a little bit," said Angelic.

Dee and Friends
Thirty-Third Day
Pilsen

The phone rang in Dee's room just before he and the others were about to go down for breakfast.

"Mr. Sanders?" said the voice.

"Yes."

"This is Jakub Vesely. I am Hana, the desk clerk's, grandfather. She said you are interested in the trains."

"Yes, Mr. Vesely, thank you for calling. And thank your granddaughter for referring us to you. We're interested in the local trains and railways and looking for information."

"So I see. Perhaps I can help you. Would you like to meet?"

"If you have time, we'd greatly appreciate it."

"Of course, there's a café near you called 'Small Balls'. It's a foosball hangout for young people. This time of day there won't be anyone there. We can have a coffee. I'll meet you in half an hour."

Dee met Jamal and Mike in the hallway and shared the information.

"Let's find directions to this café and see if we need to drive or if we can walk."

"Maybe a streetcar or a bus," added Jamal.

Stopping at the desk to ask, they found it was a little over a mile away.

"Let's take the car in case we need to follow up on something," said Mike.

A few minutes later they were en route and shortly afterward parked in front by the door and entered the café. It was empty.

"Gentlemen?" said the man behind the counter.

"Three coffees please," replied Dee.

They sat at one of the tables and watched the door.

"You're expecting someone," said the man.

"Jakub Vesely."

The man nodded and turned to the kitchen. They could see him preparing some sort of drink. There was a screech, the door opened, and an elderly man with a cane shuffled inside.

"Gentlemen," he said and begin coming toward them. "I'm Jakub Vesely."

The man behind the counter appeared and placed a mug in front of Jakub. "Thank you Otto." The man nodded and turned back to the kitchen.

Jakub shifted in his chair.

"Did you have to come far? We could have come to you," said Dee.

"It is no problem. I like to get out and as you can see I come here often. The tram runs near my home and brings me here on its way downtown."

"Thank you for coming," said Jamal.

Jakub nodded his head. "What can I tell you about the trains…" he paused, "or do you really want to know about the tunnel?"

Dee, Mike, and Jamal looked at each other quickly.

"It's okay. It's not a happy story, but it's the only one about trains here in Pilsen that someone would come to see or hear. How did you know about it?"

"A friend, who was on a similar train, had a friend who was on this train," replied Dee.

"I hope they weren't on it for long."

"From somewhere in the Bavarian Forest to here."

"Not so far, that's good. Is this person still alive?"

"No, they've been dead for quite some time."

"Disease?"

"Untimely fall."

"It's just as well."

"Why is that?"

"May I start at the beginning, as I know it?"

"Please."

"My father worked for the railroad before the war. Most of the other workers were conscripted for military service but he remained behind to run the trains for the military. He considered himself quite lucky. When the war ended, the survivors came back but by then he had acquired a very specific knowledge of all the rail lines, as the only engineer. In the mid-1980s, maybe 1985 or 1986 the Soviets came to Pilsen. They had maps, and they wanted the person with the most knowledge of the rail lines, my father.

"The man in charge was named Gregoriy Orlov. He had a German kid named Hans Mueller as his assistant. He came from one of the other tunnel towns and was Orlov's personal assistant, obnoxious kid, the only reason my dad remembered him."

"Hans Mueller?" asked Dee.

Jakub nodded. "You heard of him or something?"

"We met him in Kufstein, when we were looking for the tunnel there."

Jakub shook his head. "You'd better be careful."

Dee nodded. "So what happened after that?"

"They searched until they located an old tunnel, just outside of town. Dad recalled it from early in his career. Told me later he knew where it was as soon as they started talking about it, but he let them find it."

"Why did he do that?" asked Dee.

"He had been involved with the Nazis when they staged the trains and blew the tunnel up. Unwillingly of course, and he slipped away right before they detonated the entrances or they probably would have killed him as they did the two other engineers that were assisting them. Time must have been running out, and the Nazis didn't chase him down."

"Did he go into hiding or…" asked Jamal.

"No, he didn't have to. The Nazis disappeared quickly after they finished blowing the tunnel and pulling the track to the main line. He went back a couple of days later to examine their work. There was a big pile of rubble to one side. Tunnel was completely blocked, but it was easy to see where the track had been because of the rail bed. It was flat. The rest of the mountain rose steeply upward."

"Did he ever tell anyone?" asked Mike.

"Only me when I was older. He said that there were only three trains, and they took two of them out, emptied them, and then burned the railcars and the engines right outside the tunnel. They blew the tunnel from the middle out every fifteen feet or so."

"Almost like they were replacing the mountain," said Mike

"Or burying something," added Jamal.

"What about the other train?" asked Dee.

"They left it inside."

"Any idea why?" asked Dee.

"Oh yes, there's more. It gets worse, at least for me. "

"What happened?" asked Jamal.

"Within a couple of days of the Soviets leaving, my father and the others who had worked with them, got sick—fevers, body aches, fatigue, and then difficulty breathing. He sat me down and told me several things. 'Just so someone will know,' was what he said and then he cautioned me. He said he thought the trains had biological, chemical, or viral experiments of some kind and that they had matured or developed in some fashion and that the trains were contaminated. The Soviets had men in hazard suits and what not but he felt like the entire tunnel was contaminated and that's why they blew it up so comprehensively and left the one train behind."

"They hoped that enough rock or earth would contain the disease."

Jakub nodded his head. "He also said there were Chinese advisors with the Soviets and that they scurried all over the trains, without the hazard suits. He thought they were the ones actually reclaiming whatever was taken. He also bet most of them would die, just as he did."

"What was it?" asked Jamal.

"The doctor said his lungs were swollen shut and choked him to death."

"Like inflammation?" asked Jamal.

"I suppose, it was something that created inflammation."

"A virus," said Dee.

"That's what the doctor likened it to although he couldn't identify it. He suspected the train or its contents as the source. There were three other cases, men who also worked on the train, all of them older."

"Did it spread?" asked Mike.

"The doctor was pretty adamant. He was a younger guy at the time. He had the bodies isolated and cremated. Made a few enemies with the families but nobody else came down with it."

"Nothing else ever happened up there?" asked Dee.

"When I was younger, I'd walk up and study the mountain from the main track, sometimes walk a short ways back on the rail bed. Probably been twenty years since I was last up there. I doubt anyone remembers it now."

"We stopped at the rail yard and asked," said Jamal. "Young guy there told us no such thing existed."

Jakub laughed. "Yeah, that's the official story. The line doesn't want anybody fooling around the tracks. I don't think most of them even know why any longer, just policy. They're big on following rules."

Boris & his Team
Thirty-Third Day
Pilsen

The next morning Boris and his men followed Dee, Jamal, and Mike to the Small Balls Café. There they met a man named Jakub Vesely. Boris knew this because his men had checked the area and determined that Dee and friends were staying at the Hotel Rango, a popular spot for tourists. Boris had spoken to the desk clerk asking about meeting his friend Dee Sanders. The clerk had offered to call Dee's room but Boris suggested he might catch Dee in the morning. The clerk advised him Dee and his friends were meeting her grandfather. From that Boris and his men observed the hotel and followed the men to the café.

They sat in two cars outside while Dee and friends spoke to the man.

"Are we going to pick them up here or what are you thinking?" asked one of Boris's team members.

"For now we're just going to observe. The old man probably knows something about the tunnels. The granddaughter said he knew a lot of local history."

Dee and Friends
Thirty-third Day
Pilsen

Jakub let them buy lunch and then drop him off at his house. He waved as he got out of the car. "It was good talking to you fellows. I'm glad I got to tell someone that story before I die. Would have been a shame to have taken that to the grave."

They waved and drove back to the Rango.

"Didn't Anna say something about sharing her story?" asked Mike.

"Yes, very similar to Jakub," replied Jamal.

"People have events in their lives that they never quite get over. They bottle them up inside and their thoughts eat away at them. Maybe it helps to get it out, to share it with someone else so they can carry it for a while and you don't have to anymore. I think they call it history, learn from it or repeat it."

"Like viruses," said Jamal.

"Yeah, like that," replied Dee.

Boris & his Team
Thirty-Third Day
Pilsen

Boris and his men followed Dee and friends after they dropped off Jakub. In a straight stretch, one of the cars pulled in front of Dee and the other closed in behind. Then the front car stopped. Boris got out and walked back to the window. When Jamal didn't roll it down, Boris motioned with his hand and Jamal complied.

"Follow us. We just want to talk. There's a parking lot up ahead, very public. We'll chat for a minute and you can be on your way."

Jamal, Dee, and Mike looked at each other as Boris walked back to his vehicle.

"What could they possibly want?" asked Jamal.

Dee shook his head. "I guess we'll find out."

"Think they'll kill us?" asked Mike.

"I think they already would have, if they were going to," replied Dee.

They followed Boris's car the short distance to the parking lot. Boris slowed until he was right in front of them. The trailing car pulled right on their bumper.

Both cars shut off and Jamal did the same.

"I'll get out," said Dee. "You guys stay in the car in case we have to try and leave quickly. Roll down the windows so you can hear."

"You should stay in the car too," said Jamal.

"Boris said he just wanted to talk. I'll show a little good faith."

"Hope it doesn't get you killed," replied Mike.

Dee opened the door and climbed out as Boris and the other men surrounded him.

Dee made a quick mental note; *it's four on three, even if we'd all gotten out. But still they were four trained soldiers and we're three tourists, two football players and a swimmer. Let's talk.*

Boris stepped closer and held both hands in the air. "We just want to hear what you learned."

Olga & Hans
Thirty-Third Day
Pilsen

Olga & Hans flew into Prague, Czech Republic because it was closer to Pilsen than Munich. They wanted to catch up with Boris as quickly as possible. It was an hour to Pilsen from their destination versus three hours from Munich, plus Olga had more resources available to her in Prague than in Germany.

They had arrived in the early morning and taken possession of a heavily-armored black SUV and significant weaponry. Olga had tolerated no questions from the local contacts. She had contacted Moscow security for Boris's location and she and Hans drove to the area as quickly as possible.

Olga and Hans had tailed Boris as he tailed Dee. It was a lengthy procession with Dee and Boris unaware of the vehicles behind them.

As Boris stood in front of Dee and listened to what they had learned, a black SUV pulled into the parking lot. Hans drove and Olga leaned partially out the passenger window with a RPK light machine gun with a 75-round drum magazine.

She began spraying the group as soon as Hans made the turn. Dee saw her a second before the others, who all had their backs outward. When Dee dropped, so did Boris. Olga's fire raked across the three other men who screamed and fell to the pavement.

Dee slid under the car after he dropped. Jamal and Mike dropped to the floorboard. Olga was now concentrating her fire on Boris.

Hans swung the SUV around for Olga to make another pass at Boris or anyone else she could see. Dee observed

Boris rolling to his side, as the SUV turned, and grabbing at something on his belt. When the SUV came back around, Boris rolled again and leaned up just enough to toss something through the window above Olga's shoulder as he kept rolling to stay in front of the trail of bullets she was spraying.

There was a pause for a moment and then a great explosion rang out and a ball of fire where the SUV had been. A second or so later there was glass and metal fragments falling from the sky. Dee saw Boris cover his head and continue to roll away from the car and across the parking lot.

Everyone lay still for a moment and then Boris, who had stopped rolling, got to his knees, brushed himself off and walked toward Dee.

Dee scampered from under the vehicle as Jamal and Mike opened the doors and climbed out.

"What was that?" asked Dee as Boris approached.

Boris was still dusting himself off. "A now former colleague of mine was the shooter and I think the driver was Hans Mueller."

"Hans from Kufstein?" asked Jamal.

"The same."

"What did you throw in there?" asked Jamal.

"An MK3 grenade." He held his jacket up. They could see a belt around his waist. There was a pistol on one side, a stun gun on the other, hand cuffs and a flashlight in between. There was also one canister and an empty hook.

"It's like a policeman's belt," said Mike.

Boris nodded. "It's handy. That was an armored SUV. The strength of its body intensified the impact to them and minimized it to us, although the subsequent explosion and the debris were unfortunate."

"What were they doing together?" asked Dee.

Boris paused. "More important question, have you talked to the women in Amsterdam, whom you travel with?"

The men glanced quickly at one another. Jamal and Mike both grabbed their phones and began to call.

"What are you telling us?" asked Dee.

"The woman in the SUV, Olga, was sent to contain your wives in Amsterdam."

"Why was she here?"

"I don't know. Let's see what your friends learn," said Boris, turning toward Jamal and Mike. They were both still waiting for a reply and then there was a click on Jamal's phone.

"Hello." Dee recognized Angelic.

"Baby what's going on? Are you alright? What's happening?" asked Jamal. He hit the speaker button.

"Slow down, Jam, it's alright. We're all alright," said Angelic. "Keno and Gina are right here beside me, I'm on speaker phone."

"Keno," called Mike.

"I'm here," she replied.

Dee followed, "Gina?"

"Hey baby, I'm okay," she replied.

The men visibly sighed and leaned back.

"Tell us what happened," said Dee.

"There was a couple and two other women," started Angelic.

"They took us hostage," interjected Keno.

"But we escaped and they fled. Something about 'Boris'. The two women were killed by the Dutch police," added Gina.

"You're okay?" asked Dee.

"Yeah, we're in a hotel and we tried to call you guys earlier," said Gina.

"Sorry, we were in a meeting, but we're here now with Boris. Hopefully we'll be out of here soon. Stay put, unless you hear from us. One of us will call back shortly. We need to clear up some things here," replied Dee.

Jamal ended the call.

Dee and Friends & Boris
Thirty-third Day
Pilsen

They turned to Boris. "What's going on?' asked Dee.

"Well, first I'm glad your wives are okay. I meant them no harm. Olga was only supposed to contain them until we learned who you were and what you were after."

"We're tourists, nothing but curious tourists."

"That's what I thought."

"Is that why you didn't kill us up on the mountain?"

Boris nodded. "You didn't seem to know much then. There's been enough death, but I couldn't convince Gregoriy."

"Who's Gregoriy?"

"He's a high ranking Russian official and billionaire."

"Why would he care?"

"As a young officer he was in charge of locating and evacuating these tunnels. We, the Russians, Soviets at the time, knew about these tunnels. We had heard of them from some of the Nazi defectors and deserters. Eventually we got around to checking the stories out."

"Thirty or forty years later?"

"Things moved slowly in the Soviet empire and only slightly faster in Russia. But Gregoriy had gathered information. There was a political angle with the Chinese and a personal angle with Gregoriy. He had heard about the art and the personal property, a large portion of which was gold."

"What did the Chinese want?"

"They had heard of the biological, chemical, and viral research the Nazis were conducting, and they were interested, at a price of course. So Gregoriy finally got the green light he had been pursuing for almost a decade. In fact he had plans of his own for locating the trains had the Chinese opportunity not come up."

"What happened?"

"There were six tunnels, including the three you know about; there were two more in what was East Germany and one in Poland."

"All Soviet bloc made it easier."

"Yes, Gregoriy marshalled some troops and with the assistance of the Chinese went tunnel hunting."

"What did they find?"

"Pretty much the same stuff as on the three trains you know of—art, personal property, gold, guns, research labs, supplies of various kinds—anything the Nazis thought might be helpful if they could recover or strike again, or just to keep anyone else from having it."

"So what happened?"

"Gregoriy ran the teams. They recovered what they found and moved on to the next tunnel. The one here in Pilsen, the last one, turned out to be the most interesting. It's where he found the lab cars the Chinese were looking for. But, more importantly to him, the search was winding down and less attention was being paid to the other items as the Chinese were inspired by the research discovery."

"And Gregoriy did what?'

"He managed to slip out a Degas that hangs in his office today although most of the art was heavily monitored by the Soviet higher ups at the time. What they didn't pay attention to were the crates marked 'property'."

"What did he find?"

"I could never prove it, but I think the basis of his fortune, gold."

"Why do you say that?"

"He blew up the front side of the tunnel, where we first met you, all the way back to the mountain. But on the back

side he stopped about two thirds of the way out. He blew a
solid wall there but left the balance of the tunnel. Then he
blew up the access to the tunnel on the outside, the mountain
side, so that no one could reach the tunnel. You had to climb
down from the top of the mountain or climb up from the
valley floor. I saw him do that and when I asked why, he said
'It doesn't matter.' I suspected then he was up to something."

"What about Hans?"

Boris smiled. "He was this smartass kid from one of the
other tunnel towns that Gregoriy took a shine to for a time.
They did stay in touch over the years but Hans never seemed
to prosper the way Gregoriy did, so I never could figure the
exact relationship."

"So why were Olga and Hans here?"

"Don't know. Gregoriy may have sent them to kill me. He
and I never got along. That's why I feared for your wives. My
only other guess is that maybe Hans knew something and he
convinced Olga to act on it."

"You mean like killing you or killing you and going after
the gold, if that's what it is?"

"Yeah, things are never what they seem."

Dee smiled.

Boris looked at him. "What?"

"Our friend that rode the train used to say that."

"You live long enough that becomes clear to you."

"If there was gold, it seems like it should be donated to
one of the Holocaust Museums or something similar. It was
mostly fillings from people's teeth, wasn't it?"

"In some of the earlier trains, there were boxes full of
fillings. I always thought the Pilsen train might have been
different."

"Why's that?"

"I followed Gregoriy here several times. It was some

years after the excavation when I became more curious. He got rich quickly, it didn't make sense."

"So what happened?"

"I followed him here twice. He was alone both times. He climbed to the tunnel, stayed for a while and then climbed back out. He had backpacks coming out that he didn't appear to have going inside. I felt sure he was retrieving something."

"Why didn't you approach him?"

Boris smiled. "He's a powerful man, my boss. It wasn't a wise career or life choice to ask. I let him leave. The second time I followed him and climbed in the tunnel myself, but I couldn't find anything. Like I said, Hans may have known something, but perhaps not the location. That could be what he pitched to Olga. She didn't like me or Gregoriy. I don't think she liked anybody, maybe not even Hans."

"What do you do now?"

"Go back to Moscow and explain the entire thing, including your escape, as a colossal screw-up on Olga's part, and then see how he reacts."

"How can you prove anything?"

"I can't, but just knowing might make it a little easier."

Boris stuck out a hand. "Be safe, but maybe you should get out of Europe for a while."

"What about you?"

"I'll go back to my life and I'll keep watching." He turned and walked away.

Dee and Friends
Thirty-fourth Day
Amsterdam

They flew back early that morning and were in Amsterdam before lunch. Their wives met them at the airport and they taxied back to the house.

When the men entered, Ate ran up to them and jumped on their legs. His tail was wagging furiously.

"He really likes you guys," said Gina.

"I guess he can travel with us," replied Dee.

"I hope so, but I told my sister about him and she'd love to have him if he doesn't travel well."

"He should be fine," said Angelic. "He traveled all that time with Anna."

"Oh, by the way, Diego texted me, he couldn't reach you," said Gina. "He says that he'll be here tomorrow to pick up the Aldo paintings. He suggests we hold the Picasso abstract, with the portrait, and he will search what he called 'a myriad of lists of stolen art' to see if it can be identified. In this fashion he hopes to determine if there was an owner without opening the painting to the multitude of claims that will arise on the other three. In that fashion, if no claim or identification can be located, we can present both paintings to Anna's great-granddaughter in some kind of timely fashion."

"If nobody has laid a claim on it, he's willing to let it go to the great-granddaughter?" asked Jamal.

"In a word, yes. His opinion was the painting was in the subject's possession, that had been painted, and that was the strongest form of ownership other than a reported claim of loss."

"That Diego is a clever man," said Mike.

"You've said that before," added Jamal.
"Yeah, and I'll probably say it again."
"History has a way of repeating itself," added Dee.

Boris
Thirty-Fourth Day
Moscow

Boris went to Prague where he caught a flight for Moscow. He didn't get in until late in the day and elected to go to his apartment rather than meet with Gregoriy.

The following morning he showed up in the outer office, where he asked Ekaterina if Gregoriy was available.

"Is Gregoriy in today?"

"Yes." She glanced at her computer screen. "He doesn't have any appointments until after lunch. Shall I tell him you're here?"

"Please."

Ekaterina rose and knocked on the inner office door, then stuck only her head inside. Boris couldn't hear what she said.

She turned to Boris and said, "You can go in now." She pushed the door open and stepped aside.

Boris entered the office and stopped by the door for a moment.

Gregoriy waved him over and pointed at a chair.

Boris sat.

"I was beginning to wonder why I hadn't heard from anyone," said Gregoriy. "Nor could I reach anyone."

"I lost my phone," replied Boris. "My men were killed as were Olga and her team and I think Hans Mueller."

Gregoriy sat back in his chair and raised his head in Boris's direction. "What did you say?'

"I said, all my team, Olga and all her team, and possibly Hans Mueller were all killed."

"By a bunch of tourists?"

"No, Olga's team by the Danish police in Amsterdam, my team by Olga and Hans, Olga and Hans by me. The tourists disappeared."

"How?"

"Not sure, I was pursuing them when Olga and Hans arrived unexpectedly and shot up my team. I overheard one of the tourists, on the phone prior, talking to his wife in Amsterdam. There was an incident with the National Police and Olga's team was killed."

"Unbelievable!"

"That's what I thought. So, did you send Olga to kill me?"

Gregoriy turned sharply to stare at Boris.

For the first time, Boris noticed that Gregoriy was beginning to sweat profusely and that his eyes were watery and pale. He had a slight twitch in his movements and then he sneezed and followed it with a cough.

"I'm so tired," Gregoriy sighed. "While we might not always get along, you have been a good soldier to the state and I would never order anything like that."

"Didn't seem that way. She shot up my team, my vehicles, most of a parking lot, in broad daylight, in a downtown area. She was pretty much in a frenzy."

Gregoriy looked at him for a moment. "She was so intense, I always suspected some type of drugs or stimulant. That's crazy."

"You know what I think?" asked Boris

Gregoriy shifted in his chair, now visibly shivering.

"You're sick."

Gregoriy's face grew harsh.

"I mean look at you, you're shaking. How long has this been going on?"

"I was in the country for a few days and it started after that."

"The country, like say outside Pilsen, Czech Republic?"

Gregoriy gave Boris a harsh look. "It will always be Czechoslovakia to me."

"So, you went back to the tunnel?"

"What are you talking about?" Gregoriy coughed again.

"You know where I'm talking about and you've been back a number of times, to whatever you left there."

"How dare you?" Gregoriy shivered and coughed again.

"The tunnel leaked, didn't it? Or whatever you have stashed there is contaminated. That one rockslide in the later portion of the tunnel didn't seal the contamination. You should have filled the whole tunnel."

"Nonsense, I've just caught a cold. I'm getting too old to go out in the countryside."

Boris stood up, leaned forward and extended a hand. Gregoriy drew back. "You're burning up, I can feel it from here. You should go home, die quietly. Don't contaminate everyone else around you."

"How insubordinate! Get out of my office."

"Happily." Boris rose and turned for the door.

"This is not over," called Gregoriy.

Boris looked back. "It will be shortly."

When Boris stepped into the outer office, while he wasn't fond of Ekaterina, he saw no reason for her to be stricken. "You should go home, take a few days. Gregoriy is very sick. You don't want it."

She looked at him blankly and then heard Gregoriy hacking and coughing through the open door to the inner office. "You're probably right." She grabbed her purse, stood, and took him by the arm. "I'll walk you out."

Dee and Friends
Thirty-fifth Day
Amsterdam

Diego arrived the following morning and taxied to the house. He caught them finishing breakfast.

"Ah, it's good to see everyone again. I can't leave you alone for a moment and you're in the middle of something else."

"I keep telling them that too," said Keno.

Diego winked at her. "Could I see the paintings? This is exciting."

"Have a seat and I'll get them," said Dee. He pulled the trunk from a nearby closet and unloaded them.

When all five of them were leaning against the bookcase, Diego still hadn't moved. "It's amazing, such fine works of art, all five of them." He pointed to the Picasso abstract. "I'm surprised that one survived. The Nazis considered modern or abstract art to be 'degenerate' art and destroyed most of it they came into contact with or sold it off to the Swiss. Perhaps someone in the Reich liked it."

"Don't really know the story. Anna said that the four of them, excluding the portrait which was hers, came off of various Nazi art trains."

"Unbelievable. There will be a long line of claims submitted for those three." He pointed to the Monet, the Degas, and the Renoir. "We'll handle the abstract separately. Most Picasso abstracts were burned. People didn't even turn in claims for them because they knew the work could never be returned."

"What about insurance or reparation?" asked Jamal.

"That's always a possibility, so we'll look at the lists and see what we find."

Dee repacked the paintings while Diego got on the phone to make arrangements for their safe passage to Seville.

When he was off the phone Diego continued, "We'll hold the opening next week. Give us time to clear the calendar of other exhibits, set it up, and promote the opening widely. It will draw a large crowd. If there's an owner out there, we'll find them."

"What if there's not?" asked Gina.

"Then the museum will hold the piece, unless you," Diego raised a hand and waved it past them all, "the owners, want something different. She left the pieces to you."

"I don't know what type of ownership Anna might actually have had, given the circumstances, I'd think it best for any of them unclaimed to stay with the museum, and be identified as 'found'."

"That'll work for me, but I doubt any of them go unclaimed," replied Diego.

Boris
The Following Week
Pilsen

Several days later Boris found himself in a Russian KA-52 attack helicopter armed with LMUR missiles. It was rather bold to fly into the Czech Republic but this mission needed to be done and no one would be harmed, forgiveness would be easier than permission.

Boris directed the pilot to the back side of the mountain outside Pilsen. Approaching the empty and uninhabited valley from the west they lined up on the open tunnel halfway up the mountain. At Boris's signal, the pilot launched two of the LMUR's into the hillside. There was rock, smoke, and dust in the air for several seconds. After it settled slightly, there was no remaining trace of the tunnel, just mountain side.

"There, sealed off for all time, the end of an era, final chapter of history," said Boris.

"What are you talking about?" asked the pilot.

"Doesn't matter. It's time to go home, hit it!"

Dee and Friends
The Following Week
Seville

The opening was held, and Diego was proven correct. There were multiple claims already made for each of the three paintings. It would take some time to sort them out.

Diego and his associates had spent many hours researching for a Picasso abstract titled 'Anna'. They had found nothing.

"I say any claim of ownership is lost to time and the Reich," said Diego.

"So, can we give it to her great-granddaughter?" asked Gina.

"Since she gave it to you, I think you can give it to anyone you want. If that was her request, so be it."

"We'll make the arrangements," said Angelic.

"Seville to Sophia."

"Seville to Vienna, we have an appointment on the river," said Dee.

Dee and Friends
Two Days Later
Vienna

They flew to Vienna and made a brief stop at St. Stephens Cathedral where they said a few words in remembrance of Anna. They honored her life, her efforts, and her experiences. Then they thanked her for her kindness, her generosity, and her honesty. They concluded by wishing her well on her next journey.

Afterwards they boarded the longship for a single day, from Vienna to Budapest. They sat on the sundeck throughout the afternoon and deposited Anna's ashes along the way, as she had wished.

———

Arrangements had been made and contact established with the great-granddaughter who had in fact become a prima ballerina for the National Ballet. She was initially leery of the call but finally agreed to it.

"I'll meet you in front of a restaurant called Le Rose on Vitosha Boulevard near the Palace of Culture."

They arrived in Sophia and taxied from the airport to the restaurant. The six of them settled on some benches by the curb in front of the restaurant to wait. Dee, Jamal, and Mike stayed close to the trunk while the women scouted the immediate area.

Ten minutes after the appointed meeting time a slender young woman in blue jeans approached them. She wore a sweatshirt with the National Ballet logo and had her hair tucked up under a cap.

"Mr. Sanders," she said haltingly.

Dee smiled at her and nodded. "Yes. You are Tatiana?" She nodded.

He introduced each of the others. "We were friends of your great-grandmother."

"She never mentioned you, but then she never mentioned many things."

"We only knew her for a short time before she died."

The young woman visibly stiffened. "What, when?"

"A little over a week ago. We were on the next-to-last day of the river cruise into Amsterdam. I think you'd call it natural causes. She was quite old, as you know, and she just got tired."

The young woman brought a hand to her face. "Does my grandmother know?"

Dee shook his head. "You great-grandmother requested us to do certain things for her and we agreed. She wanted to be cremated and her ashes spread along the Danube near Vienna."

The young woman smiled despite the tears beginning on her cheeks. "She loved those river cruises, back and forth and back and forth, and she loved Vienna. The dog, what happened to…"

"We have been caring for him." Dee pointed to the smaller crate beside the trunk of paintings.

"Oh, are you keeping him or …"

"Anna wanted you to have him if you want?" injected Gina.

The young girl's hand fell from her face, and she nodded. "Yes, please." And she cried in earnest.

"He's a wonderful dog. We've enjoyed caring for him," said Gina.

"But there's something else," said Dee. He pointed to the trunk.

"The Picassos?" asked the girl.

Dee nodded. "Anna wanted you to have them."

"And you're giving them to me? They're quite valuable."

"They're also quite beautiful. But she wanted you to have them."

The tears were really falling now. "I'm sorry." She pulled the hat from her head and a long stream of thick blonde hair fell out. She shook her head slightly. "I'm Tatiana, and I see you were my great-grandmother's friends. Thank you."

"I think you'll find the portrait looks very much like you, and what Anna must have looked like as a young woman."

She hugged Dee first and then each of the others. "My apartment is near here. Can we take everything and go there?"

Dee nodded and flagged down a couple of cabs.

———

They spent the remainder of the day in Tatiana's apartment admiring the paintings and answering questions about Anna. She asked them about dinner and they agreed.

"The paintings are so beautiful. You were right. It's as if I posed for the portrait myself. She must have been something."

"She was, right through to the end of her life. It was an amazing cruise on the river with her. Each place we stopped she had a story, from a different time and different circumstances."

"I'd love to hear them all sometime."

"I'll write them down for you."

Dee and Friends
The Following Day

They flew back to Amsterdam and settled into the house. Diego texted them the next day and said that all three paintings had been identified by heirs of the original owners and would be returned to them. One family planned to keep the work and the other two planned to auction them off. Their ownership will be short he'd said. Circumstances had changed for the families; for many, the past is never where we leave it.

They sat around the large kitchen that night enjoying a dinner they had all taken part in making.

"Man, I didn't know I could cook this good," said Jamal.

"You didn't cook nothing, you peeled potatoes," replied Mike.

"Crucial ingredient, this wasn't possible without it."

"You're dreaming, you do that a lot."

"No, that's Dee. He's the dreamer."

They both turned to look at him.

Dee paused for a moment, as if collecting his thoughts. "Hey, maybe I am a dreamer, but we got to not only hear a slice of history, we got to see it. We got the real world the way it was then and the way it happened. You can't get that from a book. You can't watch the past evolve into the present. She lived it. Anna was a gracious, generous, and resourceful lady. She was a survivor. That's how we should remember her."

"Besides, we're $750,000 richer, with a gold bar we'll donate to charity, a fine home on the grand canal in Amsterdam, and lessons for a lifetime. That's not a bad reward for thirty days on a historical river cruise. Where we going next?"

THE END.

ENJOY THIS BOOK?

A note from Author LP Snyder

If you've enjoyed this book, I would be very grateful if you could spend just five minutes leaving a review (it can be as short as you like) on the book's Amazon page and on Goodreads or BookBub.

Thank you very much.

ACKNOWLEDGMENTS

From Author L.P. Snyder

Thanks to all the readers who have made my books successful. That has encouraged me to continue writing, and here we are. I hope you enjoy reading the books as much as I enjoy writing them.

I want to thank Vince Conti for the beautiful cover. I especially want to thank my editor, Lisa Lee, whose invaluable assistance helped me pull this book together from a concept to a finished product. I also want to thank Jamie Lee Scott for the maps.

Also, thanks are in order to my friends and fellow authors Kelly Utt and Shannon Brown for their extensive insight, support, and patience, and finally to my wife, Diana. She told me I could do this! So I did. She's also a great beta reader.

ABOUT THE AUTHOR

LP Snyder is a life-long reader who, at the last minute, decided to become a writer. It's been a great experience, and he wonders why it took so long to decide! Having read a little of most genres, LP decided to stick with his favorites—adventure, espionage, and crime thrillers! If you like fast-paced, humorous, action-filled, suspense thrillers, he's your Huckleberry!

Newsletter subscribers receive bonus content, including short stories and extended epilogues. Don't be afraid to ride that train!

Sign up at www.lpsnyder.com.